Hunted

James Kipling

Hunted

Copyright 2013 James Kipling, Dipasha Tara Raj Publications House

License Note:

Table of Contents

Chapter 1

August 17ʹ 2008

Dev walked along the gravel road and the small stones like old friends, spoke to him. They weaved a tale of times gone by when this same gravel path carried two sets of shoes.

Pastel colors of soft candy-floss pink and burnt orange cut swathes through the sky, the last threads of the fading sunset and he recalled better times when he and his wife, Alka, had strolled the path, watching, at peace. The sunset had belonged to the two of them as if only they were seeing it, as if it were a scene unfolding just for them.

Dev's life had changed much over the years and tonight was the first night in a long time that he would spend away from his sugarcane factory. He had lost track of how many weeks had passed since he'd enjoyed a warm meal with his family. It was as if he was living at the factory these days, but Dev knew he was providing his family with a life they deserved. Granted, they still lived on the outskirts of Kamgar Putala slums near Pune, but they were much better off than most other families that resided in the neighborhood.

Turning towards the northeastern sky, he saw the clouds beginning to form into a grey cluster that bulged with the promise of the rain to come. He could smell the rain that the month of August always brought here. Pausing a moment, he took it all in before making his way towards his home. He was excited to be going home to spend a weekend with his family and he tried to picture the look on Alka's face when she saw him return at long last. He could just imagine seeing her eyes light up the way they always did whenever she was jubilant. He wondered what his son Raj would do when he saw that dad was home. The thought of Raj was painful because Dev knew one day his son would learn the truth about him and Alka, and he would even discover more about himself. He would eventually discover the secrets he and Alka had kept from him. It was inevitable that Raj would uncover the truth but that fact didn't alleviate the pain Dev felt when he thought of the calamity that such a discovery would bring.

Pushing away those thoughts, he focused instead on the good things that were happening at that moment. Despite his best efforts, as always, those negative thoughts continued to linger in the back of his mind; nagging at him. Giving way to those thoughts, he finally wondered if he should tell Alka about the threats he had received recently. Perhaps it was for the best, but he knew the moment he mentioned it to her she'd be filled with fear from that point on. He knew he would have to act to protect his family sooner rather than later and that could possibly mean he could never see them again; just like the others. His actions were causing this and he would suffer the consequences but so long as they were safe, nothing else mattered.

The closer he got to home, the heavier the realization became. His shoes began to drag against the gravel road sending stones skittering in all directions as the weight of what he must do almost brought him to his knees. She needed to know. They would have to go for help whilst he attempted to fix this mess. As he made it to the next bend, he looked towards his home which was about 100 meters in front, he paused. Something was wrong. Over near the front of his home he saw a luxurious black SUV parked.

Shaking his head, he knew whoever it was they were not here for him. He was not expecting anyone, so perhaps one of the neighbors was entertaining some important guests. That wasn't unusual but as he stared at the silent, still vehicle something else occurred to him. Paranoia had been his constant companion for a little over a decade now and he wondered if all his fears – all those nightmares – were finally coming to pass.

As Dev continued to walk past several other homes, he peered over his shoulder and he couldn't help but feel a trickle of fear run down his spine. He had to get home at once. He had to make sure that his family was safe and well.

Almost home now, he rounded the corner and saw one of Raj's friends, Mahi, standing towards the back of the house. His expression was indifferent and seeing him there gave him the reassurance he needed. Raj was indeed home, he was safe, and sure enough everyone else was safe as well. He anticipated seeing his beautiful wife making conversation with his younger sister. The two of them would be making a small meal and tonight he would be there to enjoy their company.

Upon reaching the black SUV, Dev attempted to see in through the windows, but he was unable to do so. The windows were tinted as if to conceal the occupants within.

He began to walk up the small steps to the veranda but once again, he paused on the top step struck by the silence. He was used to returning home to the sounds of laughter or at least the excited chatter of Alka through the papery thin door, but today there was nothing – only an ominous void that dragged the fear from within him and left his heart racing. That was when he found his courage and entered through the front door before making his way along the corridor, his breath in his throat. On his immediate right was the living room and what he saw made him stop dead in his tracks, his blood turning to ice.

Three men dressed from head to toe in black. Their faces were covered in masks, but despite that, he knew who they were and he knew why they were here. In the corner, he saw his sister struggling to break free, but she was unable to do so. A noose was tied around her neck and he saw the panic in her dark brown eyes. He saw the familiar warning gesture she used to give and knew that she wanted him to run away and save himself but he couldn't. He was the reason they were here and he refused to run off like a coward.

Then, all of a sudden, his sister flailed her arms and he watched as she broke away from the man restraining her. She was heading towards the open window when the man grabbed the end of the noose and yanked on it. He watched in silent horror as his sister was forced backwards and he watched as if frozen in place as her head hit the floor with a loud *crack*. He watched in horror as blood began to ooze from her skull and mingle with her black locks.

Dev finally snapped out of his stupor and knew what he had to do. He saw the knife sitting there beside the plate of fruits. Its blade was dull but he knew it was enough, it had to be. It was all he had. He knew he was outnumbered, but if he could kill at least one of them then maybe this would not all be in vain. He felt something take over him then and whatever it was, it gave him the strength and agility he needed. He lunged for the knife, gripped it in one hand and turned to face the three intruders. There was no time to formulate a plan of any kind. He was acting on pure instinct now and it drove him to leap at the nearest man, the knife held out before him. When the gun went off and a sudden searing pain exploded in his shoulder, he knew he had failed. Dropping the knife to the floor, he took a step back and placed his left hand over the steadily bleeding wound in his shoulder. Blood poured freely from the wound and he frowned as he watched it, thinking how impossible it seemed that so much blood could come from such a small hole. The masked intruder who had shot him walked over to him and reached out, squeezing the wound until he cried out and dropped to his knees, the pain almost unbearable. The room was a blur but as he sought out his sister and the others, his fluttering eyes settled on the crumpled form of his sister. She looked dead but his eyes wouldn't respond to his instructions so he couldn't know for sure. Perhaps she soon would be anyway, once they'd finished with her.

He slumped to the ground, letting himself hang when he realized his wife and son were probably dead by now. He had failed them all.

"You're looking for the others, aren't you?" He heard the mocking in the man's voice and that was when he was picked up by the arm and yanked to his feet. "Well your beautiful wife is at rest now," the voice continued, the pleasure the speaker was taking in telling him, clearly evident. "She put up quite a fight, but when I was finished with her she welcomed death. Hey—" he said as he shoved him to the third man. "Show him to his dearly beloved."

Dev felt himself shoved into the hallway and dragged to the next room along. His wife lay in a pool of freshly spilled blood. She was wearing a light yellow sari that was now partly stained crimson. Her unseeing eyes were pointed heavenward. He wished right then that he could undo everything.

However, there is no reset button in this game called life.

He was ripped from his despair for a moment by the shriek of his sister down the hall in the next room – she was still alive. All three men were there now and Dev wished he could do to them what they had done to his family. He could not though and so he remained sprawled next to his wife's lifeless body, devastated, but Raj was nowhere to be seen.

"Dev," the obvious leader of the three said. "Do you see what you made us do to your family? You should have accepted the deal that was presented to you. If you had done that one simple thing, your family would have been safe. But you thought you were smarter than us didn't you? Now you will die for your arrogance and your son too shall face the same fate."

Fury built up inside him at the mention of his son and he lunged at him. Forcing him against the wall, he was only able to get a punch in before he was dragged backwards. "You leave my son out of this! If you ever touch him the gods will curse you and all of those who follow in your ways!"

Laughing in his face, the leader lowered his head so that their eyes were level. Dev could see the man's eyes through the mask and he could make out the architecture of his face. He knew who this was and he knew why he was here. "Please, spare me that nonsense! Your gods have no power here. If they did, they would have been here to save you and your family. Your gods are cowards who sit upon their thrones and enjoy the danseuses as they flaunt their curves," he spat. "If your gods exist, then you should start praying now."

Dev was then pushed into the wall and a gun was shoved in his face. His mind flashed images of his family, of his son. He hoped Raj would survive this – and he also hoped when Raj learned the truth of him and Alka he would not show enmity towards them.

There was an explosion, then nothing.

Chapter 2

The wind was howling through the canopies and Raj felt at ease as his curly black hair brushed against his face and neck. He sat on the soft grass and felt as if he could remain there for all of eternity. He was reflecting on his day and he knew it was easier to be away from his mother and his aunt along with everyone else in the slums. However, he knew he could not always run away from his issues, but for now he needed to get away – he needed to clear his head.

Closing his eyes, he listened to the thunder overhead and he could tell that a strong storm was brewing and it would be upon him soon. The heavens seemed to snap in two then as an ear-splitting sound like shattering wood ripped through the air and signaled the beginning of the deluge to come. The pain of the heavy rain drops like bullets upon his skin was invigorating but soon it faded and he felt nothing.

He opened his eyes and watched as the lightning flashed threateningly across the black sky above. Most people were afraid and he knew that sometimes the monsoons became too much for the earth. Sometimes they had mass flooding that killed and whisked people away. Anyone caught by the floodwater would not be able to survive it, no matter how strong a swimmer they were. People in the slums did not usually take to swimming – the waters were dangerous and if one of the creatures that lurked in depths did not get you, something on the edges of the swollen torrent most certainly would.

As Raj remained there, he felt a sudden power surge through his entire body. The rain continued to fall and crash against him like a sea, but he was not cold nor was he in pain – he was more alive than he had ever been these past seventeen years of his life. Then he felt something primitive stir inside him and he heaved himself up to his feet and raised his hands to the heavens above. As the rain cascaded down his body in rivers, he was consumed by a feeling of oneness with the universe.

Exhilarated, he felt a sense of power wash over him and he could not help but savor this feeling. One day he wanted to be a powerful man – a man that others respected – a man that did not have to succumb to living in the slums. He did not want any part of his father's sugarcane business. If he was to ever inherit it, he would pass it to his father's right hand man. As he looked up to the heavens, he knew he wanted something entirely different with his life, but he was unsure of what it was. He had time though, but in the meantime, he knew he had to return to his family. He knew he could not stay out here forever.

Tearing himself from his reverie, he saw the silhouette of someone standing nearby. He wondered how long they had been there and he immediately felt abashed. The stranger approached him and he suddenly felt paralyzed, rooted to the spot. That sense of power had fled his body and he remained there drained and ordinary once more. Squinting in the dim light, he was able to make out the figure before him and he saw that it was a boy. His skin was darker than his and his eyes were hazel in color. Raj saw a scar above his left eyebrow and his nose was crooked. It was Mahi. He remembered clearly how Mahi had received the wounds. It had happened on the day they met.

Raj saw the expression on Mahi's face and he had a sinking feeling – something was terribly wrong. However, the question that surfaced in his mind lodged in his throat, unable to come out. He pushed away the morbid possibilities clamoring for attention in his mind. As real as those possible scenarios were for the slum dwellers, he didn't want to face them. They were nobodies and they were easy targets, but that couldn't be why Mahi appeared horrified – there had to be something else.

"You need to come with me, Raj," he said as he struggled to catch his breath. His eyes were wild and refused to meet his and Rodger began to feel as if that morbid thought was not just a thought, but reality. Without warning, Mahi grabbed his wrist and they started running through the sea of vegetation splashing through the grounded rainwater. As they ran, Mahi pulling Rodger behind him, Rodger knew he would soon have to face those horrible thoughts fighting for attention in his mind.

"What is the matter, Mahi?" he shouted as he pulled Mahi to a halt. Raj had always been stronger than Mahi and as he pulled, Mahi staggered and almost fell. As Mahi turned towards him, speechless, Raj felt as if he was going to break down.

Mahi paused for a moment and the expression that came over his face was one that Rodger had only seen on one occasion. Raj's mind involuntarily went to his family. He waited several seconds but Mahi said nothing. Raj felt the tears stinging at his eyes, but he could not cry – he would not cry. He still did not know what was wrong and that was when he looked back to Mahi.

"Please just tell me what's wrong," Raj shouted. He was desperate now.

Standing there frozen he noticed how Mahi could no longer look him in the eyes. He was silent and his head hung low upon his chest.

That was when he finally spoke. "It's your parents," he said. "Something has happened."

"What has happened?" he demanded, but Mahi remained silent. It was as if he was too afraid to speak.

Raj shook his head in frustration. He could still feel the tears stinging at his eyes. No, this couldn't be happening! Not his family. He was merely dreaming, but he knew better. Dreams did not feel this way. Before he knew what he was doing, he took off running. He ran blindly down a familiar path and as he trampled through gardens, he couldn't tell if anyone had seen him but he didn't care; right now, nothing mattered. As he ran, he felt his heart throbbing in his chest and just as his home came into sight, he knew something was wrong and stopped in his tracks.

Not too far off, he could see his home and he could see the people as they gathered in front of it. It seemed dreamlike, as if he were merely observing from another reality. He was frozen – he was afraid.

He didn't want to see them like that, but he had to know.

Maybe they were okay – maybe they were just injured. But the likelihood of that was nil and he knew it.

He took a few tentative steps towards his home. His feet were like lead and splashed through the puddles of rain at his feet, kicking up water that struck his shins – but he felt nothing. Then he heard the heavy breathing of Mahi behind him. Moving towards the gate, he could hear the low whispers of the onlookers and he wondered why none of them had put a stop to it.

They all feared for their own wellbeing of course. It was obvious.

Pushing past them he heard someone shout out, "You can't go in there," but Raj wasn't listening. Driven by the need to know if his family was alright, he ran headlong up the stairs and through the front door. When he entered his home, his nostrils immediately filled with the heavy stench of death. The air was thick and stuck to his body like wet clothes and as he staggered along the hallway, he knew. He didn't need to see the bodies of his family to know that they were all gone but there they were, laid out before him the sheets covering them stained with blood, thicker in places, revealing the injuries beneath. There were several other people inside canvassing the area, but Raj knew it was a waste of time. The local police force was useless, only showing up when the killing was done. They didn't serve and protect. Rather, they were little more than cleaners, waiting for the deed to be done before moving in to clear up the mess.

There would be no investigation, Raj knew.

Kneeling beside them, he felt sick. His father was there – home at last, as if he'd returned to die with his family. Raj wondered if he was here tonight to surprise them. It was a rarity, but this time, the surprise had been on him. Raj leant down and fingered the edges of the sheet covering his father. He knew who was who from the shoes protruding from the bottom or feet in the case of his mother and aunt. There was no danger of him breaking down at this point. His body was no longer his, as if he were merely an observer, not attached to the feelings within it. It was only a matter of time before the floodgates opened however. He pulled back the sheet covering his father's body, looked into his lifeless eyes and saw the gun-shot wound in the middle of his forehead. Another wound in his shoulder had stained his shirt a deep red.

Next, he moved on to the body of his mother. A single bullet had penetrated her chest and a surprisingly small amount of blood had spread outwards from the entry point, staining her dress. He remembered helping her make the outfit and they had only finished it yesterday afternoon. His eyes saw the rips and tears covering her clothing and he felt sick as he wondered what had happened to her. Was she afraid – did she cry? When she gasped her last breath, did she still believe that her only son despised her? He wished he could tell his mother one last time how much he loved her.

Finally, his eyes settled on his aunt. She never married because she was different from most other people. She was as wildly independent as any woman could be in the slums, especially a woman with her limitations. His eyes lingered on the bruises around her neck.

There was a faint tremor of feeling within him but it slipped away as he gently placed the sheets over his family once more.

There was something growing within him, a storm brewing. He could feel its edges reaching out like fingers, pulling him in slowly and mercilessly. At its center, in the eye of the storm feelings raged, as his mind knitted the facts together. Despair, grief, despondency, each had their moment but the one that overcame all the others, smothering them easily was dark and monstrous. While he had been away, dealing with his anger his family had been slain in cold blood. Had he been here, maybe things could have been different. He could have protected them – or so he hoped – but none of that mattered now because they were gone and he was here. He was still breathing – why was he still breathing?

His thoughts turned to the perpetrators of the crime then and he clenched his fists until his knuckles ached.

Getting to his feet, he turned towards the crowd outside. Their blank faces were streaming with rain yet they made no move to find shelter, as if they were dumbstruck by the violence on their doorstep. Raj knew though that their distress was for themselves and their own families. They didn't care that Raj's family was gone. He didn't feel the rain as he stepped outside to address the crowd. He didn't bother to hide the hatred he felt for those people who hadn't lifted a finger to help his family as he spoke.

"What happened here? One of you must have seen something – someone, anything?"

Their heads bowed, the crowd began to disperse silently. Regardless of who was murdered in the slums, no one would ever speak out. They all lived in fear because the moment they stopped being obedient nobodies was when they were executed. As he looked back at his house, he thought of how they had been obedient and had done more for this slum than any other family.

And it had all been for nothing.

He looked back at his house and realized it was all over. Whatever it had once been, was gone now, wiped away in a hail of bullets. He wasn't sad though. He was enraged but the emotion was in a controlled state ready to be channeled when it was needed. When he found them, whoever had done this, they would suffer, of that there was no doubt.

He heard someone approach. Mahi was standing before him. His eyes met Raj's for a brief moment then darted away as if fearing the contents. Instead, he looked down as he reached out and took Raj's hand, pulling him away from the house. Begrudgingly, he allowed himself to be led and soon they came to the gravel path – this was the path his father used to walk home on.

"I am sorry," Mahi finally said. "They surely did not deserve to die."

"How did you know what was happening?"

After being silent for a moment, Mahi finally spoke. "I was going to see if you were home. I wanted to talk to you, so I went to the back of the house where you usually were. That was when I saw them," his voice began to shake.

"Who – who did you see?"

Shaking his head Raj could see how fearful he was. "I don't know who they were. They wore some sort of black stocking over their faces. I was afraid they had seen me so I hid in the bushes and it was as if I couldn't move. I watched as they shot your mother, but before they did, she saw me. She wanted me to help her but I was too afraid, Raj. I'm..." He paused as if about to say something profound but then a single word burst forth in a bluster of air. "Sorry..."

He saw Mr. Tarun Banik, Mahi's father, walking towards them, moving quickly. The look of devastation was in his eyes and Raj knew why. Raj's father had given him a job in the sugarcane factory after he had lost his former job. If his father had not done that, there was no telling what might have happened to the Banik family. As to how he already knew about the fate of his family, the answer was simple; word travels quickly, but that didn't mean he was innocent, not to Raj anyway. Everyone was now a potential murderer in his eyes. He couldn't trust anyone.

As he stopped in front of Raj, he bore an expression of apology. "I am terribly sorry, Raj. When your father said he was leaving work I should have gone with him. Maybe if I had, this would all be different."

Raj's head dropped to his chest and stayed there. This wasn't helping one bit. He didn't need apologies. He needed answers but still, from somewhere inside the twisted mass of his tormented mind he managed to find words, if only to fast forward the moment so he could be free of them all. "It's not your fault. You couldn't have known. You couldn't have stopped this." *Yes, he could have, they all could have if they weren't so damn cowardly.*

He was struggling to hold it together, the rage mixed with grief still as fresh as the fallen rain at his feet. Wrapping his arms around himself, he turned away from Mahi and his father and that was when he saw his father's factory off in the distance. It was a specter haunting him, a skeletal husk of a building and it had taken his family from him. He didn't know what to do now; it was not as if he could stay here where his family had been brutally murdered. He knew he was a Shudra, an unskilled worker. He didn't even know how to operate his father's business because he had never expressed any interest in it.

Looking back on it now, he knew he should have. His father had built the sugarcane factory from the ground up. He never knew what inspired him to do it or even where the money had come from, and now he wished he had known. He was a terrible son for not caring about that and now he would never know the story about his father or how he became the man he was.

He looked to the darkened skies above. The rain had ceased for the time being but the clouds loomed overhead as if watching the scene unfolding below. Closing his eyes, he prayed to Shiva and prayed that the destroyer could help him on his new path. He vowed he would not stop his quest for vengeance until he had fulfilled it. He would kill the man responsible without hesitation or remorse. Who gave him the right to take away his family? By taking them from him, he had sealed his own fate and Raj would gladly hunt him down and make sure he suffered before he died – as his own family undoubtedly had.

As if giving voice to Raj's conviction, a clap of thunder then sounded violently and angry white forks of lightning tore a rift in the dark canopy of the sky. He was filled with that power again and he was no longer afraid of what lay before him. He could endure anything from this point forward.

"Raj," he heard Mr. Banik say. "I believe the police would like to have a word with you."

Turning on his heels, he saw them watching him. He had nothing to say to them. Nothing he said would help. He began to walk away, but Mahi stood in front of him, his brow furrowed. "I know that look, Raj – don't get involved."

"Wonderful, you can read the expressions on my face," he said acidly.

He made to push past him but Mahi wouldn't budge. "Do not take these matters into your own hands Raj. Let the police do their job and think about your future."

"I've already made my decision and we both know the police don't care about us. They are Vaishya and they're higher up on the totem pole than we are. People like us don't matter to them. So long as they remain in their caste, they'll be content. Besides I think we both know they are the ones orchestrating these – these killings!"

"You will lose out on your entire life by seeking revenge, Raj. Why would you waste your years trying to find someone who might as well be invisible?"

"Because they deserve what's coming to them."

"You are a Hindu," Mahi said, his voice pleading. "You and I believe in Karma and this act of treachery will affect them in their next life."

"I can't let them get away with this," Raj spat.

"Raj, how do you know they won't find you first? Why would they let you try to find them? Lay low and go about your life."

"Let me ask you this." Raj stepped forward so that his face was inches from Mahi's. "If it was your family, would you just not care? Would you let it go?"

"I would never forget, but I wouldn't waste my time trying to find someone who doesn't want to be found. If you go ahead with this, it's your life, your future on the line. Are you willing to give that up to embark on this ridiculous vendetta?"

Raj pushed past him, a bad taste in his mouth. Walking towards his home, he watched as the bodies of his family were removed. Three policemen watched him approach. Only one of them caught his eye. He towered over his colleagues and something about his manner set him apart, maybe it was his clean cut appearance or the cap that sat precariously balanced on his head, khaki with black and red stripes running along it.

He stopped in front of them and waited for them to pretend to give a damn. He swept his eyes from one to the other and finally settled for the taller one in the middle, hoping that he might simply cut to the chase and skip the pointless questioning. Even if he were to answer all their questions, he knew it would be for nothing. They didn't care. They were pawns in a dark game of chess, playing for power and prestige. The only killers they'd be bringing in were those who refused to share their ill-gotten gains. This 'appearance' was all part of the veil of deception.

"I am Inspector Kumar," the one in the middle said. His voice was not as deep as Raj thought it would be. "And if you don't mind, I have a few questions for you. Come with me please." It was a command, not a request.

Raj *did* mind. He wasn't going to waste his time playing their game. He held his ground and stared at the officer, his face blank. As if used to such treatment, Inspector Kumar softened in his approach.

"I can only imagine how much pain you feel now, but you need to help us. You must know something that could point us in the right direction. Without your help we might never catch the killers?"

The lie filled Raj with rage but he held the storm in check – for the time being. As culpable as they were for the death of his family, his rage was better spent elsewhere. Instead he said nothing. Seeing that Raj wasn't going to cooperate, Inspector Kumar said, "We can ask you the questions here."

"What could I possibly tell you that would help you figure out who did this to my family?"

Raj watched as his brow furrowed and he shook his head. "I know most people like you don't believe in people like me, but you must understand that your kind hardly ever tell us what we need to know. So if you want our help, you should answer the questions to the best of your ability."

"My *kind*," Raj spat. "It's little wonder that you can't do your jobs properly, we're little more than filth to you. Trust me, one day my *kind* will be your leaders."

An ugly smirk wound its jagged way up the right cheek of the inspector's face and he stepped forward to lean in close to Raj. "That's a lot of talk, but I do understand where your hostility comes from. You are an orphan now and you are taking all your anger out on me." His index finger wagged before Raj's face like an irritated insect. "I'll give you one more chance to cooperate. Just answer the questions." The inspector retreated and regarded Raj, his body stiff, waiting for Raj's next move.

The police could make his life hell, correction – would make his life hell, what was left of it and if it wasn't for his desire for vengeance Raj would have toyed with them. He had no choice but to cooperate. He nodded for the inspector to begin. "Did your father have any enemies that you knew about? Was he ever threatened by a former employee or anyone at all?"

"No, my father did not have any enemies. He never let anyone at the factory go either. He did everything he possibly could to keep them."

"At any given point, did your father seem stressed or upset about anything?"

Pausing, Raj thought back to two weeks earlier. He had heard part of a conversation that he shouldn't have been listening to. It was between his parents, but that bit of information was not something he was keen on sharing. He had no idea what they meant as they spoke, but it must have held some significance.

"No, well yes, but it was just because he was working very long hours at the factory. As a result, he came home only once every two weeks or so. He always said how much he wanted to spend more time with us – he wasn't even supposed to be home this early. I think he was trying to surprise us."

The inspector's dark eyes narrowed. "Is it possible your father killed your family?"

"No!" Raj knew what was happening. "My father would *never* do such a thing. He loved us."

"Well, what if he came home and went after your mother," he began with his story telling and Raj's worst fears were given life. "And after shooting her in the chest your aunt grabbed the gun from him and shot him in the arm. He then pushed her backwards and she hit her head and he got the gun again…" The inspector paused and Raj watched him as his mind concocted the lie he would feed his superiors. "He hung her and out of guilt he shot himself in the head." He straightened, nodding.

"Of course you would think up a story," Raj said anger raising his voice. "You don't want to find the truth do you? How do you even sleep at night?"

"Quite peacefully – but you should know that you are nothing. What I say is more likely to be believed than a boy who denies that his father cracked. Now thank you for your time, kid."

Raj remembered something and though he knew it was pointless, went after the police. "There is a witness, someone saw what happened here. The murderers were seen waiting here for my father to return. Why don't you investigate that?"

"Your kind should know your place," he said. "Your lies won't convince me or stand up in court. I am sure your friend over there saw something but he twisted the story to suit your agenda. This was nothing more than an enraged husband taking things too far…happens all the time with you people."

"Maybe to crooked cops like you but I'll find someone who will help."

"You know nothing of this job, boy."

"Cops are supposed to know people – I bet you couldn't even tell me what my name is."

The inspector looked him up and down, his stare icy. "Your name doesn't matter like you and everyone else in this slum." As if to drive home the message, the inspector closed the space between them and whispered, "Raj Varma, they will be watching you."

Then they were gone in a cloud of dust that obscured their vehicles. They wouldn't be back. Their work was done, whoever they were. Raj's work however, was just beginning.

Chapter 3

The rain picked up again within the hour and Raj watched it from the window. Mahi was sitting in the corner and he seemed to be in another world entirely. Raj had told him about the conversation with the inspector. His father had not murdered his family and whoever it was knew Inspector Kumar. Hell, whoever was responsible for all this death must have been higher up, someone who could be considered untouchable for the simple fact that they had the ability to buy whatever they wanted, whether it be information or a hit man, it would not matter.

"You're still going to seek revenge aren't you?" Mahi asked in a low voice.

"Yes, and you should know that nothing you do will persuade me to do otherwise. I mean, what good is it to be a righteous person with a good heart if that still gets you killed? If you ask me, this is all about survival of the fittest. All of us need to be on our toes, alert, and sharp. You kill or be killed."

"Look around you! No one else is lashing out like that. You are not the only one who has ever lost someone by the hand of another. Half the people we know all lost members of their family and they are not seeking revenge. Karma will handle everything. I mean, don't you want to be reborn into a higher rank?"

"That's not important to me any longer! What is important is that my family is gone!"

Raj wanted to tell Mahi what else Inspector Kumar had told him, but that would not accomplish anything. Over the years, he had learned to be careful and to keep certain things to himself. Not everyone can be trusted. In fact, it seemed as if most people were self-absorbed and only cared about their immediate selves and no one else. He hated it being that way but he wasn't a magician, he couldn't change the world – but he could ensure his family's killers were put to justice.

As he sat there in silence, Mrs. Rita Banik walked in. She wore a blue sari that was too big on her petite figure. Raj knew that the sari had belonged to his mother long ago. His mother was the most loving and the most giving of any woman he had ever met. She did all she could do for the people here. His aunt would accompany her as well. Now they were gone and he wondered if the others felt their absence as much as he did.

"Raj," she said softly. "Would you mind following me?"

Looking over to Mahi, he shrugged, nodding. She placed her hand on his shoulder and walked him into the hallway. Standing there, she seemed rather uncomfortable and looked down at her feet before speaking. "I know how hard it is losing your family. That's how I met my husband actually, but that's beside the point. Your mother and father were good people."

"I already know that."

"Of course you do. I just want you to know that not everyone is perfect. Your parents hid things from you – things you don't even know about."

"Are you trying to tell me my parents had a double life? I don't believe you." He was tired of the lies. First the police and now so-called friends, it was getting beyond ridiculous now.

She didn't seem to be fazed. It was almost as if this was the reaction she was expecting from him. "Believe what you want Raj. In the morning I would like for you to go to the factory. What you will find there might help you understand more about what is going on. In the meantime, try and get some sleep."

Raj nodded. He felt awkward as she put a comforting hand on his shoulder – it was a mother's touch and something his own mother would never be able to do again. He returned to Mahi's cramped room his mind and heart at war. He knew he should be breaking down at this point but he wouldn't allow it. He needed to stay focused.

"Is everything alright?" Mahi asked when he returned.

"I suppose so. Goodnight, Mahi."

Picking a spot near the window, he laid down. He noticed the rain for the first time, now that he was alone with his senses. Though the downpour was almost done, the raindrops striking the tin roof rang out like bullets, each liquid explosion a bullet for his family. When the rain finally stopped, releasing him from the torment of seeing his family die in his mind over and over again, he drifted into a deep sleep, the kind of sleep one falls into after several nights of insomnia.

*****

Watching from a distance he wondered if the boy could sense his parents' killer. He doubted it and now it was his turn to die. This time the boy was alone while the others scurried back home to their own families. As he watched the people in the slums, he remembered when he was one of them. He was orphaned at the age of seven and that was when he was taken in by someone powerful – someone who ought to be feared.

Killing the people of this area was not a difficult task. It was as natural to him as preparing a meal. He showed his loyalty to his father and he did everything he was told without question. The boy had to die in order to complete this assignment.

The boy had been taken in by a neighbor and that good deed was prohibiting him from doing his job. He watched as they were all getting ready for bed and wondered if perhaps he should just kill them all. It didn't bother him morally. If it wasn't done right, he might leave evidence or living relatives and that would only anger his father.

Pulling the phone out of his pocket, he called the man who he owed his life to, his savior. This was a man who knew no love. He didn't need love to command his army of crooks. He got by just fine as the most feared crime boss in the slums.

"Is there a problem?"

"The boy, he's being sheltered by another family. How should I proceed?"

"Kill them all however you need to. Just make sure you leave no survivors. This boy could be dangerous someday."

He placed the phone back in his pocket and wondered just how this boy could be dangerous. He was only angry and over time that would calm down. He would eventually forget this anger and he would go about his life. Then again, he didn't know anything about him, or his family. All he knew was the father had not agreed to a deal, but what was entailed in that deal he didn't know.

With practiced ease he scouted the area. There was only one way in. Good. There'd be no escape.

*****

Waking from his dream, Raj sat upright and looked around. There was something wrong, but he was unsure of what it was. He

28

looked over to Mahi and found him sound asleep. He listened and waited for the noise again. He heard it again and knew what it meant. Someone was skulking through the house, their footfalls disturbing the loose floor boards. A muffled shriek filled the silence before the sound was cut off like a bad phone line.

Someone was in the house.

Quickly, he moved to Mahi and shook him awake. Mahi awoke with a start. Raj put his finger to his lips. A strange sound came at them from along the hallway then, several low clicks in quick succession and a tremor ran through Raj's body. Someone had come for him but not just him, Mahi's entire family – a clean sweep. They meant to wipe all trace of Raj and his family away forever even if it meant slaughtering Mahi's family too.

Raj motioned towards the window and Mahi nodded. As silently as they could, they slipped out. The only difficult part of it was they were on the second floor and the coolness of the night left the windowsill slick with condensation.

Raj let Mahi go first, he was more awake now and Raj could see the panic in his eyes. As Mahi dropped from the window, there was a loud *thud* as he hit the metal roofing of the home underneath them.

"Where do you think you are going?" A figure appeared in the doorway of Mahi's bedroom.

In that moment, Raj wanted to kill him, but he couldn't. There was no way in the world he could win this fight. The shadow raised its hand and Raj scrambled over the window sill and dropped, hitting the tin roof before bouncing off it to land on his back on the damp earth below. Winded and stricken with the shock of the impact, he watched as the killer leaned out of the window and fired, the muzzle of his weapon discharging its deadly load with barely a wisp of smoke.

The first bullet missed, kicking up dirt beside him but the next struck home, only it didn't hit Raj. Mahi wrenched Raj to his feet and dragged him away from the house, his shirt over his shoulder a crimson swamp. With Mahi beginning to sag against him, Raj's instincts took over. Dragging his friend with him, his own vest soaked with Mahi's blood, he fled into the slums, knowing the killer would hunt for them until they were both dead.

Raj knew this slum better than anyone. There were hundreds of places to hide and he knew which one would be the safest. Running into the thick vegetation, he knew it would be easy to track him with the mud being as thick as it was but if they could just keep moving, they might lose their would-be killer.

"Stop," Mahi gasped. "Stop, Raj! I – I can't go any further."

Eyeing his friend, he saw his shirt was soaked in blood and his wound was still bleeding, the blood running along his arm to drip off his fingertips.

"I'll fix you up when we get there. C'mon!"

"No...I'm done. I've lost too much...blood."

Mahi's eyes were glassy and unfocused, his skin taut and pale and Raj sensed he didn't have long left. A pang of sorrow opened him up briefly, reaching into his heart as he realized he was about to lose someone else. As he lay Mahi down in the sodden mud, he felt the first tears of the day emerge at the corners of his eyes. There was no one left for them to take now. They'd robbed him of his family and best friend.

"Go...on," Mahi gasped, a coughing fit doubling him over, stealing more of his waning strength.

"I'm sorry, Mahi." Raj rose and sprinted away knowing that he had to survive. He was the only one who could avenge their deaths but he had to survive the night first. Mahi had been against vengeance but Raj wondered how he would feel now that his family had also been taken. He briefly thought about blaming himself but pushed it aside for another time. Later, there'd be plenty of time for self-pity, but Raj preferred the idea of channeling every ounce of rage into finding and slaughtering every last one of those who had brought this upon him.

They would pay dearly.

He ran, mud hindering his progress, sucking at his bare feet and splashing up into his face, a wall of ever moving liquid that threatened to blind him slowing him down like an ally to his pursuer. He knew where he was going, but he didn't dare look over his shoulder. If he fell in the mud, he was as good as dead. Pushing on, he cried out as a blur in the dark struck his legs and sent him sprawling to the ground. Instinctively, he raised his hands as the figure towered over him. His mission for vengeance was over before it had begun.

"Follow me," a voice said and Raj whose eyes had been squeezed shut finally opened his eyes and saw the man standing before him wasn't his pursuer.

The stranger reached out and offered his hand, gesturing for Raj to get up. Realizing he had no other choice, Raj took the proffered hand and climbed to his feet. Without another word the stranger beckoned for him to follow and led him along a gravel path to a parked car and there he hesitantly climbed into the back seat. Someone was already in the driver's seat. The stranger climbed in beside him and shifted in his seat, turning to face Raj.

"Raj Varma, my name is Hari Singh Sidhu and I am here to protect you from the men who killed your family."

"How do you know me?"

"I'll explain everything to you when we are in a secure location. In the meantime, you can't know where we are going, so please accept my apologies for what I'm about to do."

By the time Raj realized what was happening, the chloroform soaked cloth clamped to his mouth and nose was already ushering in darkness. He welcomed it and it gladly accepted his invitation.

Chapter 4

He woke up with a jolt, a feeling that something wasn't right lingering in his mind. He pushed off the blanket covering him and rubbed the sleep from his eyes. Sunlight was casting angular shapes upon the floor around the room as infant sunlight invaded the room, ray by ray. He lay there in the semi-darkness that remained below the windows and thought back to the night before. So much had happened in so little time. He knew he ought to be broken right now, a bubbling mass of tears and snot but he felt nothing. Good.

Pulling his knees to his chest, he reflected on everything that had happened. The events of yesterday evening ran through his head as he remembered what Mahi had done for him. At the thought of how Mahi had saved him and sacrificed his own life he felt a flicker of emotion but he pushed aside as it was useless to him at that moment. He needed answers to what was going on, because the man who took him knew his name as if he had known him before, but Raj had no recollection of a man named Hari Singh Sidhu in his life. However, the last name seemed vaguely familiar.

Finally, he stood and moved to the door. A knock at the door stopped his hand half-way to the doorknob and it froze in midair at the sound. The door opened to reveal a boy about Raj's age with hair so unruly its curls hugged his ears, neck and shoulders like armor.

"Good morning," he said in a voice that was pleasant without trying. "I'm Sai and I was just coming to wake you up for breakfast…but I see there's no need." Sai shrugged, his shoulders jerking with the movement and Raj saw he was a rather skinny kid.

Pausing for a moment, Raj wasn't sure how to react. This place seemed safe and it looked to be secure, but he didn't understand why or how this was happening.

"Is everything okay?" Sai asked.

"I guess so," Raj said slowly. "It's just that everything is so – weird. I don't even know where I am."

"This is the compound and a few of us live here. Hari should be waiting for you if you wanted to ask him any questions."

"Do you know why I was brought here?"

"No. All I know about you is your name and that you arrived here last night. But follow me and I'll take you to where you need to go."

"Alright," Raj said as he began to follow Sai. As they were walking down the corridor, Raj realized just how big the building was. They passed several more connecting corridors, each one brimming with doors and Raj felt like he was taking a stroll through a prison. It was perturbing but at least he wasn't being hunted by a merciless killer that slaughtered entire families just to get to one boy. He hoped, as he watched the boy walking ahead of him casually that he had found some allies at last.

They turned left at the end of the hallway and more doors greeted them but in this part of the building, he saw just how beautiful the place was. He'd never set foot in such a building and tried to imagine what it must look like from the outside. He'd once seen a governor's mansion in town, from atop a hill. To a slum boy like Raj the mansion was like something out of a dream where you could fly and there was no limit to what you could do. That's how majestic it was, all white stone and arches and gardens stretching off into the distance almost touching the sky. That's what it must look like, he thought. How then, had a slum boy like him come to be here? The beige walls were covered with framed articles, as they walked but Raj didn't manage to see what they concerned. All he knew was that the finery of the place meant he was in the home of someone very important.

At the top of a flight of stairs they came to a large room where three people were sat around a table, presumably waiting to meet Raj. Two of them Raj did not know and sitting in between them was Hari. He seemed tired as if he hadn't slept the night before.

"Hi Raj," he said with a smile. "It's good to see you awake and well. I was afraid that I used too much chloroform, but you seem okay. Now, I would like you to meet Ash and Jadu. They are the early risers and, of course, you've already met Sai."

"Yes – would you mind telling me what this is all about? I really don't like being in the dark like this."

Hari nodded and stood up. He was several inches taller and considerably bigger than Raj. He had a thick beard and Raj could not help but notice the Kirpan sword he wore around his waist. Raj waited for Hari to answer but Hari was in no rush and motioned to the food on the table. "Help yourself to some food and then we can talk," he said.

"I'm not hungry."

"Come now, Raj," Hari said. He spread his arms and nodded to the food again. "We both know that's not true. Last night must have taken a lot out of you."

Raj had to admit he was rather hungry. His stomach growled in response as if issuing an order and Raj gave in. The food spread across the table was every Indian boy's dream and included both vegetarian and non-veg dishes. Raj would never eat such a variety of foods in the slums. He filled his plate with some of everything and looked to Hari. He was struggling to contain the saliva that threatened to spill over his lips.

"Ash, Jadu, I will be back soon so we can resume our conversation." Hari motioned for Raj to follow.

Raj looked to the two boys and they nodded. They seemed indifferent about being interrupted and were soon deep in conversation with Sai.

Hari led Raj down two flights of stairs and down a hallway until they came to a lavishly decorated room with arch windows high up in the wall. Hari seated himself on a couch and motioned for Raj to do the same on the opposite couch. Raj sat down with the plate in his lap. He felt a little awkward being in such luxurious surroundings but the food on the plate was too much to resist so he began to pick at it as he waited for Hari to begin.

"So what do you want to know?" Hari asked finally.

"I want to know where we are, for starters."

"We are not in the suburbs. We are almost half-way between Mumbai and Pune very close to the Mumbai-Pune Expressway. In fact we are not too far away from the Kamgar Putala slums where you were. This place is not accessible to anyone other than me and those I trust enough to allow inside the walls."

"How did you know who I am?"

"I knew your entire family for several years. When we heard what had transpired yesterday, I was sent out to retrieve you."

"How could you possibly know my family without me ever seeing you around before?"

Shifting in his chair, Raj could tell that Hari was becoming uncomfortable. It was almost as if he was afraid to answer his question. "The last time I saw you, you were about three years old. I was in the slums with a friend of your father's and we were discussing your future. Your mother did not want us there any longer and she sent us away. Ever since then I have only interacted with your parents through letters."

"Why were you talking about my future?"

"That is not something for me to say, Raj. The man who knew your father the best should be here this weekend and he will be able to talk to you then."

"No, don't give me that. I want my answers now because there is nothing keeping me here."

"Well that is a lie," Hari snapped. "This is a compound and the only person who knows their way out of here is me."

"So, what you're saying is this is a prison?"

"This is not a prison! This is a home for kids like you...for children who have lost their families – like you."

"And none of them want to leave?"

"All of you eventually leave," Hari said. "But you leave when you are deemed ready to. We educate you and get you ready for the real world. Many children here will eventually leave and go on to attend university. There's no reason why you can't do the same."

"You want me to sit around twiddling my thumbs while you decide what to do with me?" Raj snapped. "I need to figure out who did this to my family and when I find the man responsible..." Raj stopped there. He still wasn't sure exactly what he would do but he knew it was something unpleasant.

Hari shook his head. "Seeking revenge is not the answer here. Plus finding the person who wanted them dead is close to impossible. Usually, the people responsible for these deaths are people who sit higher on the political ladder and they are almost untouchable."

Raj put his plate down on the table. "I am highly motivated and what would you do if it was your family? What would you do if it was your friend and his entire family? They were all good people and they didn't deserve to die."

"You are correct. They didn't deserve to die, but it happened and nothing is going to change that."

Raj was silent as he slumped back on the couch. He disliked the fact that Hari was right. Nothing he could do now would be able to change the deed that had already been done. He did not know why they all had to die though. He remembered what Mrs. Banik told him. She disclosed that there was something at his father's factory that could help him, but how was he going to get out of here?

"How did you know where to find me?"

"I arrived in the slums late last night. I got to your house when I saw you were jumping out of the neighbor's window. I stayed back and watched you go into the forest and I followed you. I was supposed to protect you and I succeeded."

"My friend and his family died and my entire family died hours earlier! How, by any definition, is that success?"

"My mission was to protect you. If I had gotten there earlier I am sure I would have been able to get you out before the Banik family was slain, but you are safe now. You just need to lay low and wait until the time is right before striking back."

"You won't take any action...will you?" Raj said.

"What makes you so sure?"

"You are a Brahmin. Brahmin don't do violence."

Hari was quiet for a moment and he nodded. "I won't have any part of violence, you're right. I will help you get justice though. Just like the others. And if that is something you are not interested in, then maybe you should leave."

It was tempting to walk away from this place, but Raj was not able to do so. He needed help, he needed information, and he needed to be clear headed.

"That is a good decision, Raj. Now, what do you know so far?"

"I don't know anything."

"You're lying." Hari eyed him unblinkingly.

"Lying, what makes you say that?"

"I study people and that is what I have been doing for years. Now what do you know?"

Raj was not sure about the significance of what he overheard, but he felt as if it was something important. Letting out a sigh, he looked to Hari who seemed to be expecting him to answer already.

"A few weeks ago I overheard my father talking to my mother. He was really upset and he told her that they were there again. That even after he had apologized they still wanted something from him. My mother told him she didn't think that making an agreement with them was a good idea. Then my father told her that they might come after us. My mother started to cry and she said she didn't want to lose me the way she lost the others."

"Do you know what she meant about the *others*?"

"No. That was the last time I heard them talk about it. Afterwards, my father stayed at work a lot. Even if I wanted to I wouldn't have asked. I wasn't supposed to know."

"Do you think your father hid things from you?"

"We were never close," Raj admitted. "It was as if I wasn't the son he wanted me to be. Almost as if I had already disappointed him. He always wanted me to run the sugarcane factory when I was older, but my heart was never in it."

"What about your mother? Was there anything different about her over the past few weeks?"

"She was restless and irritable. She was always checking out the window as if she was looking for something. I don't know why, we never expected company. Yesterday she told me I couldn't leave the house. She told me I needed to stay home for my own safety," Raj paused for a moment, the memory once more stirring up emotions he didn't want to feel yet. "She was afraid, but I lost my temper and left her there. She ran after me and begged me to stay…but I didn't. I told her I just needed space away from her and now I wish I had stayed home like she had wanted"

"Don't beat yourself up about it. You have no idea what it could have resulted in had you stayed. Maybe all four of you would be dead. And was there anything strange going on with your aunt?"

"She was quiet, the way she always was. She always looked at me like I was precious. Nothing about her was ever wrong, to other people she was a freak because of her deformities and her inability to speak, but she was wonderful."

Hari was silent for a moment and he nodded. "Losing the people you love is the worst thing someone can endure. While you're here you'll be safe and we'll be able to figure out who did this to your family. You can trust me Raj, and the others here."

"Are they all like me?"

"They...*we* ...have all lost our families."

"Are you all seeking revenge?"

"No, because not all of us had our loved ones murdered. Raj, I know how badly you want to get your revenge, but for now, lay low. I know that's difficult to hear and to even do, but you are going to have to do that for me. Whoever did this to your family still wants you dead."

"I'll lay low," Raj said and as he spoke, he wondered if Hari could tell it was a lie. This time though, Hari seemed to believe him or at least wanted him to think he believed him.

"Feel free to finish eating your breakfast here," he said as he was getting up. "If you need anything, ask one of the others. They'll be able to help you and they all know where to find me."

Raj nodded and looked down at his breakfast. When Hari left, Raj began to eat, but as he chewed the food, it dawned on him that it didn't taste as good as it had looked. Was it the food or was it the fact that his mind was somewhere else, erecting plans for the future. He shoveled the food in anyway. He would need his strength.

Chapter 5

Picking at his food, Raj sat there in silence unsure of how to proceed. His mind kept flashing back to the memories of the previous night. There had been so much death and he couldn't help but feel that it was his fault. He wondered if anyone had found the Banik family or if they even found Mahi's body in the forest. His friend had made the ultimate sacrifice and Raj wondered if it was all worth it, if he didn't act, if he merely hid within this fortress like the other kids, it would all be for nothing. Alone now, he was the only one left who could act, not to do so would be an injustice to those who had been taken from him.

Setting the plate down on the small table he looked outside and saw the rolling undersides of the clouds at the window-tops like dark zeppelins carrying his inner rage waiting to expel it at his order. In the distance, a pocket in the dim cloud filled-sky harbored forks of lightening as they thrust to the earth below, seeking targets. Yes, he would take his vengeance no matter what the cost. He had nothing to lose now anyway.

Leaning back, he wrapped his arms across his chest and watched the light show in the sky, but someone was coming. He heard the pitter patter of light footsteps. Sai appeared with a girl. As they stopped before him, he was sure they were brother and sister. The similarity was all too clear.

"Hey Raj," he said. "This is my little sister Rani."

Raj waved at the girl and she returned the gesture.

"Hari sent us up here. He said we should give you a tour of the compound, if you would like."

Getting to his feet, he nodded. "I guess that would be okay."

Sai smiled and motioned for Raj to follow him. Rani walked past him and picked up his plate, now bare of food. "I can take care of my dish," Raj said as he reached out to take it from her. He'd always been taught to take care of himself and the last thing he wanted was for a girl he'd just met to be cleaning up his mess, it didn't seem right.

"No," she said, her voice was somewhat shaky. "I can take this. You just go with my brother."

She looked at the floor as she spoke and Raj wondered why she was so timid. Was she as damaged as he was? He knew it was even harder for a poor girl in the slums. He left her then, not wishing to bother her and fell in step behind Sai. They began to walk downstairs. After a few minutes went by, he spoke. "How many people live here?"

"There are only seven of us, you, myself, Rani, Ash, Jadu, Priya, and Hari. There used to be more of us, but the others were able to get into university so they left the compound. Soon there will be only six of us because Jadu is about to start university from next week."

"Do you ever want to leave?"

Sai shrugged. "I'm unsure of what I want. I might wait until Rani is older and able to leave before I go."

Raj nodded. He didn't know how to respond to that. He had never had a plan, but he did know he wanted to be successful. And with whatever he earned, he was going to help his slum and ensure that they were all safe – safe from the same corrupt forces that took his family. Though he wasn't sure how he would achieve it, he wanted to make sure the people of the slums were afforded the same rights as everyone else. No one cared about those who resided in the slums. They were treated like livestock and he hated it. He wanted to change it.

"What about you? Do you have any plans?"

"Not yet," he said. He thought it best not to share his desire for revenge with Sai.

Sai nodded. "Alright, well anyway—this is a four level building. The level we just came from is the second floor and on the third floor is where all of us have our rooms. And the fourth floor is where we study and do other activities."

"What's on the first floor?"

Sai shrugged. "No one other than Hari knows. We don't even know how to get down to the first floor."

"Doesn't that bother you at all? You're being kept in here like prisoners."

"We can leave," Sai said defensively. "None of us want to leave though. We have everything we could possibly need here. Plus no one here has anything outside this compound so there is no point in leaving."

As they walked through the building, Raj scanned each and every hallway, making note of the doors and staircases. It was a big place and one could easily become lost. "How come there are so many different hallways and doors? They all look the same to me."

"If there was ever a break-in, we'd be safe. We learn how to walk through the hallways and we know where the best places are to hide, whereas a complete stranger would get lost in this labyrinth. There's safety in uniformity, I guess."

"I thought Hari said it was safe here."

"It is. We've never had an incident with someone getting in over the wall, but this is just a precaution."

Raj nodded, but he didn't understand why anyone would take all these safety measures. He didn't even understand why anyone would want to kill any of them. They were slum kids and they were nothing of importance to anyone. If they were, people from the suburbs would be coming into the slums more frequently to help out instead of taking everything they believed they were entitled to.

"And what if one of us wanted to leave?"

"I guess we could if we wanted to, but there's nothing we can do for ourselves, not yet anyways."

Walking down a winding hall, Raj saw a staircase and he continued to follow Sai. When they reached the top of the stairs, Raj stood there stunned. There were hundreds of books, three rows of computers, desks, and more things than Raj could process. The entire room was designed for students. Raj began to see the possibilities for himself immediately and wondered about his plan to escape and get to the sugarcane factory. If he left would he be allowed to come back? If he stayed here he could excel and become successful. He could change everything in the slums and be the person he always wanted to be. His own needs would have to wait however, he decided. He needed to go to the factory to try and find out what Mrs. Banik was talking about.

"Sai, what happens if one of us wants to leave, just for a short time to get something?"

"None of us have ever needed to go back out there. If there's something important I am sure you could tell Hari. He's a good guy and I know you've only known him for a few hours, but you can trust him."

Raj wanted to believe that he could trust Hari, but he couldn't afford to risk it. Somehow, today he needed to find a way to get to the factory. Maybe the people responsible for the death of his family were going to incinerate everything, maybe they already had but he had to know either way. They would make it so there was no connection back to them, because for whatever reason, his father had crossed paths with a deadly enemy who would stop at nothing to get his own way.

Nodding, Raj began to think about how he was going to take action. He didn't want to admit that he needed help, but there was no doubt in his mind that he was going to need it.

Chapter 6

Hari was sitting in his room alone sorting through his mail when the phone started to ring. He didn't recognize the number but he had a vague idea of who it might be or should be.

"Hello."

"Hari," the caller said. "I won't be able to make it to the compound this weekend and I just wanted to let you know. I also want to see what you know about Raj. Does he suspect anything?"

"No. He has no idea and I don't know if we should keep it that way or not. I'm not sure if telling him wouldn't only harm him more. He's been through a lot already."

The other man sighed and Hari knew he was most likely deep in thought. "He needs to know the truth about everything. It's not like that son-of-a-bitch is gonna give up the chase anytime soon. He stands to lose too much if Raj lives."

"Who is the man responsible?"

"You know him very well," he said slowly. "I won't give out the name over the phone. I'll mail you the information. You should have it Monday afternoon."

"Is there anything you are at liberty to tell me now?"

"Yes," he said. "Some time before his death, Dev Varma discovered some pertinent information about the man responsible for his death. He has it hidden somewhere in his factory, but as to where, he did not disclose that to me. All I know is that the man responsible will attempt to find that information so he can destroy it."

Hari fell deep into thought as his mind filed through a list of names, searching for the man responsible. "And do you want me to go and retrieve it?"

"Yes, and be sure Raj does not read it. If he finds out the truth there is no telling what he'll do. I'll tell him when the time is right."

"Alright, I'll be sure to keep him close where I can keep an eye on him."

"Good. And Hari, I heard that the Banik family had also been killed, is that true?"

"Yes sir. After the Varma family was killed, the Banik family took Raj in. What significance are they to you?"

"Find out about Rita Banik and you will surely understand the significance. For now I must go. If anything else arises, be sure to let me know."

"Yes sir, I surely will."

After hanging up the phone, Hari pulled his laptop in front of him and turned it on. The name Rita was familiar but he had no idea why. As he was typing her name into the database, he heard a knock on his door.

"Come in," he called and turned around to see Raj standing at the door with Sai behind him.

Peering over his screen, he thanked and excused Sai and gestured for Raj to take a seat and he did so. "What can I do for you?"

"Last night before the Banik family was killed, Mrs. Banik told me there was something at the factory that could help me find the killers and learn the truth about my family. She said my parents hid things from me and that I would find all my answers at the factory. I was wondering if you could help me."

Hari closed his laptop and thought about it for a moment. How had Mrs. Banik known so much? He knew the answer was on his screen, but he had no time to read it now. "I will help you, Raj. However, you need to promise me something."

"What?"

"That when we leave the compound you'll stay close and do as I say. If anything should happen, your safety and security comes first…no heroics, please."

"I can do that," Raj said. He was not too sure he could live up to that, but he was going to pretend he could.

"Good. Now I'm going to get a few things together. I'll come for you soon."

Raj nodded and left the room without any other questions. Hari opened up his laptop again and looked at his screen. Rita Banik's information was on the screen before him but as he read it something occurred to him. Her case was almost identical to that of Raj. Rita had been the youngest of five siblings and like Raj, grew up in the slums. Her entire family was massacred and everything they had owned had been stolen. Two of the children went missing presumably having escaped, herself, and her older brother. When Rita resurfaced six years later, she told authorities she and her brother had been hidden away by several men and when her brother had fought to get away they had killed him. She didn't know why she had been released, but no one believed her story. By that time she was seventeen years old and was living in the slums where she met Tarun Banik whom she later married.

As Hari continued to read he began to wonder about the link between the two families. Then he saw it, the clue that tied them together. The year Rita and her brother were abducted a man named Mr. Rajesh Chaudhry adopted a young boy, roughly the age of her brother. Mr. Chaudhry was a politician and a corrupt one at that. He was untouchable and none of his crimes could ever be tied back to him. Hari had met his adopted son, Vikash "Vik" Chaudhry, who had taken over the business since Rajesh passed away two years ago.

Pulling up the picture of Rita and Vik, he could see the family resemblance with the strong chin and prominent cheek-bones. It was clear that Vik was Rita's brother and had allowed someone to kill her, but why? Did he not remember that Rita was his sister, and if he did, did he not care? Hari was unsure but he was going to find out eventually.

Shutting his laptop down, he went over to the drawers to the left of the window and rummaged within. Where they were heading, he knew they had to be inconspicuous and that meant they were going to be doing a lot of walking, and with the way the weather was he knew they couldn't leave without the proper preparation.

He took out two vials of polyvalent serum and put them in his pocket. If the Naja Naja, Indian cobra, was out they could very well cross paths and he wasn't about to die from a snakebite.

After a few minutes had passed, he opened the door, bag in hand, ready to leave. Sitting across the hall was Raj, and Hari could not help but feel the pain he felt. Family is everything and when it's gone it leaves an empty space that can never be filled. That was why Hari had built this place. He would give orphans like Raj the life they deserved and make sure they were reintegrated into society rather than forgotten and abandoned as they otherwise would be. Seeing the look of determination in Raj's eyes, he knew it wasn't going to be so simple with this one.

Chapter 7

As they walked, Raj wanted so badly to ask Hari what was happening. He felt as if he was hiding something from him as if to protect him. He was going to find out eventually, so why not just tell him now? It was frustrating that they were holding back the information he needed to trace those who killed his family. He deserved answers and he shouldn't have to fight to get them. What was so dangerous about the truth?

"You seem bothered," Hari said. Once again, he seemed to be reading Raj's mind.

"I am," he admitted. "I sense that you know something, but you are refusing to tell me. It's driving me crazy! I have every right to know what is going on. Surely, not knowing is worse than knowing? Wouldn't you want to know if your family was slaughtered in cold blood?"

"How would knowing help?"

"Because," Raj said, attempting to find the words he needed to win this argument. "If – if I know everything you know it can help us figure out who is behind the death of my family and the Banik family. Maybe with all that information, I can get the closure I need."

Hari stopped and turned towards Raj. He couldn't deny that he had a point, but he was not going to tell him anything. Now was not a good time. "Right now I know as much as you do. I also know that you're not looking for closure – you are looking for revenge. Don't be foolish and become a killer. The moment you become responsible for another person's death, it will haunt you for the rest of your life."

"There isn't much of a life left for me anyway; I've lost everyone I ever loved." Raj didn't let his head drop, he held it high. He knew what he wanted. "Something tells me you understand what I'm going through – do you?"

"I haven't always been this way," he admitted. "Everyone has a dark side and sometimes people let that part of them loose and before they know it, they are consumed by it. What starts out as a one-off, an act of revenge or self-defense becomes them and they can't stop. Lucky for me that never happened, but I have seen and done…things."

Looking down at the muddy path, Raj wondered whether to believe Hari or not. After everything that had happened, all the lies and the secrecy, he was done putting his trust in others. For all he knew, this was just another lie to convince Raj to stop what he was planning.

As they walked, the sporadic rain drops increased in tempo and size, running down his forehead and over his lips like tears and Raj looked up at the ever present clouds blotting out the sky. They reflected the gloom in his heart, he supposed.

"Have you ever wanted to – to *kill*?" Raj looked up at Hari and waited for a reaction to what he knew was a sensitive question, but his face, glistening with the light film of rain remained expressionless.

Raj had already given up hope for an answer when Hari spoke next. "Yes I have and before you ask the obvious – yes I have and believe me, I still remember it as clearly as if it happened minutes ago. It never leaves you."

"Whoever you killed must have deserved to die."

Raj stopped walking and stared off across the fields towards a wall of rain in the distance that hit the ground at an angle. It would soon be upon them but Hari didn't seem to care as he said, "We as men should not be the judge of who lives and who dies. The fate of another is not our decision and the moment we commit the act of murder we tip the balance in favor of chaos. The more chaos we allow to reign, the worse things will get. Wrong deeds breed more wrong deeds – someone has to break the cycle or we're all doomed."

Raj said nothing and a silence settled over the two of them, the only sound the hiss of a light rain as it fell about them. Raj pondered what Hari had said. Hari had a point, but to him he felt that by killing the man responsible for all this death he'd be helping to restore the balance, not unsettle it further. Once the threat was eliminated, the danger would be gone and people would no longer live in fear, at least that's what he hoped.

They pushed further and further into the vegetation and soon the grass they fought through towered over them a sea of dark green. Dangerous animals lurked within the jungle and the surrounding grasslands and Raj trod carefully as they moved, praying that they made it to the factory in one piece. They made it through the grassland unscathed much to his relief and soon, the factory appeared before them, silent and still as if it were in mourning for the loss of its master. His father never allowed him back in this part of the forest because he declared it was much too dangerous, but they arrived without any issues and he knew that the answers he so desperately wanted were inside.

To his surprise the factory was deserted. His father's right-hand man would normally have overseen the factory in his stead but there was no drone of machinery to greet them. Perhaps they were in mourning.

Regardless of what it was, Raj didn't have a good feeling about it. The rain was turning to a misty haze around them, coating their clothes with the fine droplets as they stopped at the entrance and listened. The air was loud with the absence of life. Raj looked up to the top of the worn metal staircase and blinked as his mind superimposed an image of his father on the scene, descending the stairs towards him, a smile on his face. This was the life his father wanted for him, but Raj turned his back on it. He wished he could tell his father he was sorry for how he had acted, but he knew that could never be.

"Where's your father's office?" Hari asked his voice low as if afraid he might attract attention in the silence.

Raj pointed to the stairs before leading the way. Each step they took on the metal stairs echoed throughout the rest of the factory, a dull, mournful sound. They came to his father's office and Raj paused on the threshold, staring into the room. His father was a meticulously organized person and seeing his office in such a state of disarray was disconcerting. His father had always told him that being clean and organized was the key to success. His father would never leave his office in such a state. Someone else had to have made the mess, but why?

"Do we even know what we're looking for?" Raj scanned the room, not knowing where to begin.

"Documents…papers," Hari said over his shoulder as he began to search a filing cabinet. "He may have hidden them well so this could take a while."

Raj remembered something then and moved to the wall, searching it for the panel he knew his father hid his secrets behind. He'd seen his father closing the panel one day but kept it to himself, knowing he was not meant to know and thinking it didn't matter anyway. It did now.

The panel was beside the window and Raj moved to where he thought it should be, running his fingers along the seams of the wood-paneling searching for a trigger of some kind. He found it easily, and pulled away the panel to reveal a single folder stashed within but as he reached out to take it, he heard car doors slamming. Looking out of the window, the hair on his arms prickled as he saw a black SUV, exactly like the one Mahi had mentioned.

"It's them, they know we're here!"

Hari pulled Raj away from the window, pushing him against the wall. "Is there another way out of here?"

Raj shook his head slowly, fear and anger fighting for precedence within him. They couldn't find him, not now, he wasn't ready. "Not from here," he said staring at the doorway.

"In here, quickly," Hari hissed. They climbed into a cupboard and managed to pull the door shut just as a voice echoed throughout the factory.

"Burn this place down. Leave no trace of the Varma's."

Through the crack of the cupboard doors Raj saw a man enter the room and begin emptying a can of gas over the contents of the office. He stopped to answer his phone a moment later.

He greeted whoever it was. "Yes sir, we're here and we're about to burn it down," he paused for a moment. "No we couldn't find the file, but it was not at the Varma residence either–yes, well if he hid it here, it will be burned and all the evidence will be destroyed. That is, if he actually found anything."

He slipped his phone into his pocket and continued to pour the gas throughout the rest of the room. As he was leaving, Raj looked down at the folder and wondered what was so important about its contents.

The voice from earlier rang out suddenly, "Burn it down."

It took only seconds to feel the warmth of the fire as it began to lick at the building. Raj watched as the fire made its way into his father's office and he was paralyzed with fear. With the fire blocking the exit, they were trapped. Hari threw the door open and leapt out, before turning to Raj.

"The window," he said heading for it, Raj's hand in his.

"But what about them, they're out there.

"They won't hang around for the police to arrive, they'll be gone soon."

Once the sounds of the SUV's engine had faded, Hari took him by the forearm and they ran across the blazing room at the window. Raj couldn't have hesitated even if he wanted to. Hari pulled him through and they fell amidst a shower of glass to the ground below.

They landed on the gravel below just as the rest of the window behind them shattered from the build-up of heat. Hari tugged Raj after him, and they ran into the jungle leaving the raging fire behind them. Raj hugged the folder to his chest knowing it was his last chance of finding out the truth. They could take everything from him, he didn't care anymore. He had what he wanted – the means to find them and punish them.

When a burning pain flooded Raj's shin, he wasn't too concerned. It was probably just a graze from the fall to the gravel but as he looked down, his eyes spied a Naja Naja slithering away into the jungle, from where he stood.

"Oh no!" Hari caught Raj's limp body as he fell. The snake's deadly poison was now working its way through his veins, filling him with death.

Chapter 8

Everything around him had suddenly gone dark and cold. He felt as if he was falling into an abyss and his heart was beginning to race. His chest was gripped within a vice that refused to let go and he wanted badly to be free from the pain. He stopped fighting it then and a golden shaft of light appeared before him. In it he saw his family standing watching him. They were smiling.

"Mom," he stammered. He couldn't believe what he was seeing.

"Am I dead?"

His mother shook her head and smiled warmly at him. "No, son, you are alive, for now. You can make the decision to stay here with us or you can go back to living."

He thought about what she was saying. He looked to his father who had his arms wrapped around his mother and saw his aunt sitting there smiling at him. It was tempting to stay here with his family forever. The serenity of this place was something he had never felt before and he had nothing to live for anyway. He had everything he needed right there with him but something tugged at him.

"I don't know what I want," he admitted. "There is nothing for me in life other than the pain. I'm so sorry about what happened to you all. You didn't deserve it."

"No one deserves to be murdered," his father said. "But we cannot control the actions of another, now can we? And you are wrong, Raj; you can mold yourself to become anything you want to be if you go back. The sky is not the limit, because if it were there would be no footprints on the moon."

Raj smiled and he looked to all of them. "Do you know why you died?"

His parent's shared a look and he knew they were not going to tell him. Why would they? Then his mother spoke to him, her voice soft. "Everyone makes mistakes and sometimes their decisions lead to worse things. If you were to know why we were on that hit list, it would destroy you. Some questions are better left unanswered."

"Why did the Banik family have to die then? Was it because of your choices or the fact they were being hospitable to me?"

"The person responsible for all of this would kill a person without a second thought. He hides behind his power and his mask of good intentions. But behind closed doors he is a monster and he is not someone you ought to cross paths with."

"I swore I would seek revenge and destroy the person responsible for your deaths."

"Don't go on the path of revenge my son, for all it leaves is constant anger and sleepless nights. You have a bright future in front of you and you should use it to your advantage. Find a beautiful woman while you go to school, start your career, settle down, and then start a family. That is the life you can have if you put aside your need for revenge"

"And if I want to stay here?"

"That is a decision for you to make." His mother smiled.

He pondered his options. He had risked his life for a file his father compiled and it was worth killing over. He had come so close to knowing the truth and he was going to find it. He might have a chance to find happiness, but he was going to eliminate the person responsible and afterwards he would get on with his life.

"This is not my time," he said after a few minutes had gone by. "I'll be back and we can be together again."

His mother smiled. "I love you," she said. His family faded away then, like a departing morning mist.

Back in the darkness for only a moment he awoke to a faint light shining overhead. After a moment, he realized he was in a room and he could hear someone snoring. Sitting up, he looked across the room and saw Hari sleeping.

Attempting to get out of bed, he found that he was unable to. He felt weak and began to wonder why. They had been running in the deep vegetation and then he remembered trying not to pass out. He had succumbed to unconsciousness however.

"Hari," he called out.

Hari stirred and opened his eyes. "Hey Raj, thank goodness. I was getting worried."

"What happened to me?"

"You were bitten by a snake while we were running, you passed out and I had to carry you here. Thankfully, I packed polyvalent serum but you've been unconscious for several hours. I wasn't sure if you'd recover but it looks like it worked."

Raj lay down and thought for a moment; then he remembered the file. "Did you look at the file?"

Hari was silent for a moment before speaking. "I did Raj and you should look at it too. Maybe you will see something I did not."

Perplexed, he wondered what he meant by that. Everything in that file should be obvious and they should know immediately who was responsible. Otherwise what was the point?

When Raj tried to get up, he found he was much too tired and weak to even want to get up. He felt as if his eyelids were weighed down with lead and soon, he began to drift off.

Hari watched as Raj drifted back to sleep. He waited a moment while Raj settled and then got up to leave the room. He was exhausted and needed his own bed. When he opened the door he saw Sai and Ash in the hallway.

"Is Raj going to be alright?" Sai inquired.

"He'll be fine." Hari rubbed at his eyes which were uncomfortable from extreme tiredness and lack of sleep. "Listen, I'm exhausted. I'm going to get some much needed rest. If I am not up in a few hours be sure to wake me up."

They didn't ask any more questions and he was grateful for that. He needed to be alone for a few hours without any interruptions.

He made his way down the hall and down the stairs, returning to his room. The file was hidden in one of the drawers and he had not yet looked at it. His first priority had been Raj and now he had the ability to work without the worry.

Sitting down at his desk, his fingers traced the bottom of a drawer. He found the outlet and pulled down. When he felt the file on his fingers he pulled it out and closed the hidden door. He flipped the file open and the first thing he saw was a picture of Mrs. Varma, only she was bruised and it appeared she had suffered a dislocated jaw. The picture was stapled to a few sheets of paper. Shaking off the urge to close his eyes, he began to read.

April 10 1990

Alka Varma was brought to our facility today after a brutal attack in her home. She has suffered a dislocated jaw, two fractured ribs, and a broken wrist. She also appears to have been raped. We have prescribed medicine for Mrs. Varma and she will be back next month for a check-up.

Hari shook his head, dismayed at the injuries. He stared at the date for a moment his tired mind forming a connection. Raj was born on December 28, 1990. The dates didn't match up. That meant that Raj was not Dev Varma's son or so it appeared. But perhaps that wasn't the case. There was more though so he continued to read on, hoping he was wrong. It was the last thing Raj needed to hear after everything he'd been through.

May 12th, 1990

Alka Varma has returned for her check-up and she is healing up quite nicely. We have given her a pregnancy test and she has tested positive. This would be her fourth child. She had requested the DNA test from the rape kit, but the sample went missing in the lab. We have requested that she checks in with us bi-monthly so we can check up on her baby.

He began to piece together the facts in his mind. Were Dev Varma and his family murdered because they figured out who was responsible for raping Mrs. Varma? His eyes hovered over a section of the page, *"this would be her fourth child,"* – Raj had never mentioned any siblings. His hand closed around his phone as a realization struck him wiping away his tiredness as if it hadn't existed.

Picking up the phone, he dialed the only person he knew would have the answers. On the fourth ring the call was answered. "Hello Hari. Is everything alright?"

"No, everything is not alright," he snapped. "You have three children right now don't you?"

There was a slight pause before he answered. "Yes, I have two boys and a daughter."

"Those are *not* your children are they?"

"Excuse me, Mr. Sidhu," he said harshly. "But where do you get off making such accusations?"

"Raj Varma and I went to Dev's sugarcane factory and we found the evidence Dev had compiled, but one of the first documents in here is that of Alka Varma. In here it says she was raped and that she was going to be having her fourth child. How come Raj of all people does not know he has siblings?"

There was nothing but silence and that was when he finally answered. "Dev and his wife were put into danger because of decisions that Dev made."

"And how are those decisions related to Mr. Vik Chaudhry?"

"It does not start with Vik," he said with a sigh. "Back when Dev and I were at the university, we made an investment with Mr. Rajesh Chaudhry and he took us for everything that we had. Dev was unable to recover from that since he was wiped out of everything, but I survived because I came from a wealthy family. Anyways, Alka was expecting their first child, and after Dev lost everything, they had no other choice but to go back to the slums. Later they found out that Alka was carrying twin sons, and Kavi and Varun were born in 1982.

"Dev wanted to be able to provide for his family and so I gave him money to start up his business and the sugarcane factory was officially up and running in 1985. Even after getting his feet back on the ground and being given a second chance, he was still wanting revenge from Rajesh since he stole his money, but there was no way we could prove it. But Dev was persistent. He realized Rajesh had been laundering money to the underworld criminal gangs – and that Rajesh was the leader of the Silas gang.

"He worked relentlessly to get more proof, but he took a break from his crazed desire when his daughter, Siya, was born in 1987. Alka was becoming sick though and he took time off from everything to tend to her. During her year of illness, Rajesh paid them a visit, but Dev had prepared in advance. He had the kids go over to the Banik residence for the day. His suspicions were confirmed when Rajesh threatened him and his family.

"After that he came to me with the favor of a lifetime and seeing as how my wife was unable to have children, we accepted. We took them in, we home schooled them, and now they are studying at the university. All three of them know the truth."

"So why would the Varma's keep Raj?"

"Of their reasoning I am unsure especially because Raj is not a Varma."

"So you don't want him to find out about it?"

"No. See Dev and Alka did not want any more children and Dev was heading back to work. I would send them constant updates of their children, with pictures, and even report cards. The summer of 1989 Dev and Alka visited us and it was a happy family reunion. But Dev pulled me to the side and told me he wanted to go back after Rajesh and I told him not to, but he still had this obsession with getting even. Then Rajesh's son, Vik, made a visit in April – he raped Alka…maybe to punish Dev I guess. That made Dev stop for several years, but he started digging again in 2005 and he told me he found something."

Hari thumbed through the papers as he listened, seeing the evidence before his eyes. "Well now that Rajesh is dead, isn't it pointless to seek vengeance?"

"Well Vik took over after Rajesh died, he was killed by a hired gun. Anyways, Dev found something other than the illegal gang activity; he found out they were also trafficking women and children. He knew too much. They couldn't let him live."

"How did they know that he had learned something?"

"Someone must have been watching him and maybe tracking his activity."

"What am I going to do now? Raj is going to want to look at this file."

"Take out all the important documents and give him the rest."

Hari shook his head – he did not feel right about this. "He deserves to know the entire truth."

"I guess that is up to you then. Just know the truth might destroy him, especially when he learns his biological father raped his mother and that they kept that from him."

"I'll decide whether he should know or not. Thank you for your concerns. And if you want to meet Raj, feel free to do so. He might want to meet his family."

"Just call me when that boy knows the truth and tell me how he reacted."

There was a click as the line disconnected and he shook his head. He was going to do the right thing, but he began to wonder if the truth was the right thing in this instance.

Chapter 9

Stirring from his sleep once more, he realized he was alone. His strength was returning now and he managed to sit up. There was a file on his bedside table and he recognized it. It was the same one they had taken from his father's office. Despite the all-consuming need to know the truth about his family and his part in all this, he was hesitant to open the file and see what lay inside. Now that he finally had the chance, he was fearful of what he might find.

He had to know. After everything he'd been through, to turn away now would be foolish. He pulled the file towards him and opened it. The contents of the folder were confusing and at first he didn't understand what he was reading. The name had been blacked out and was unreadable. There were only about twelve sheets of paper along with a few notes his father must have taken.

Reading his father's notes, he began to understand what might have happened. There were no names mentioned or any idea of how the information had been obtained which was unusual. Whoever it was, they were laundering money to human trafficking and to a gang in the suburbs. So this was why his father had been killed. Somehow though, it felt like it wasn't enough.

He set the file back down and got to his feet. He felt lightheaded initially but managed to steady himself while the feeling passed. Picking the file up, he slipped it underneath his mattress and limped over to the door. As he pulled it open he was half expecting to see someone, but he was alone.

He walked then, not knowing where he was going or why. Rounding a corner, he came face to face with Hari who seemed preoccupied, almost as if something was on his mind and Raj wondered if he knew something more.

"Raj," he said, surprised. "Are you okay? You know you should really be in bed for the next two days. Do you need me to get you something?"

"I think I'm okay, just a little confused."

"About what?"

"The file you gave me. It's just a bunch of transactions. Did my father really investigate something so ridiculous that it got him and the rest of my family killed?"

"What your father uncovered was not ridiculous. He found out that women and children were being trafficked and he was compiling evidence to prove who was behind it so they could be stopped."

"Why would my father even care? I mean, that sounds awful and all, but he could have just looked in the other direction."

"As to why he would care and continue to dive into it I am unsure. That's just what was there even if it seems like it wasn't worth it. It obviously meant something to your father."

Raj's head dropped. "Well thank you for helping me," he finally said. He began to walk away, feeling like they wasted their time but then something occurred to him. "You'd be able to figure out who this person is, right?'

Hari shrugged. "All the important information was blacked out and we can't really do anything without a name."

Hari looked down at his feet and Raj knew then that things weren't going to get any better as far as finding his family's murderer. There was nothing else to say on the matter. "Thanks though. I guess I am going back to my room then."

"I'll bring your dinner to your room later if you'd like…"

Raj nodded and walked away. He needed to be alone. He felt this sinking feeling in his gut as he remembered his father's factory being burned to the ground. Everything was gone, and for what? Just a few pointless documents, the trail had gone cold. Raj couldn't help but feel there was more to the story, but maybe he just wanted there to be something more. Or maybe Hari was hiding something from him, but despite only knowing him for a few short days, Raj had his doubts about that. He seemed to have Raj's best interests at heart – but was that a good thing? Was he still protecting Raj from the truth because of that?

Back at his room, he slipped underneath the covers and stared up at the ceiling his mind racing. Somewhere out there, the man responsible for killing his family was still on the loose and there was nothing he could do about it.

Chapter 10

November 14, 2008

Several months had passed and for Raj it seemed like a lifetime. So much had changed and he felt powerless to do anything, so he did his best to get on with his life. Sitting in the library, a book lay open before him and he scanned the contents. He had never had an education like this before in the slums and he knew he was on the path toward bigger and better things. It still felt wrong though, to put everything behind him as though it hadn't happened. He remembered the dream and how his parents had urged him to get on with his life. Were they right? Should he just forget what happened to them? It was just a dream, wasn't it?

Sitting between Sai and Ash, he felt their eyes on him. They were itching to talk, but Mr. Khanna, their teacher, would have none of it. He often told them that talk and study didn't mix well, not if you wanted to get anywhere in life. Raj was inclined to disagree but he wasn't going to argue with a man in his twilight years.

As he was looking for the answer to Mr. Khanna's latest question, Raj began to feel a throbbing behind his eyes that spread to his temples, on and off, on and off like someone was crushing his head between two giant hands. This studying lark was new to him and his brain wasn't yet used to it, he guessed. When Mr. Khanna cleared his throat in his usual manner, Raj was relieved.

"Pencils down, children," he said. "Now you have all being doing rather well in these past few weeks…" he said with a pause and Raj felt the entire class analyzing the meaning of his words, their tired minds working together for one last push. "You deserve a little break." A murmur of cheer sped through the class.

"Tomorrow is Saturday," Ash chimed in. Mr. Khanna smiled and nodded. "Yes. See, by taking breaks from your studies, your mind turns to pudding. No one wants a mushy brain now do they?"

Everyone shook their head and he nodded. "I will see you all here on Monday, but first I have a task for each of you to complete. It is due by the end of class on Monday but trust me when I say you don't want to slack off. On Monday you will not have any time to finish this whatsoever. So I'm giving you the choice to manage your time wisely or to suffer the consequences when Monday arrives and I find you've been neglecting your studies."

Just like that, he handed out some sheets and Raj waited until his back was turned to roll his eyes. This was a complete waste of time, but then again, he didn't have anything he needed to do this weekend. As he was reading the first few questions, he wondered what it would be like to have a head filled with pudding. As Mr. Khanna walked away, Sai nudged him.

"So, we've heard a rumor."

Raj looked at them, waiting for their answer. When Sai remained quiet, Raj pressed him. "What rumor?"

"That Priya has taken a liking to you."

Looking across the room to where Priya and Rani sat, he shook his head. Priya was a girl he figured most boys would fight over like dogs over the last bone. It wasn't her long black hair or seamless skin though that attracted Raj. It was her eyes. They seemed to drink you into them – but there was also something powerful in those dark eyes and Raj wondered why such a beautiful girl would like him.

"Liars," Raj finally said after he tore his gaze away from her.

"Why would we lie?" Ash asked.

"I don't know, but that is Jadu's younger sister. I bet he wouldn't want me anywhere near her."

"Last I checked, Jadu was accepted into the university – he isn't even here! Plus I'm sure he wouldn't mind if you two started dating."

Shaking his head, he couldn't help but admit he would love to date her, but he couldn't. He'd lost too much. He was not about to develop feelings for another person, not after he'd lost everyone he'd ever loved. Something about the way his heart sped up when he looked at her told him it was too late for that. As he was thinking, Sai and Ash stood up and gestured for Rani to follow. In doing so, Priya realized they were alone and she smiled shyly.

Raj felt as if he was paralyzed from the waist down and he couldn't move or breathe. As she approached him he realized they'd never really spoken until this moment. He panicked, then, his mind freezing and turning all thoughts to ice.

She sat down across from him and smiled. She didn't like the traditional garb of typical Indian women and instead, she preferred jeans and a V-neck shirt. Today she wore one that was bubble-gum pink and it looked good against her skin.

"Hey Raj, you alright?" she asked, her voice small, eyes on him but lowered slightly.

"Fine I suppose. What....what about you?" Raj groaned inwardly, he sounded like a damn robot.

She smiled at him not bothered by his monotone reply and Raj's heart almost jumped out of his chest. She didn't seem to mind how awkward he was. He began to tremble as her right hand touched his. Her touch was electrifying and he wanted to get up and run away.

"I'm better now," she purred. "I have a question for you though."

"Okay," he said slowly. "What's that?"

"Do you want to," she stopped and Raj's heart rate accelerated, drawing beads of sweat out onto his brow. He would do anything she wanted, he knew. "Would you want to date me?"

He was still in shock that such a pretty girl was into him. "Sure, but how does that work in the compound? I mean I don't really know how to be romantic in the first place and this sort of limits things, you know?"

Priya nodded. "I understand. How about this? You come and get me from my room and we will just hang out like you would with the guys, but different."

"Different how?" Raj realized just how amateur he must have sounded but Priya seemed delighted by his naivety.

He couldn't help but notice how she thrust her chest out as she straightened, withdrawing her hand from his. "You will see."

She began to walk away and he watched her go. She was beyond gorgeous and maybe she could be something to him. However, he wasn't sure if he was ready for a relationship quite yet. But when a pretty girl approaches you for a date, you don't say no.

After several minutes had gone by, he finally got to his feet and pushed in his chair. Walking to the other side of the room, he sat down at a computer and started looking at the local news. It was as if the encounter with Priya had awakened a need within him. He sifted through the murder and trafficking reports, knowing that somewhere there must be a link to his family's murderer.

As his eyes roamed the pages of news, scanning for keywords he heard someone enter the room. "Hey," he heard Ash say.

"Hey Ash. What's up?"

"Nothing," he said as he walked over towards him. He pulled out a chair and he sat there watching Raj as if he was something of interest. "I was just curious to know if Priya asked you out."

Raj turned towards Ash. If he wasn't mistaken, Ash seemed too interested almost as if he was jealous. "She did and it was kind of awkward to be honest. I really don't know what to think about all of it."

"Well, you should know that Hari really doesn't approve when the boys and girls mingle."

"Mingle? You don't mean just regular interaction, do you?"

"No, I mean…sex."

Raj rolled his eyes. "I don't plan on *mingling* with Priya. I guess she just wants to get to know me better and I agree with that. I can assure you I'm not really looking for anything else."

"Well, what happens if that is something she wants?"

Taking his eyes away from the monitor, he looked at Ash and shook his head. "I don't know what will happen then, but I can assure you I really am not interested in that sort of thing - especially not now. I need to get back to this but if anything were to come up, you will be the first person I contact, okay?"

Ash nodded and walked away. Raj wondered just how much Ash liked Priya. He hoped it didn't come between them in future. He brushed the thoughts away and continued to scan the news. A news report leapt at him from the screen. A single mother and her two daughters had disappeared from their home and were reported missing. Raj wondered what the whole point of this was, but he was beginning to understand why women were the targets. They were sold like livestock and probably treated worse. He wondered how his father began his search into this, but he was going to finish what he started.

Printing out the news report he decided the best person to show it to would be Hari. He was hoping this last piece of information would be enough to get Hari to help him. Thus far Raj had learned that Hari was not the head of this organization, he was just the face. He wondered if the person in charge would be able to help him.

Pulling it from the printer he began to walk down the winding halls until he arrived at his bedroom door. He pulled the file from underneath his mattress and slipped the report inside with all the others he'd gathered. He felt the urge to find Hari then and went to the one place he knew he would be. He found him in the small study, a book propped on his chest and he was reading.

"Hey," Raj said to get his attention.

"Raj, what's on your mind?" Hari asked as he sat up. He placed his bookmark and closed the book before setting it down.

"How did you know something was on my mind?"

"Call it a lucky guess. What is that?" he gestured towards the folder.

"Well, ever since we got the file from my father's factory I've been looking into the trafficking and I'm trying to figure out which gang might be involved."

"So what information have you gathered so far?"

"I really don't have too much information. All I do have is a list of missing women and children and a few murders of people who were related to the missing people."

Hari reached for the file and took it. He began to read through it and Raj watched as his brow furrowed. "This is very elaborate, Raj," he said, his voice filled with surprise, "it seemed like it took you weeks to piece it all together. My only question for you is what do you want to do now? I mean, you still don't even have an idea as to who is behind all of this."

"No I don't," he admitted. "But I am sure someone who has a lot of connections would be able to figure it out. Plus, I already did the grunt work."

"True," he said slowly. "I will talk to someone about this, Raj, and I should give you an answer by Monday."

"Thank you, Hari."

Raj headed for his room and on the way he saw Priya standing in her doorway and she smiled warmly at him. "Where are you going?"

"To my room," he said.

"Before you go there, would you be able to help me with something?"

Raj noticed she was fidgeting with her shirt and he wondered what she really wanted. "Uh, sure I suppose." Stepping inside, he saw her room was very similar to his own, but she had a few other personal touches. "So what am I helping you with?"

That was when he heard her door lock and he turned towards her. She was biting her lower lip and he was not too sure what was happening. "Do you really not know what I'm hinting at?"

As she approached him he began to feel excited and yet very uncomfortable. "I suppose I don't."

She was only inches from him, her moist lips brushing against his, invitingly. His heart was racing madly and he flinched as he felt Priya's weight against him, pushing him down onto her bed. He landed on her bed and she wasted no time in meeting his lips with her own, her legs straddling him, holding him in place. Raj's mind fought hard to resist her but as she pushed against him, wanting him, he gave in to the rush of desire taking over his body. His hand slid down her back, caressing her flesh and he began to kiss back, letting himself slip into the well of passion.

Chapter 11

Hari read through the entire file and when he'd finished he wished he could just convince Raj to stop, to make him believe this was not worth pursuing. The only issue was this *was* and he understood the importance. However, he was not too sure any of this could be solved. Regardless if all of this information led back to Vik Chaudhry it could still mean that the secret Hari decided to keep could get out. He didn't want Raj to get hurt in this process and yet he felt as if there was no other way.

Putting the file back together, he headed to his room. He knew he would have to make this phone call, but he didn't know what would happen after he got everything off of his chest. Part of him didn't want Raj to go down this path, but even if he tried to prevent him from doing so, he knew Raj wouldn't stop. It was something very human, the need to know, the search for answers and in Raj, the need was stronger than most, he saw.

Setting the file down, he looked at his phone. He really didn't want to pick up that phone. He wished he could just sweep it all under the rug and walk away. Finally he got up his courage, picked up the phone and dialed the number.

A man answered.

"This is Chandu speaking."

"Hi Chandu," Hari said. "Would I be able to speak to your superior please?"

"In just one moment," he said.

Waiting on the line, it seemed as if several minutes had gone by, but in retrospect it was only about thirty seconds.

"Hari," he heard him say. "What's wrong?"

"Raj is relentless," he said. "He's been researching and scouring the news reports. I think he's beginning to connect the dots. I am unsure of what we are going to do."

"I think you should distract him from what he is trying to accomplish. This is not a path he should be going down."

"You don't think it's time to tell him the whole truth?"

"Not now. Honestly, I don't think he will ever have to know."

"Don't you think he deserves to know about his heritage?"

"I think that boy deserves the kindness that only lies can give, regardless of whether you feel the same or not, I couldn't care less. As for this information he uncovered, you can fax it to me and maybe we can do something about it."

"You just don't want Raj's help, do you?"

"No. He seems to be a very smart young man and he has potential to do other things. Obsessing over this is not good for him."

"Do you plan on making an appearance?"

"For now, no, I would rather remain behind the scenes for a little while longer. I will come when I feel it is the right time."

Hari nodded as he put the phone down. He didn't really like all these games but he knew this was what needed to be done. Hopefully with Raj accepting this place he might become distracted. If all went well, Raj might realize his own potential and maybe he would stop on his own, but Hari knew he was not going to force him to do anything.

*****

Raj was gazing into Priya's eyes and she smiled warmly at him. Now that it was all over he somehow felt as if it had all been worth it. He moved closer to her and kissed her neck. She giggled as he deftly slipped on top of her.

"This was not what I was expecting for a first date," he admitted.

"Hopefully we'll have more dates like this then."

"You do realize I shouldn't even be here, right? I mean. I did not even ask Jadu for his permission or anything."

"We don't need his permission to do anything. He technically isn't even my brother either. His mother took me in after my grandfather passed away. I was seven. So don't feel too bad about it. Plus I am sure you didn't even care about the rules anyway."

"Well initially I wasn't really *thinking* about anything. You sort of distracted me."

"Seeing as how I'm a girl, I guess that's my power to wield as I may…and I may just use it again." She ran her finger along his jaw, stopping at his lips.

Smiling, he kissed her jaw and made his way up to her lips. "How come you wanted me?"

"You are different from the other guys. You have something that drives you and you have goals you want to accomplish. The other two are clueless, and besides they aren't nearly as attractive as you are either."

"Where does that leave us then?"

"We are in a relationship," she stated. "But Hari can't know. He has this rule that we aren't supposed to do anything, but it looks like we just broke that."

"Why does he even have that rule?"

"I'm not too sure. Maybe he is afraid it could distract us or something. I really have no clue. It is what it is though."

"I guess we should be getting ready then. Dinner will start soon."

She nodded and he moved away from her. Retrieving his clothes from the floor, he looked at her and smiled. She was beautiful and she was his. As he was putting on his pants, she walked over to him and he paused. His eyes were transfixed below her neck and she smiled. Her forefinger went to his chin and he looked into her eyes.

"Maybe after dinner you can have some dessert."

"Well we will surely see."

After he got dressed, he crept out of her room, checking to make sure the corridor was clear before leaving. Heading down the hall he made his way to his room and opened the door. That was when he saw Sai walking down the hall towards him and he waved casually.

Raj waited for Sai to approach, not wishing to arouse his suspicions but Sai clearly wasn't born yesterday. He looked Raj up and down, his eyes widening before pushing past Raj and walking into his room. He turned as Raj closed the door.

"So I guess you and Priya did it then."

"Did what," Raj said as innocently as possible.

"Seriously? You are glowing dude and I'm sure it is not for any other reason."

"Well, you're right. Is there a problem with it?"

"No. It's just that Ash sort of has a thing for her."

"Then why didn't he tell me anything?"

"Because he blew his chance with her and plus Jadu didn't want the two of them together."

"Jadu isn't technically her brother so I don't see where he gets off making those sorts of decisions for her."

"It's the principle and you just fucked up. I mean, if Jadu finds out about the two of you, he will have your head on a spike."

"Yeah, sure. Look, he's not here and ever since he left he hasn't even tried talking to her. So I really don't give a damn and I'm sure he is with plenty of girls. I mean certain things are traditional, I know, but not everyone abides by that anymore, things are changing."

"Well maybe you should. I mean, can you even see yourself with Priya?"

"See myself with her how?"

"If you were her husband and she was your wife. I mean do you ever want something like that?"

"Truthfully I haven't thought about it long term and maybe now I should. I mean she is beautiful, smart, and into me. I mean what else is there?"

Sai frowned and dropped his head dramatically. "Jeez, I have no clue. If you can list anything else, you know where to find me."

Raj watched as Sai left and he rolled his eyes. He didn't understand why he was getting so upset about all of this. He really didn't care at this juncture. He had more important things to attend to like getting ready for dinner.

Chapter 12

Sitting at the table, he poked at his peas. He wasn't that hungry this evening. That was when he saw Hari standing there and he seemed to be very concerned. He motioned for Raj to follow him with a wave of his hand.

Pushing his plate to the center of the table, he got up and strode over towards him. He wondered if Hari had somehow learned about Raj's actions that afternoon, and if so, he wondered what his punishment was.

He suddenly realized just how stupid he'd been. What had he been thinking, just jumping into bed with Priya? He hoped Hari was lenient. In Hari's room as Hari seated himself, Raj wondered if he should just tell him. Raj wanted to blurt out everything that had happened but he didn't have a chance because Hari began to speak. "I have made a phone call and right now it is being looked into. I faxed them copies of your findings and I should be hearing back soon."

"So what I found was important?"

"Yes, and you did excellent work might I add. And now there is another reason I brought you here," Hari paused and it seemed as if he did not know what to say or how to say it. "Is there something you are not telling me?"

Taken aback, Raj felt his cheeks redden. "That depends. I'm not sure if I should, I might get into trouble."

"Ah, so the rumor is true. You and Priya have done the dance then."

Raj remained there, frozen. He was surprised how nonchalant he was about the entire ordeal and he wondered why his head was still attached. "I thought we got in trouble for having, uh – relations with someone of the other gender."

"That was an old rule, plus the two of you are going to be heading to the university by next year. It's okay to have a distraction." Hari seemed pleased.

"I have been told it is not the traditional way of doing things and frankly I feel bad for that. How do you even know?"

"I cannot say. Just know, Raj that you should marry before you have children."

Raj looked away, ashamed. If Hari knew and Sai knew then that meant the others knew too. "Well obviously, I just – I thought you would have been angrier, and I really don't know where I stand with her. It's just crazy really. One minute we were friends and the next we were..."

Hari nodded and even grinned which was unusual for him. "I'm glad you found someone. Now, anyways, I also brought you in here for another purpose. I'm going to be leaving the compound for the evening. There is something I must address in the slum and if something is to go awry this is the number you can best reach me at."

"Why do you need to leave?"

"I will tell you tomorrow afternoon. Now, go and take care of the others."

Raj didn't move. "How come I am the one being left in charge?"

"Because they look up to you and I know I can trust you to get the job done."

"Ash has been here the longest."

"Ash is not as reliable as you are. Plus, he has a hot head and doesn't always think things through. At least I know I can trust you."

Raj left the room and headed for his own room then but something about the way Hari had acted played on his mind. He was hiding something from him, he knew it. Raj was determined to find out what that was.

*****

Several hours had passed since Hari left and Raj had finally broken free from the dozens of questions the others were asking him. As he made his way into Hari's room, he sat behind his desk making himself comfortable in Hari's chair. He needed to think like Hari for a moment. If he had to hide something where would he put it? The desk was in the center of the room and it faced the door. There was a picture of a family, most likely Hari's, and there were several other things it was obvious he kept dear to his heart.

If there was anything of importance, it would be on this side of his desk, surely. He ran his fingers along the edges of the drawers feeling for a trigger but he felt nothing. Next he started opening the drawers of his desk. As he opened a drawer there was a knock at the door. Raj froze. Why would someone be knocking at Hari's door? Hari was not here and they all knew that.

Before he could hide, the door opened and Priya stood looking in at him in her nightshirt.

"Raj," she said. "What are you doing?"

As she walked in, he got up from the desk and he shut and locked the door behind her. He watched the way she was playing with her hair and he knew he could not be distracted by her. However, he knew he could trust her and that was when he spoke.

84

"Hari is hiding something from me and I'm going to figure out what it is."

"What could he possibly be hiding from you?"

"I don't know truthfully. All I do know is that it is here somewhere and whatever he has hidden is worth lying to me about. I mean, the night we left here together we found a file my father had and I swore there was more to it than what he later gave me."

"Do you mind if I help you look?"

He shrugged. It couldn't hurt and another pair of hands was welcome. Raj went behind the desk again and he began pulling out the rest of the drawers, until finally he was at the bottom. As he pulled it out, the drawer snagged on something almost as if there was something prohibiting it from sliding all the way out.

Getting on his hands and knees, he traced his fingers on the bottom part of the drawer and he found a place he could slip his forefinger into. As he pulled it down, paper came crashing out. Picking it all up, he put it on the desk and that was when he saw Priya was watching him intently. It was obvious she had more than sex on her mind.

"What? Why are you staring at me like that?"

"Nothing…I just want to know if you see this relationship going anywhere."

"Of course I do. I mean, I am slightly confused by it all, but you are terrific and I don't think any other person will make me happier."

"Do you really mean that?"

"Yes, of course I do."

"Alright, so, can you promise me something then?"

Raj felt uncomfortable making promises. He was unsure of what she could possibly want from him, but he nodded anyway knowing she was about to tell him. "Whatever you find, can you promise me it won't ruin our relationship?"

"Why do you think it would be something that would ruin our relationship?"

"I have been here since I was eleven," she began. "If Hari hides something from us, it is to protect us."

"Protect us from what?"

"From destroying ourselves of course. There have only been a few that have lost someone by the hand of another. When that happens, you cannot help but want revenge. If Hari uncovered something that is of any importance and he hid it from you, it is to protect you. Plus, the person Hari answers to has great influence over him."

"So if there is something revealing about why my family was murdered, you don't want me to get angry about it, you mean?"

"You will get angry about it. There is no way to avoid that. I am just saying not to be rash about it. I mean, I know we haven't really got to know one another as well as we should have, but I care about you. I don't want you making the same mistake."

Raj paused and looked at her. "Same mistake…"

"Yes," she said. "When I found out the truth about my father I escaped the compound and I was on this crazed mission to kill the person responsible, but it was futile. The people who are in control of this are untouchable and I just don't want you to be out there all alone with hatred in your heart."

Glancing at the stack of papers, Raj made his decision. He was *not* going to look at the files today, but one day he hoped Hari would be able to disclose the truth to him. Granted, Raj was angry though he knew that he shouldn't be. His parents hid these same secrets from him and the only reason Hari did the same was because he cared for his well-being.

"I promise," he finally said. "Plus I don't think I am ready to know the truth yet."

Priya smiled and kissed his forehead. "Thank you," she whispered.

Chapter 13

Hari was deep in the suburbs. There was little light in the streets at midnight and every shadow and outline seemed to leap out at him. What he was about to do was making him jumpy and he wanted to get it over with as quickly as possible. When he had been summoned to meet this person, he knew at once what they'd be asking of him. He would be making no such deals. The man he was meeting this evening had once been something else until he had been corrupted and molded into an obedient puppet.

Arriving at the door, he saw two large men standing outside. They both had their guns ready and he stopped before them. "I'm here to meet with your boss," he said to them.

Without saying a word, the two of them stepped aside and he walked into the room. This place was spacious and he felt as if there were others here, but of course none of them would be here of their own free will.

Before him, he saw a grand living room and he stepped inside. Already sitting was Vik Chaudhry and he was accompanied by a woman. She was wearing little to no clothes and she looked terrified. Hari felt sorry for her. She was clearly a slave and Hari knew that if he were in her position he too would be terrified considering present company.

"Why did you call this meeting, Mr. Chaudhry?"

"I know you are the one harboring Raj."

"What is it that you know of Raj?"

"I know he is my son. After all, his mother and I had a splendid day together. Actually two nights, and pleasurable they were indeed. Right before she died she remembered who I was. Too bad she struggled though. Maybe she would have chosen me instead of that fool Dev if she relaxed and had the full experience."

"I realize you are a sick individual. Especially after you had your sister and her family murdered, but you have no right to Raj."

"I don't have a sister," he said simply. "And I have every right to my own son."

"He doesn't even know you are his father. Dev Varma raised him as his own. As far as Raj is concerned, Dev is his father. And you had a sister. Her name is Rita – Rita Banik and you had her and her family killed."

"What makes you believe I have a sister? I mean, you must have me confused with someone else."

"No, there is no doubt. Maybe you should read this and then make your decision," Hari said as he tossed the papers on his desk.

"I'm not interested in knowing who she is or claimed to be. Now there is another reason I asked you here today. This is a message for your boss. If he decides to continue getting in my way I'll hire someone to hurt him where it hurts the most – his family. I'm not afraid of ordering the death of those who stand in my way and he of all people should know that."

"He's untouchable to even you and you know that. And here is my message for you Vik, if you have any goodness left in your body you will stop these abductions. I see what you're doing and I promise you, it won't end well if you continue in this vein, I'll find a way to bring you down."

"Give me Raj and I'll stop all of this."

"You think I'd be stupid enough to trust you?"

Vik smiled wryly and shook his head. "At least you recognize my lie. I just hope you realize that Raj *is* my son and he is going to end up like me given time for his birthright to germinate, a cruel man with an unquenchable hunger for power and success. Raj is my spawn and as such, I'll see to it that he becomes every bit as charming as me. I'm a dab hand at manipulation, I'm sure you'll agree."

"Raj is a better man than you will ever be. You've already taken enough from him. Now, if this meeting is over, I believe I should be leaving."

"It is not over yet. I have a gift for you Hari." Vik smiled, his veneers gleaming like rows of straight white tombstones.

"A gift…" Hari said, straightening. "What could you possibly have to offer me?"

"Your sister," Vik replied, the smile dropping away in an instant.

Hari froze. He didn't want to believe it but knowing just how despicable Vik was, it was possible. His sister had gone missing eleven years ago. She had only been sixteen when she and her friend had disappeared. Hari had prayed that she had simply run away for a better life and was now living in safety and comfort. Seems his prayers had gone unanswered.

Vik snapped his fingers together and one of his thugs appeared, dragging his sister into the room. She was so much thinner now and her hair was cut short. She appeared to be drugged and to his horror, pregnant. His heart twisted as he looked at her. The things they must have done to her, he couldn't imagine. She looked miserable and he just wanted to reach out and tell her everything was going to get better from now on.

"See, she is no longer of use to us. Besides, she always fought back. Now this is my offer. I'll give her over to you if you give Raj to me – come now, you shouldn't have to ponder the value of such a trade, it's obvious you want her back. My son for your pregnant sister, it's the easiest deal you'll ever make"

Hari felt trapped. His sister, Hema raised her head to stare at him, a flicker of recognition drifting across her drug-sunken face. She was nothing like the girl he'd known, full of life and adventure with dreams of being like her mother, running a household, caring for a family – her dreams had been simple, yet Vik had crushed even them. There was still hope for her though. He wouldn't abandon her, not now. Little did he know but Vik had sealed his own fate this night. Hari would play him at his own game.

"Fine, you can have Raj, but don't hurt my sister."

Vik smiled, the thin line lacking any sort of mirth. "I can assure you that I won't harm her so long as you keep your word. I want Raj here on Sunday night. Bring him here. If you lie to me or attempt to trick me, your sister will pay the price. Are we understood?"

"Yes," he said.

Vik motioned for someone to escort him out. Hari pondered his options and knew that he had no other choice but to tell Raj the truth now. There were two lives at stake now and he would need Raj's cooperation if they were both to be saved. Raj had to know the truth. Somehow, Hari thought that even if this hadn't happened, he might have told Raj the truth eventually. Who was he to withhold such information? Who was he to decide what Raj felt and didn't feel? The appearance of Hema had changed everything. Vik was going to pay dearly.

Free from Vik's goons, he began the long drive home. He knew he would have to take the long way around to ensure he wasn't being followed. The journey would take a couple of hours but Hari didn't mind. He would also use the time to develop a plan to take Vik and his scum down. His jaw ached but he couldn't stop biting down, every muscle and sinew in his body was taut and bunched like the surface of an oak tree yet he found it was impossible to relax. Hema...after eleven years of hard labor, being used over and over again by all those men until she was nothing but a slack-faced waif, she was ruined. He wondered if she would ever be the same again, if she would even remember who he was. Like a bulldozer, driverless and unstoppable, he crushed plants and small trees, inflicting his anger on them again and again. He would kill Vik and all his men. There was no other way. Now he understood Raj.

After driving for about fifteen minutes, Hari parked his vehicle in a secure place and like a lunatic free from his strait-jacket, he ran through the night, the veins in his temple undulating as his heart pumped adrenaline soaked blood around his body. Revenge would be his...

Chapter 14

Hari was nowhere to be found. Raj had waited for hours but it seemed as though he had vanished from the face of the earth. When Hari finally appeared, he was wild-eyed and moved in a shuffle. His face was lined with grime and there was a hollowness to his eyes that Raj didn't understand.

"Is everything alright?" Raj asked.

Hari answered, his voice distant and lacking its usual strength. "I suppose everything is fine for now. I just need some sleep. I'll be awake in a few hours and you will be the first person I talk to."

He watched as Hari slinked towards his room and he wondered what was wrong. He wondered if Hari had finally realized he should be telling him the truth about everything, and Raj was still upset with him for not being entirely forthcoming, but there was nothing else he could do.

Walking up to the fourth level he wondered if he should do some more research, then again he also had an assignment that was due on Monday. Homework was such a drag, but he knew it all had to get done eventually.

He sat before the computer and powered it up, promising himself that he'd only briefly scan the news before moving on. Then an article about a regional businessman caught his eye and he stopped to read it.

Mr. Tapan Butala has been popular in the media for over three years but had fallen off the radar for the past six months. During his interview with the press last Wednesday he explained that he got away from the limelight to recover after the recent loss of his family. He was reported to have mentioned that the weight of the loss had become too much to bear and that he needed some time out with his pregnant wife, Katherine Butala, whom he met in the United States a year earlier.

After he was bombarded with questions, Mr. Tapan Butala announced his imminent partnership with Mr. Vik Chaudhry in a business venture that would bring in more income to poor areas as well as jobs which would greatly help slum dwellers in Mumbai (Dongri and Dhavari) and Pune (Kamgar Putala). They know the slums have been struggling with crime and both men believe that with a strong focus on redevelopment and restoration, brought about by their new venture, crime in the slums might be reduced and better homes and sanitation provided for the poor in the area.

Mr. Tapan Butala also announced that he would be a candidate for the upcoming elections in 2010 and would be a candidate for the Prime Minister's post. This sudden change in direction has left many shaking their heads. Once a successful entrepreneur and philanthropist, he now surprisingly aims to delve into the political melting pot which is equally perturbing when one considers his background. Accused of murdering his own parents three years ago, it beggars belief that he is now even considered as a serious candidate for the seat of Prime Minister. His main potential competitor is Krishnaji "Krish" Wasimrao, a respected political figure and this will surely add to what is already an intriguing story. We'll keep you posted on further developments. This is one election that will be scrutinized carefully.

Raj finished reading the article. There was something about it that bugged him but he wasn't quite sure. He also wondered who all these people were. Raj barely knew anything about the very successful and powerful men and women in India, and maybe it was time he knew.

Recording each of their names, he searched for Mr. Tapan Butala first. The name was vaguely familiar. He found another article and clicked on the hyperlink.

One is only to assume there is no such thing as coincidence and now we put that theory to the test. With the untimely death of Mr. Mahesh Butala and his wife Tanu, one is to wonder if their ambitious son, Tapan, is to be held responsible. We must remember that four months earlier Tapan's only brother Rohan Butala and his whole family was killed in a fatal car accident. And now Mahesh and Tanu have been brutally murdered in their own home. This leaves Tapan as the sole inheritor of the Butala fortune.

According to police reports it seems as if the only person responsible for these murders would have been someone working on the inside. The security system to their beautiful home had not been alerted and it was Tapan who had called the local authorities claiming he walked in on the murderer, a man wearing a black stocking over his face.

Authorities claim that this is a sensitive matter and as of now they will not be pressing any charges against Tapan. Instead they are looking for a suspect even though they have one right under their noses.

Raj shook his head. He did not believe that Tapan Butala was innocent because it appeared he gained a lot from all the deaths in his family. It also seemed he knew someone who controlled the police department. Raj remembered what Inspector Kumar had told him. How he said they would be watching him and Raj's stomach twisted itself into a knot. He did not know how to react or how to feel. All he knew was something was not right here.

He pulled up an article on Vik Chaudhry and began to read:

Today Mr. Rajesh Chaudhry adopted an orphan boy from the Kamgar Putala slums and he has named him after his great-grandfather, Vikash "Vik". He said he had been walking through the slums for charitable purposes when he found the young man starving and orphaned. It appeared his parents and younger sister had been murdered and no one had the heart to care for this young boy.

We mustn't forget about the cruel side to Mr. Rajesh Chaudhry. Granted, all of the reports filed against him were dismissed but it is curious that several dozen individuals took the time to file reports against him, especially seeing that one of them was from his late wife's brother who has mysteriously disappeared.

Raj went on to read an article that had been published years later.

Mr. Rajesh Chaudhry has been receiving death threats from a young Dev Varma. He claims that Mr. Chaudhry swindled him out of his life's savings and now he has absolutely nothing. His wife, Alka Varma, is expecting twin sons and now they have moved from Dongri in Mumbai to Pune's Kamgar Putala slums. As of now, Mr. Chaudhry denies ever stealing or scamming money out of anyone. We decided to speak with Krish Wasimrao, another young man who had reportedly lost most of his money to the same scam. He reported that he too invested in a business that Mr. Chaudhry was about to launch, but it turned out to be false.

As of now, there have been no further investigations into the matter.

When he checked the date, Raj felt sick. The article was first published was March, 1982. He was not even born until 1990. He had a sinking feeling in his stomach. He was not an only child. How much had Hari held from him? It seemed he had so much more to learn but part of him was beginning to regret even bothering. It only made him feel worse and after everything, that was the last thing he needed.

He hugged his knees to his chest and pondered his next move.

Chapter 15

Hari stirred from his sleep. He realized it had only been about two hours since he'd collapsed on his bed exhausted. Regardless, it was enough, there wasn't much time. He had to make a phone call, before he could do so though, his own phone began to ring.

Picking it up, he waited for a moment before speaking.

"Hari, I'm waiting down here. Please allow me access to the compound." It was Krish.

"Yes sir," he said as he hung up the phone. He wasn't expecting any visitors, especially since hours earlier he'd told him he wouldn't be visiting for a while.

Rubbing the sleep from his eyes, he opened the false wall and walked downstairs to the first level. He peered through the peep hole and saw that Krish was not alone. He opened the door and was stunned when he saw Hema standing before him, her eyes clear and drug free but quickly filling with tears.

"Hema," he mouthed and embraced her, pulling her close but he was careful not to hurt her. She was barely more than a bag of starved bones. When he pulled away from her he saw a gash across her forehead and she was cradling her wrist.

"How…how did you…" Confused, he closed the door.

"It was easy. Vik called one of my lines to speak to the obvious mole I had in my nest. I learned where he was hiding from what I gathered from the conversation, and sent my men in to dispose of the vile snake."

"So, is Vik dead?"

"No he got away, but he's injured. He will resurface eventually and now I must know why you would agree to meet with him without consulting with me first."

"There was no time to inform you. I needed to see what he was offering. He offered me an exchange - Raj for Hema."

"Well now you shouldn't worry. Vik has gone in to hiding for now and when he resurfaces, I'm sure he'll be out for revenge so we need to be ready. Of course, there is always peace before a typhoon, so don't let your guard down. He'll be waiting for that."

Hari nodded. "Alright, I'll be careful." Hema was not looking well and appeared to be getting worse by the second. Picking her up in his arms he motioned for Krish to follow him. "So do you want to meet Raj then?"

"I might as well get this all over and done with. There is no reason for Raj to face all this in the dark, especially since he is going to university next year."

Opening the false wall once more he set his sister down on the bed and motioned for Krish to sit down. "Did you find anyone else there?"

"You mean those abducted women? Yes, yes we did indeed. I alerted the media first and foremost so now Vik's name will be smeared throughout the media. They found missing women and girls in his home and I wonder if he is going to be able to get out of this."

"I doubt it."

"Only time will tell. So tell me what there is to know about this young man, Raj?"

"He is smart and independent, has real initiative. He's even gone as far as to start a relationship with one of the girl's here in the compound."

"What, he's gone against your wishes and you aren't pulling your hair out over it? What's gotten into you, Hari?" He laughed.

"Well seeing as how this is the first person to make him truly smile, yes."

Krish nodded. "When would I be able to meet him?"

"Now, if you would like."

Krish agreed and Hari took him to the library where he knew Raj would be sifting through news reports as always. Hari remembered when Krish built this complex. It was to be a refuge for those who had nowhere else to go. Krish had once run this place himself and when Hari was experienced enough he had taken over from him. This was a safe haven and this was the one thing Hari had done right.

As they walked along the corridor, they came face-to-face with Rani who still seemed to be half asleep. Hari greeted her and she grunted in reply, not looking up. Her nose was buried in a book and she was making her way to the dining room for breakfast. Hari smiled as he watched her go, pleased that she was so focused. She'd make something of herself one day. It was nice to feel hopeful for a change and Hari began to feel an unfamiliar lightness to his step that had been missing for a long time.

Ascending the steps to the library they saw Raj sitting at a computer. He was pillar-like, rigid and frozen as he stared at the screen in front of him. He glanced over his shoulder at them as they approached and Hari saw concern in his eyes.

"Raj," this is—"

"Mr. Krish Wasimrao."

"How did you know that?" Krish said; his voice a whisper.

"I know because I found an article about you written in 1982. My father and you invested with a Mr. Rajesh Chaudhry and he lost everything, but you were fine since you came from a wealthy family. It also said there that my mother was pregnant with twin sons. So I must know - the twins you adopted a year later, are they my brothers?"

Krish sighed and nodded slowly. "I adopted Kavi, Varun, and your sister Siya."

"Why?" Raj pressed; his voice harder than granite.

"Because when Dev was seeking revenge on Rajesh Chaudhry it put him and his family in danger. They asked for my help."

"And how come they didn't do the same for me?" Raj was relentless.

"I'm unsure," he answered.

"Why are you here?"

"Because there is someone outside this compound who is looking to harm you and those you love in order to manipulate you."

"Who exactly would that be?"

"Your biological father," he said.

Raj looked him dead in the eyes and he shook his head. "You're lying?"

"We are not lying to you. Your father Dev upset Vik Chaudhry and not only that; he found information about him that would bury him for life," Krish took a deep breath before continuing.

"He raped your mother to prove a point and when she had you, it was clear that Dev was not the father, the tests proved that."

"I don't care if he was my biological father or not. He raised me like his own! Why are you choosing to tell me this now? Why does Hari have to listen to everything you tell him? How do we even know we can trust you?" Raj's voice filled the library, echoing through the space and into the corridor. He was growing angry.

"That's up to you," returned Krish. "Either you trust me or you don't. It is that simple. I own and fund the running of this complex, protecting you and the others from harm." He stopped speaking then as if changing his mind about justifying his position.

"If you want any more proof about anything, go to Hari. I'll be staying at the compound for the next few days so when you calm down I'll be more than happy to talk to you."

"You were afraid I would walk the same path as my father," Raj said evenly. "You thought if I learned the truth that has been masked that I would become some villain. Well you are wrong about that and I will prove it to you."

"You are not mistaken. And the reason we are telling you this now is because of something that happened last night. You should tell the boy," Krish said turning to Hari.

Hari hesitated, ashamed that he was about to reveal yet another lie. "Yesterday I was asked to go to Mumbai to meet with Vik Chaudhry. He knew you were in my care, but he did not know your exact whereabouts. Anyways, he told me he was going to get to you and ensure you emulated him. He was very sincere about it. He wanted you in his palms so he could mold you like clay. He knew I would not agree to his terms if there was no bargaining chip in it for me." He paused for a moment. "He had my sister who he had been using as a sex slave. That was who I was to get if I traded you in."

"So what happened?"

"I happened," Krish said. "I got rid of most of those working for Chaudhry, but he disappeared. For now, everything is alright until he comes out of hiding."

"You should look up Tapan Butala. I read he is aiming to become the Prime Minister following the upcoming elections in 2010, and Vik Chaudhry is helping him. If he was to go anywhere, I would put my money on him hiding in a property belonging to Tapan Butala. I mean where else can he go?"

Raj fell silent waiting for their reaction. He hoped they'd act on his advice and in fact he felt they owed him. Though he was relieved they'd finally told him the truth about his father, he was angry that they'd kept it from him for so long. It didn't surprise him that he wasn't Dev Varma's son or that he was the son of a crook and a murderer. Nothing surprised him anymore and perhaps that was for the best.

"So are you going to act or not?" He asked Krish.

Krish nibbled at a fingernail. "I suppose we've no choice but it's a delicate situation. Tapan Butala is a highly respected man."

"The money going to Tapan Butala for his election is dirty money, isn't it?"

"Yes it is, but still, we need to tread carefully."

"Then I'm going to help you guys however I possibly can."

"Good, then stay out of my path, Raj. I know what I'm doing and this is a mess Dev and I got into years ago. We'll be the ones to fix it."

"We'll?" Raj said, shaking his head. "Dev was my father and in case you're forgetting, he's dead, remember? Killed by that animal on the loose out there..." Raj fell silent, his emotions welling up for once, rising to the surface like trapped air finally released, pushing outwards to freedom. He held them in check. It wasn't time.

"I need to think. I'm..."

"I know Raj," Krish said. "This can't be easy."

Raj stood up and left without saying goodbye. It wasn't that he was angry, he was. It was that he could feel a wetness threatening to spill over onto his cheeks. Not now, not yet, it was too early.

Chapter 16

Raj sat on the foot of his bed as he began to think about everything that had been said to him. He'd finally heard the truth and now that he had, he didn't want it. It hurt too much to know that he'd been fighting for a lie. What he thought had been his life had been nothing more than a cover up, a charade. It wasn't all bad, he tried to convince himself. His mother had loved him all those years despite the knowledge of how he had come to be. His father cared genuinely for him despite the fact he was not his own. And now he understood why his aunt looked at him the way she did. He was the only one they kept and his family died because of the man who was responsible for all the original pain.

He let himself fall back onto his bed. Everything from his childhood seemed to make sense. Certain times he had overheard his parents speaking and it had never made sense to him until now. He wanted to know his siblings and he wanted to get a fresh start in life, but he was unsure how to do that. A knock at the door interrupted his thoughts.

"Come in," he said somewhat bitterly.

Standing there was Priya again. Despite the feeling of happiness she brought to him he did not want her there, not today. However, he wasn't going to make her leave because in that moment she was the only thing that made sense to him.

"Is everything alright?"

"No, but you don't need to know what's going on in my head."

Sitting down next to him, she reached out and took his hand in hers. "I care what's in your head, Raj. You can't go on bottling up your emotions, if you do, they'll tear you apart one day and everyone around you."

"Well I learned the real reason my family were murdered. I know now that I'm not an only child. I also know the man I called my father all these years is not my biological father. I just feel like something exploded in my chest and I honestly don't know how to feel. Usually I get angry and break things, you know, like a toddler, but now I realize how ridiculous that is."

"Raj you've grown up a lot in the past few months you've been here. When something tragic happens we all change inside and see the world through new lens. We perceive things differently and now you know things you never did before."

"I vowed to get revenge," he admitted. "I still want to, but the only thing is I don't know how to go about it. I'm so lost right now."

"How about you focus on the present? Right now there is nothing you can do but focus on the present. You will even the playing field out eventually, but for now, just relax and take your time. What you do today will prepare you for tomorrow. You should know that by now. Mr. Khanna only says that twenty times in a class."

Raj couldn't help but smile. He had to admit he had never felt this way about anyone before. He could barely open up to his own relatives yet here he was and here Priya was and she was still a stranger, but he trusted her. He looked into her eyes and couldn't help but notice the feelings he had – feelings he once swore he would never have. Maybe you can't control who you fall in love with – it's deeper than that.

"Priya, you know you make the world seem a much nicer place than it really is right?"

"I hope so," she said and smiled, "because you deserve to see things brighter and better. Plus you are not in this alone either. I am sure Hari and the others would be there for you. We are sort of a family."

Raj kissed her gently. "I like the sound of that."

He took Priya's hand in his. This young woman beside him was the reason he wanted to be a better person and now he was beginning to understand why they told him about his heritage. In war the leverage someone has on you tends to be those you love. Sociopaths, however, love no one. The only way to defeat one is to completely and utterly destroy them. That was something Raj was not yet prepared to do but he was considering it. He might not have a choice. It was that or be hunted down and harried for the rest of his life.

"I think we should go get something to eat," Priya said, searching his eyes trying to pull him back to reality.

Nodding, they both got up together but Raj's mind was elsewhere. There was too much to process, but he knew he would understand it all by the night's end.

As they walked into the dining room he saw Ash sitting there. He was poking at his eggs. He seemed upset about something. He had no idea how Ash had ended up in the compound but he wanted to know. Maybe there experiences were similar, Raj thought, maybe not.

Sitting down beside Priya he got a plate and put some parathas and scrambled eggs on it. He wasn't that hungry, but he knew he was going to have to eat eventually. He heard someone else coming up and turned to see Krish, Hari and a young woman entering the dining room. Raj wondered if the woman was Hari's sister. She was a person Hari was willing to rescue no matter what the cost. They exchanged smiles as they sat down near Raj.

"Raj, are you feeling better than you were an hour ago?"

"Yes," he said. "It's going to take a little time for all the information to settle in."

Krish nodded, as if he understood what it was to deliver bad news. Raj wondered how his siblings were despite the fact they were older, of course. He wanted so badly to meet them because they were all that was left of his family. He even wondered if they knew about him and about how he was conceived.

"What do my siblings do?"

"Well, Kavi went into politics and Varun went to America to start his career as a doctor. Siya just started college a little over a year ago and she is planning on becoming a nurse."

Raj could not help but hear the pleasure in his voice. "What do they know about all this?"

"They know nearly every detail, except for the name of the man who harmed your mother."

"Is that for their protection?"

"It's for the protection of everyone, of course. Your siblings are just as headstrong as you are so being forthcoming with them about every detail was not wise. Or so I believed."

"Do I have any nieces or nephews?"

"As of now you do not. However in a few years' time that should change."

"Would I be able to meet them?"

Krish looked over at him and nodded. "When you leave the compound to go to university I will make arrangements."

"Does anyone know that your children were adopted?"

"No. We altered your mother's documents to make it look like it was my wife. She's never in the public eye because she enjoys staying at home and working there. The media didn't focus too much on the children because there were more pressing matters at hand."

"Why are you running for Prime Minister?"

Krish chuckled. "You have dozens of questions, don't you? Well, it's because the time is right in my career to make a go of it. Nearly twenty years ago I vowed to never become a politician and look at me today…Anyway Raj, who is your friend?"

"This is Priya and she's more than just a friend."

"Is that so? Well you are astonishingly gorgeous, young lady. Now, what do you want to do for schooling?"

"I want to be a nurse. I feel that is something very important, and someone ought to take care of the sickly."

"That's very true, and what about you Raj?"

"I want to go into business like my father did, but I don't have any plans to rebuild the sugarcane factory."

"So go where the wind takes you, young man." Raj liked the sound of that.

Chapter 17

July 30th, 2009

Sitting in his room, Raj realized this was going to be his last night here and it seemed so surreal. He hefted his bag and stared at the contents until a shadow fell over him. He looked up to see Sai standing in the doorway. Earlier, he had attempted to convince him not to go, but Raj wanted to leave. This was going to be a fresh

Chapter   in his crazy life and it was going to be starting off wonderfully. His girlfriend was going with him to meet his siblings and he was becoming the kind of person he'd once only ever dreamed of becoming as a boy in the slums.

"So is there anything I can do to make you stay?"

"No." Raj smiled. "And remember, you are the one making the choice to stay here with Rani. I mean if you want to change your mind you can still submit to the university and they might be able to take you."

"You're right, but Rani is my only blood relative and I don't think I can just leave her here. What if she falls in love with another student? How would I be able to stop it from outside the compound?"

"Put cameras in her room," Raj teased.

Sai rolled his eyes and put his hands in his pocket. "So is there anything you're going to do before you head out?"

"Actually I'm going into the Kamgar Putala, Dongri and Dharavi slums with Priya and Hari for a final good-bye. It's about time I face my fear and get over everything that happened."

"Even if you never get over it, at least you're stronger now than you ever were before."

"Damn straight," Raj said with a smile.

Raj got up on his feet and decided to take one last stroll throughout the compound. He found Priya and went to her. She had a bright smile upon her face and Raj saw Hema's baby girl in her arms. She had been named Amla, which meant *pure*. Hema had started her life over here and it seemed as if everything was looking up for the better. Thus far no one had found Vik Chaudhry, but Raj knew it would only be a matter of time before he resurfaced. He was honestly hoping Vik had died somewhere; that way, this feeling of serenity would last. Raj was dreading the day it ended, but he had Priya and they were going to be there for one another.

"I want five," she said as she cuddled with Amla.

"Are you sure?" Sai asked. "I mean, babies tend to make people fat."

Priya slapped Sai's shoulder with her free hand and giggled. She then turned her eyes to Raj and he nodded. "Yes, but we have to be settled with our careers first."

She smiled brightly and nodded. "If that's the only stipulation, then that's okay with me."

Raj smiled and kissed her forehead. "I'm just going to take a walk, you know, say goodbye to this place. I'll come and get you tonight."

"You know where to find me," she said and walked away.

"See," Sai said. "I want something like that eventually... a beautiful girl wanting me to father her children."

"You'll get there eventually," Raj assured him. "Plus, relationships take a lot out of you, but I promise you it's worth it."

"Yeah well you're a natural kiss-ass. But you know, I guess that's something only quality guys can do."

"Exactly," he said, with a wink.

Walking towards the living space they saw Hari sitting there. He was looking out at the bright sun that seemed to be sitting atop the canopies. He seemed relaxed, and yet he was somehow tense at the same time.

"Is everything alright, Hari?"

"I suppose so," he said. "I got off the phone with Krish about ten minutes ago. According to his personal informant, Vik is staying in Central America for the time being. He might not be able to come back here for the elections."

"And why is that?"

"Do you really have to ask?"

"Of course I do."

"Well, Krish has damaged his reputation by exposing his illegal activities, but there are other goons here that still take orders from Vik. Also, Krish has the entire file your father had been putting together. If Vik returns, that's his insurance policy. However, Tapan is still around, and if anything he's just as bad as Vik."

"Well, right now it seems to be low key, especially since there is less reported crime in the slums these days."

"I'm glad to see you're being positive Raj," he said as he was getting up. "I owe you a proper good-bye, Raj. It's been a pleasure having you here with us and we're going to miss having you around. Promise to keep your nose clean and to be prosperous."

"You could have told me that after we visited the slums."

"True, but I would rather say it now anyways."

"Do you want to eat a light meal before leaving?" Hari inquired.

"No. Not right now. I think I want some time to myself right now."

Hari nodded and left him with his thoughts. Glad to be alone for a moment, Raj dropped down onto the couch. Yes, he was sad to be leaving but it was for a life that he had once thought impossible. The pain of losing so much might never leave him but in a way, it had strengthened him and prepared him for the life before him. He had lost much, yes, but through that loss, he had gained so much and the future looked bright for him.

*****

Raj and Priya loaded all their belongings into the car and he smiled at her, an excitement he'd never felt before washing over him. "Are you ready for our new adventure?"

She nodded and grabbed his hand. As they were walking back inside for one last good-bye, Raj realized how much he was going to miss this place. He never thought he would be part of another family or call somewhere else his home, but today this was his home and this was his family. Despite the pain his family's murder brought him, it was amazing to see how he had regained what he thought he could never have again.

Finally, they were ready to part ways with the compound and he and Priya walked hand in hand behind Hari. They climbed into the car and Hari set off for the Kamgar Putala slums where Raj's journey had begun. Raj wondered whether his family was watching him from heaven as he was moving on in life. He also wondered if his siblings ever thought about him. Finally, his thoughts once again strayed back to the future: what would it be like to live a normal life?

The trip to Kamgar Putala took about two hours from the complex because of heavy traffic on thc roads and when they arrived, the slum seemed like a different place. It seemed happier and the people were mingling and speaking to one another as they enjoyed the good weather. It was a far cry from the hell hole he had once called home. It seemed like the entire atmosphere had changed since Vik had left the area and Raj was happy for everyone. It was as if everything was where it was supposed to be. Maybe this is what life was like when there was no evil in the world.

Stopping outside the gates, they exited the car. Raj looked to the place he had once called home and the feeling that washed over him was one of emptiness. It seemed as if no one dared to cross over the threshold and he wondered what was inside.

His hand tightened around Priya's as he stared at the empty shell that had once been his home. He wouldn't – couldn't go back there again. It held too many ghosts for him. He turned to Priya and kissed her on the forehead. "I'm ready to meet the rest of my family now."

They walked back to the car hand and hand but before they left, Raj wanted one last look. He turned, and as he did so, he noticed a glimmer of light flickering in the distance.

It wasn't over yet.

*****

Two hundred yards away, a figure lying prone watched his prey, his trigger finger itching to take them both out. He was pleased with himself. He had done well. When he'd received the call earlier from his inside man, telling him they would be visiting the slums, he knew it was his chance to prove himself to the boss. Vik was a hard man to please but today there was no doubt in his mind that he'd more than show what he was capable of. When he'd called Vik to inform him Raj would be visiting the slums for one last goodbye, Vik had been clear: "Get to the slums and call me when you have them in your sights."

He watched them as they climbed out of the car, arm in arm. They weren't going anywhere, just standing there ripe for the killing. He pulled his phone out and dialed Vik's number, hoping he'd give the order. He was through waiting and watching.

"What is it?" Vik sounded impatient, irritated.

"Raj Varma's here. He's with his arm candy. Who should I take out?"

There was silence for a few seconds before Vik answered. "Shoot the girl. One shot kill, you hear me? You take out the only person he loves and he's left with hatred, something I can work with. Kill her!"

"Yes sir," he said as he hung up.

Looking through his scope again he waited patiently for his chance and when he saw it, he pulled the trigger.

Chapter 18

Raj did not know how or why he reacted. Something didn't feel right. There was no time to analyze it. It just *happened*. He leapt, pushing Priya to the ground but before they reached the ground, he heard a distant *pop pop* and then they were sprawled in the dust, eyes stinging, mouths full of dirt but Raj felt something else. A searing pain in his shoulder and a dull heavy weight as his arm flopped at his side, useless. Blood splashed into the dirt at his side, making a noise like a dripping faucet, a consistent pitter patter.

Luckily they'd landed behind the parked car otherwise they'd be dead. He checked Priya and she was fine but she stared up at him, fear in her eyes as she saw the wound in his shoulder, blood running off his fingertips in a steady stream. Someone screamed but to Raj it was a distant sound as though heard through glass. He was fading fast, his consciousness slipping away when he felt himself being tugged upwards and thrown into the back seat of the car. Priya slid in beside him, staying low and as Raj fought to stay with her, the car started and accelerated, throwing him back into the seat.

He heard Hari dial a number.

"Krish," he said out of breath. "Raj's been shot, it must have been a sniper, one of Vik's. The wound doesn't look too bad but there's no way I can get him to you now. I need to get him fixed up and away from these maniacs."

Hari fell silent for a short while, listening to the voice on the other end of the phone. Then he hung up and turned to Raj. Raj, still managing to hold on to consciousness, gasped, "That bullet wasn't meant for me," he said between breaths. "It was for Priya."

Hari's brow furrowed. "Why would he…" he stopped as something occurred to him.

"He wants to remove those you love, your only weakness."

"But love isn't a weakness." Priya said, shaking her head.

"It is to Vik," Hari said, "If he removes you, the last person Raj cares about, Raj will be filled with hatred and that's exactly what Vik wants, another soldier for his army."

"Then he doesn't know Raj very well, does he," she said. Raj could hear the sarcasm in her voice. "He should have sent me a card first explaining all of this. I would have worn my best dress."

Raj smiled up at her, pleased at her strength. He could see how worried she was yet she was still strong. It was a side of her he hadn't seen.

"I'm going to need you to apply pressure to his wound," Hari said, "just to keep as much of that blood from leaving his body."

"I can do that."

"Good."

Raj was almost gone, a darkness slipping over his vision. Just before he fell away into the nothingness he told Priya something he once thought he might never say. "I love you."

*****

The sniper quickly packed away his gun and fled the scene. He'd missed and that meant he was in deep trouble. Vik would hire another hired gun to kill him, the man that never missed; unless he found a way to finish the job. Vik wouldn't take his failure very well, he knew. He couldn't return home empty handed. Then he remembered. There was still one last person he could go to for inside information on Raj. Broken hearts and money were powerful things indeed, especially where leverage was concerned.

Chapter 19

Back at the compound, Priya was on the verge of tears as she watched Hari move Raj into their small infirmary. She knew Raj would be fine, he was strong. Taking in a deep breath she wondered if this was really worth it. She loved Raj but she didn't want to be a target for some sick man's game.

Stepping away, she walked down the hall to her room and ran into Rani. "What's the matter?" Rani asked.

Priya attempted to stop the flow of tears, but she was unable to do so. There was so much going on and she wasn't sure how she was going to deal with it all. This was Rani though and she knew she could trust her with this information.

Taking her by the hand, she walked into her room and they shut the door. "Raj took a bullet for me. Someone knew we were going to be in the slums and they tried to kill me."

Rani was stunned. "Is he going to be okay?"

"Yes, but I don't know if I'm going to be okay. I love him, but I don't know if I can be with him. I don't want to be a target because some lunatic doesn't believe in love. What's with that, anyway?" Priya slammed her fist on her bed again and again, frustrated. "Why can't he just leave us alone to get on with our lives?"

"You can still beat him. You can get out of this, the two of you and start a new life elsewhere, away from that animal and his cronies."

"Maybe," Priya said, sobbing. Then she realized there was no point in hiding the truth any longer. "Rani, I went to the doctor this past weekend."

"Yes, you told me. Is there a problem?"

"I'm pregnant," Priya nearly screamed. "I'm carrying his baby and I don't know how to tell him. I want to be with him and I want to raise our child together, but how do I know it's going to be safe?"

"You don't. Look, when Raj comes back around you need to tell him. He deserves to know the truth about what's going on."

Priya nodded and got to her feet. "I need to get some air."

Priya left Rani and headed up the stairs to the library where she knew it would be quiet. She needed to think. As she was walking along the corridor to the library, Hari rounded a corner. When he saw Priya, he smiled. "Is he alright?" Priya asked.

Hari nodded. "He's perfectly fine. I just gave him some morphine and he'll be asleep for a few hours."

"Can I ask your opinion on something?"

"Sure."

"Do you think I'll always be a target?"

"Honestly, the possibility is very real as long as Vik lives."

"How hard is it going to be to get resident visa for another country?"

"Not too hard. Why, what's on your mind?"

"I'm pregnant," she said, her voice so low, Hari could barely hear. "And I don't want to be part of this game with Chaudhry. I want to raise this baby with Raj, but I don't think I'll be able to do so."

"You know if you just pack up and leave without telling him, you'll hurt him even more."

"I know, but it won't be forever, just until...the threat is eliminated."

"I'd like to tell you what to do but it's not my place, there's too much at stake."

Priya nodded, her head limp. "I know, I know. I have to think about our child now too. It's not just me and Raj anymore."

"But don't you think you should talk this through with Raj first? He's the father, surely he gets a say too."

"He almost died for me, Hari! Imagine what it'll be like bringing up a child together with that animal watching and waiting to destroy his family all over again." Priya was beginning to feel sure now about what to do. "At least if I go away for a while, he'll still have us. We'll still be together, just not in the flesh. Once it's all blown over, we can be together again."

Hari stood at the door. His mouth opened but no words came out. He looked like he wanted to say something more but in the end he looked at his feet. "You're doing the right thing, Priya but if you think Raj's going to let you disappear, you're mistaken."

"That's why I'm not going to tell him."

Hari nodded, meeting her eyes for a moment. His smiled, nodding. "That might be for the best." Then he left quietly, leaving Priya with her thoughts.

*****

When he awoke, he expected to see Priya sitting at his bedside but he was alone. That was unusual but then again, she might be asleep, he thought. He couldn't expect her to sit at his side twenty-four hours a day. He sat up, wincing at the pain in his shoulder and spotted a sheet of paper on the bed at his side. Frowning, he reached for it and started to read:

Dear Raj,

I regret making this decision and fleeing like a coward, but I cannot be with you right now and it is for the safety of our unborn child. As of now I'm going to another country to further my education and to raise our child somewhere safe.

I am sure you are sad, but until Vik stops preying on the people you love it might be safer for us all to be apart. Raj, just know I love you and I'll be sending you letters to let you know what's happening. We'll always be together Raj.

With love,

Priya

As Raj reread it and reread it again, he felt cheated. It wasn't over. Once again, his family was in jeopardy and once again he was at the center of it. It had to end.

"I'm so sorry Raj. There was nothing I could do." Hari closed the door behind him and went to Raj's side.

Raj let the sheet of paper slip from his fingers. A familiar vibration began to spread throughout his body, filling his being until it finally settled in his heart. He nodded then. He knew what he was going to do.

"There is something you can do, Hari."

"And what's that?"

"You can help me get Chaudhry."

"And what do you plan to do when you get him?"

"Kill him," he said simply.

Chapter 20

July 31st, 2008

Raj was looking to Hari for any sign that he was on his side, but instead Hari remained silent, his face a stone mask. He waited, searching Hari's eyes, hoping to find some sign that he could count on him but something was wrong. Hari seemed hesitant as if held back, as if anything he said would only make things worse.

Finally it came to him, the answer to Hari's silent plea and Raj let his head drop in defeat. Hari had become a devout believer of non-violence as a way to atone for the chaos of his past. To help Raj now, to assist him in the slaying of another human being went against everything for which he now stood. Raj wasn't about to give up so easily. Surely, Hari could see the benefit of his request, not just for him but for everyone. With the death of Chaudhry they would all find peace and there would be balance once more. Raj gritted his teeth, determined to press forward.

"I understand that this would go against your principles, but this is something that affects everyone, not just me. I'm not the only one who has been harmed in some capacity by Chaudhry. You thought Hema was dead, but she lives here now with her child," he said, arguing his case. "We both know her scars aren't just physical. They run much deeper than that. She'll never be the same again. If she wasn't going to be used as a pawn in this game, do you think Chaudhry would have kept her alive?" Raj shook his head. "We both know the answer to that. And think about all the other women and children. This isn't just about me, but about all the people he's used and tossed aside over the years."

A flicker of emotion passed over Hari's face and he pursed his lips, the muscles in his jaw bunching. Raj almost sighed with relief when he saw the change in Hari. His words had broken through Hari's defenses. Hari finally spoke up.

"He is a monster and he deserves to die. I will help you get to him, but I refuse to kill another."

That was all Raj wanted – an alliance with someone he could trust, in a world filled with disloyalty and mistrust. This was how it needed to be. Raj started to rise, pushing through the weakness but a wave of dizziness forced him down again. When the fog clouding his vision passed, he saw Hari staring at him, concern etched into his tired face.

"You need your rest Raj. In the meantime I need to speak to Krish."

"Before you go you need to promise me something."

"Tell me what it is I am supposed to promise because I refuse to promise something blindly."

"Don't keep me out of the loop. I deserve to know what's going on. Plus, if you keep something from me I'll find out, you know how thorough and persistent I can be," Raj warned.

Hari knew it was a promise he'd find hard to keep but he nodded anyway.

"I'll let you know what's going on."

Raj nodded.

"Good."

Hari stood.

"I'm going to make that phone call."

The door shut and Raj at last let himself relax a little. Hari was right, he needed rest but as he lay back he remembered the note from Priya still clutched tightly in his hand. He prayed she was safe now that she was far away from him but thinking about it caused a part of him to twist inside and a dull ache began. When it was all over, when Chaudhry was rotting underground, they'd be together again but it still hurt being apart from her.

Soon, my love... soon...

*****

Krish was sitting in his office when he heard a knocking on his door. Peering over his shoulder he saw Siya standing there. She was the spitting image of her mother with the same radiant glow about her. Krish knew she'd been withholding the news that she was pregnant from him, but he refused to inquire about it. She'd tell him in her own time.

"What can I help you with Siya?"

"Do you know if Raj is alright?"

"I'm currently waiting for a phone call. It's touching that you are so concerned about a brother you've never met."

She folded her arms over her chest and rolled her eyes. Most women would never dare do such a thing, but she was not most women. She was wildly independent and that was why she was leaving India. She refused to conform to a society that demanded she be anything but independent and free thinking.

"I ought to be concerned. He's still my brother, doesn't matter if we've met or not."

"Half-brother," Krish corrected.

"Don't give me that garbage! His 'father' doesn't fit into this equation and I wish you'd stop mentioning that bastard."

"Vik Chaudhry is a big part of this equation whether we like it not. He's the reason your brother was unable to come here this evening."

"So are there any plans in place to terminate him?"

"At this moment in time, no," he said as he sipped his tea. "I'm tracking down the person who shot your brother. When we find him, we find the information we need to finish this once and for all."

"Information about what? Where Chaudhry is? I'm sure you could do more than you are. I wish you'd just get it over with already so we can get on with our lives."

"Siya, you should leave."

"Why?"

"The less information you know the better it is for you and for your unborn child."

Krish watched as Siya's hand went to her abdomen. She looked away.

"How do you know?"

"I've seen much in my years here Siya and you should know that you are horrible at keeping secrets."

"Thank you for that observation," she said, her words laced with acid.

"I do trust you though and before I bring her here I'd like to know if you'd be opposed to taking someone to America with you."

"Who else would be accompanying me?"

"The woman your brother got pregnant. The same woman that will be used against your brother and she needs to stay hidden. Is that something you would agree to do?"

"Why choose me?"

"Because Varun lives in a large city and Kavi is not the type to protect someone. On top of which you live in a rural part of the country and you are truly difficult to find."

"You want me to support a stranger in a foreign country who is being hunted down by a sociopath who is attempting to get to my brother?"

"Precisely."

Siya thought on it for a moment and then nodded.

"I'll keep her safe."

"Good because she'll be here shortly. You'd better get packing. You'll both be leaving in a few hours."

He watched as Siya walked away. This was what needed to happen and he knew in a few moments he'd be getting a phone call from Hari with an update. A war was coming and Krish wondered how many more people were going to die.

Chapter 21

Hari stared at his phone. He was trapped in a sea of thoughts. He knew his promise to Raj would be near to impossible to keep and he knew right now, what he was going to do would immediately break his promise. But there was no other way, his hands were tied.

Picking up the phone he winced as a current of guilt traveled from his heart to the hand gripping the phone so tightly it creaked in his grasp. It was a tough call but what else could he do? He dialed the number and Krish answered.

"I'm surprised it took you this long to call me. Is something wrong?" Krish enquired.

"No there's nothing wrong. I just made a promise to Raj and I'm not sure if I can keep that promise."

"Oh? And what was the promise?"

"That I would keep him informed."

"Then don't break the promise to him. He has every right to know what we know. We don't need to keep him in the dark. It serves no purpose. We've all seen what happens when we keep secrets – people die. We don't need any more bloodshed."

Hari knew Krish was right.

"So where do we go from here?"

"You should already know the answer to that."

It was true, Hari already knew the plan. Find the shooter, find the informant and the next phase of the plan could go ahead.

"And those who still live here in the compound, what do we do with them?"

"We'll move them to a location closer to the heart of our operations."

"Are you sure that's a good idea?"

"Yes. I'm sure the mole in your company continues to gather information on Raj. It's only a matter of time before they attempt to take him out."

"You know who it is?"

"I have my suspicions and I'm sure you've arrived at the same conclusion. You know how men are when they feel they've been cheated out of something they thought was rightfully theirs."

"I'll go now then," said Hari. "When are you expecting to pay us another visit?"

"Not me. Kavi will be there shortly accompanied by escort. He'll see to it that you all reach here safely. I'll see you tomorrow, Hari."

Hanging up the phone Hari sat there in silence for a moment. He had grown accustomed to how he was living and now he was pulling up roots and taking everyone with him. Perhaps a change was for the best though, in more ways than one. It wasn't all bad. At least now he was positive of the course of action he needed to take. He was just unsure of how to approach Raj about any of it.

A knock at the door pulled him from his reverie and he turned to see Hema standing in the doorway, her features dulled by tiredness.

"Is everything okay," he inquired as she shut the door.

Her eyes refused to meet his. She looked frightened, her small malnourished frame hunched, and her arms pulled in as if to shield herself. He gave her the time she needed to compose herself. After a moment, she said, "I can't forget what happened to me and I can't just leave the others behind, suffering the same hell I did. We have to free them. I want to help you wage this war, brother."

Getting to his feet he strode over and comforted her, pulling her to him. He remembered when her biggest fear was the dark and he wondered if she ever got over that. After all she'd been through, he supposed, the dark was just that – an absence of light. He balled his fists out of sight of Hema. She'd seen real darkness, the sort that resided in the hearts of corrupted men. A slave to satisfy the perverted lusting of twisted men, she had been shoved in the dark – drugged – abused in ways he couldn't imagine, refused to imagine. And yet here she was, attempting to be strong and he would not deny her the revenge she so desperately wanted. He felt her trembling against him and he wished he could take away all her pain and all of her fear, but this was all he could do. Embrace her and be there for her in every way he should have been all those years. All those years he thought she had been dead. Pulling her close, he felt the steady simmer of rage as it switched on once more, overriding the years of avoidance.

*****

He waited, pacing the rundown shack with heavy impatient steps. The shack was a mere shell, the walls consisting of poorly placed boards, now split and worn and sheets of cobwebs undulating in the wind, just above his head. Objects strewn about the room threatened to remind him of his previous life, of what he had once been but his thoughts were elsewhere, on the future. He saw movement from the corner of his eye and turned to see the killer he had tasked with murdering Raj. The look on his face promised bad news and Ash kicked the dirt at his feet.

"What went wrong?"

"He got away but I can still finish the job – if we can find him."

"What!" Ash snarled. "He's still alive? Are you really so incompetent? I chose you out of all the assassins in the area and you missed!" He glared at the so called assassin. "I thought you were good..."

"I hit Raj, but the bullet only wounded him," he said. He knew the only reason Ash was here was to ensure Raj's death. However, his orders were to kill the woman that Ash cared for.

"What went wrong?"

"The woman, the one you love. She knew something was wrong. Don't ask me how but she pulled him away at the last minute...I had a perfect shot to his heart."

"I will no longer be in need of your services," Ash snapped, waving his hand dismissively. "I'll kill Raj myself. He's weak now and I doubt anyone suspects me of anything."

"Don't kill Raj. Someone else has a bounty on his head."

"Oh really and who would possibly want to pay anything for him?"

"Vik Chaudhry. He wants Raj alive – at least at first," the assassin said.

"Why would someone as powerful as him want trash like Raj?"

"Because Raj knows things, he knows it was Chaudhry that killed his family. Whoever delivers Raj, will be paid quite a handsome sum, I'd imagine."

"And why would I let someone else take all the pleasure?"

"If Chaudhry kills him it won't be instant. There will be torture involved and pain, lots of pain."

Ash took a moment and thought about it. He had a good point. Raj deserved to suffer. He finally nodded. "I will deliver him to Chaudhry. I'll be in touch once I've managed to lure him away from the others. Be ready."

"Good," the assassin answered and watched as Ash walked away. He could sense the tension Ash carried and it was most likely because of this house. He remembered what happened here. When he was sure he was alone, he removed his phone and dialed a number.

"Sultan, this better be good information," Chaudhry's voice was tense and sounded hoarse like two rocks rubbed together.

"Ash will be delivering Raj to us. What happens after I have Raj?"

"Kill the other boy. He is of no use to us and he is being overrun by emotions. Now do not call me again until you have more information."

Sultan hung up and for a moment his mind drifted back to the night years before when he'd torched the shack he was standing in. He remembered the nine year old Ash frightened out of his wits and he especially remembered his sixteen year old sister. She belonged to Sultan now and she had no choice in the fact. However, no one knew that fact other than himself.

Chapter 22

Raj had read the note over and over again and he wondered where Priya was and if she was alright – he prayed to whatever God was out there to keep her safe. Everything had happened so quickly and he felt as if he was losing all that he had gained. No. He refused to lose everything. He would make sure nothing happened to Priya or their unborn child.

He pondered the future for a moment; the future after Chaudhry was gone and wondered how it would be to be a father at such a young age. It was all happening too soon. Having a baby now was not right – there was so much craziness in the world and he knew he could not, in good heart, allow his baby to be born into the chaos he found himself in.

A feeling of apprehension settled over him then and he felt a shift in the atmosphere. Maybe it was just paranoia, he had plenty to be paranoid about, after all – but still, he had to investigate, he had to know it was safe. His body ached as he crossed the room to the door but he switched his focus from his aches to the door in front of him.

He slipped silently into the hallway and saw Sai leaning against a wall speaking with his sister. She seemed distraught and he wondered why. Sai noticed him then and turned to watch him approach them in his slow, staggered steps.

"You should be resting."

"I should, but something seems wrong."

"Oh really? Are you psychic now?"

"No, but something doesn't feel right, okay? I don't need to have a good explanation about how I feel. Now could you tell me where Hari is? I need to speak with him,"

Raj didn't bother to keep the irritation from staining his words. He was in no mood for niceties. If his instincts were right, and they usually were, something was afoot.

"He's in his room, I think."

Raj heard barely contained tension in Sai's voice and he wondered what was happening. As he approached Sai someone turned the corner. It was Hari. He didn't notice Raj at first. He seemed to be deep in thought and judging by the furrow that cut his brow in two, something was wrong.

He seemed to snap out of a trance upon seeing Raj.

"What're you doing up?" he asked, his voice distant. "You should be resting."

"What's going on Hari? Something's wrong isn't it?"

Raj's question was met with silence so he repeated the question.

"What's going on?"

"We're all leaving the compound to be closer to Krish. The time has come to move on. They know we're here, they're watching us even as we speak, I suspect," Hari said. "We're moving closer to Krish. It'll be safer that way."

"Why on earth would you think such a thing?" Raj said, scanning the corridor as if eyes were watching from every crevice and corner.

"No one knew what was going on other than the people in this compound," Hari said, his voice low. He looked over his shoulder. "Someone here is out to get you Raj, someone consumed with jealousy. Do you know who that might be?"

Raj immediately understood the logic and though he didn't want to believe it, he knew it had to be true. "Ash...you think he's the one responsible for the information leak?"

"He's missing from the compound," said Hari, "I think he knows how to get in and out without being detected."

"That makes a lot of sense. What do you need me to do?"

"Be on your toes, but stay close."

Raj sensed someone else approaching and turned to see the others standing nearby, awaiting instruction--Sai, Rani and Hema with Amla cradled in her arms. So this was the trouble he had sensed.

"How are we leaving?"

"Most likely a car. Krish is sending Kavi here and he should be here soon – the sooner the better," Hari added, his eyes meeting Raj's, and betraying the urgency in their depths.

They moved through the halls, each one of them eager to escape the sudden suffocating confines of their soon to be former home. A noise rang out along the corridor, catching up to them and making Hari halt and turn, his eyes wide.

"What is it?"

"Ash...he's back," hissed Raj, adrenaline beginning to pump through his body.

"Good, he can stay here," Hema said. "Let's leave him behind. He's nothing but a traitor, now."

Raj looked to Hari and the look on his face told him he agreed with his sister. Ash was crazed and this was all because Raj was with Priya and he wasn't. Jealousy made men foolish, made them do things completely out of character – then again, Raj thought, perhaps not. Perhaps it was just as well that Ash had shown his true colors now and not later. He thought of Priya then and gave thanks that it was him with her and not Ash. He was clearly unstable, jealousy or not.

Keeping up with the rest of the group was proving rather difficult. Raj was quickly tiring and as he forced himself along, his body protesting to each forced movement, he saw a movement in the adjoining corridor. It was Ash. His face was set in a determined scowl as if he had made up his mind to do something. The hint of silver in his palm revealed his intentions but Raj was breathless, there was no air left to cry out.

As Ash approached he saw the blade in Ash's hand come up before him but before Ash could get close, another body moved in front of Raj, blocking his view. It was Sai and he was moving in to attack, to help his friend. The light faded and the two scuffling figures before him were enveloped in a sheet of blackness. He was losing consciousness but he didn't want to go, he wanted to help his friend. He felt himself hit the ground and just before he lost his grip on the world, a shriek rang out, cutting through into his sense deprived world.

Then blackness took over.

*****

As Priya sat in the car with Siya, questions formed a queue in her mind, clamoring for precedence but words eluded her. She was frightened of what was coming and she wanted to see Raj. She wanted to believe that he was safe, that it was over now but somehow, she doubted that. She felt there was yet more pain to come.

Wrapping her arms around herself she felt Siya's eyes fall on her. "Do you love my brother?"

Priya was shocked by the forthrightness of question and all she could do was nod.

"I'm sorry for the question," she said, although Priya was sure she was not sorry at all. "It's just that I never got to know Raj and now I'm told that you and he are together and are expecting a child. It's a shock…"

She knew too much Priya thought to herself and she wondered why Krish thought it wise for her to live with Siya. Siya obviously didn't like her and she wondered why. She hadn't done anything wrong and truthfully she would much rather be living off the grid and invisible to the world than living with someone so cynical.

"What's the matter, has your captivity caused you to forget how to speak?" Priya flinched at the question, the poison in Siya's inflection and words causing an injection of anger within her.

"I'm perfectly capable of speaking," she snapped. "I just don't feel like talking right now. I have other things on my mind and I would much rather think on them than speak to you. It's obvious you don't approve of me and I'm beginning to wonder why you agreed to help me in the first place."

Siya backed off, her eyes breaking contact with Priya's for a moment. She clearly hadn't expected any resistance from Priya.

Siya soon regained her confidence. "Truthfully, I don't know you so why bother trying to be friends when that's the case? And the only reason I'm willing to help you is because you're carrying my brother's child. If the only thing I can do is ensure the safety of that child than I'll do it."

"Then we have something in common," Priya replied. "We both want to make sure this child is safe. Now if you don't mind I'd rather sit here in peace than listen to you speak."

"Even if I have questions about Raj?"

Priya was silent for a moment before she finally sighed. "If you want answers about your brother…I'll give them to you."

Silence filled the car once more and Priya wondered if she was ever going to ask her questions. Siya was staring out of the window and it seemed she was deep in thought.

"What's Raj like?" She finally asked.

"He's a gentleman, kind and considerate and in case you were wondering, there's not a bad bone in his body," Priya said, knowing that being the son of such an evil man would forever taint him in some way. Raj is curious and soft spoken. His intelligence surpasses that of everyone around him though one would never know it because he doesn't flaunt his superiority. He is too modest and his mind is always somewhere, analyzing and searching."

"Did he want to get you pregnant?"

"No, of course not, we both agreed to wait until we were done with schooling, but it just…happened. I was hoping to tell him after we had met you. He was already so anxious thinking about meeting you and I didn't want to pressure him even more – he has enough on his plate. Instead I told him in a letter when it should have been done in person."

"Why was he so anxious to meet us?"

"You should already know the answer to that."

"Maybe I do have the answer," replied Siya with a shrug, "and it's possible I'm simply trying to confirm whether it is correct or not."

Priya considered Siya's answer for a moment before speaking. "He wondered if you would accept him despite knowing the truth about how he was conceived. He was afraid that you wouldn't accept him and he wanted so much to be part of your lives. He didn't want to disappoint any of you."

Siya looked away without a word and Priya wondered if she was satisfied with her answer. She turned and scanned the street outside to see a landscape of blurred lights. They weren't going to the airport – it was too public. Instead they would be going on a boat that was crewed by sellers of fine artifacts. No one was allowed to be on board other than the crew, but Krish knew the captain. Priya wondered what it was going to be like at sea. She had never seen the ocean and she was deathly afraid. Swimming was not something she had been taught – but she pushed those thoughts out of her head and raised her eyes to the night sky. Everything was going to be just fine.

Chapter 23

Hari stared at the lifeless body laid before him, emotions running amok within him. He couldn't believe it had come to this. A boy turned murderer. Krish entered the room and glanced at the lifeless body, his face grim. "There's nothing we could have done to prevent this and you should know that Hari. What's done is done now and no amount of self-blame will change that. All we can do is put things right."

"That doesn't make me feel any better. I should have known this would happen and yet I did nothing. Maybe I could have prevented it." Hari closed his eyes. He didn't want to look at the boy's handiwork anymore. In a sense, it signified he had failed in his efforts to change.

"There's no way of knowing now is there. I'm surprised the others are not as shook up as you are. Was there some animosity between him and the others?"

Hari shrugged and turned away from the body. "If there was, I didn't see it until it was too late." He had suspected that Ash might harbor ill-will towards Raj but not to the extent that he would attempt to have him killed.

"A boy became a killer today," Hari said, his voice descending into a whisper. "That was something I never thought he would be capable of."

"Sai doesn't seem to be too shaken. He was protecting Raj and that's what brothers do isn't it – protect their own?" said Krish, "you of all people should know that! You did it several times yourself and it seems to me sleep has not eluded you in quite some time."

"All of this could have been prevented! Sai did not need to become a killer."

Krish sagged visibly. He knew he was wasting his time trying to convince Hari it wasn't his fault. There was nothing left to do then but leave him to his self-torment.

"I'm going to check on Raj, anyway..." he mumbled and walked away without looking back.

*****

Sai sat and stared at Raj's unconscious form. He hadn't stirred since the attack in the corridor and Sai wished he would wake up if only to relieve a little of the tension simmering deep inside his gut, weighing him down. He knew it was selfish to wish that, to somehow pass the burden to Raj, but he didn't know how else to deal with it. The truth – he'd killed a young man and not just any man but one who he had lived with and shared sanctuary with.

If it was so bad though, why did he feel nothing? There was a knot in his stomach, that was true, but it wasn't grief, at least not for Ash. He was concerned about his friend unconscious before him and ending the stupid war they were embroiled in – the grief wasn't for Ash.

Ash was dead but the alternative would have been much worse and Sai had done right by killing him instead, he told himself. But the fact remained – he was a killer, no better than those who had sought to end Raj's life and taken the lives of so many before him.

He was a killer...

He looked down at his hands and noticed that they were now clenched into fists. He wanted to break down into tears but he couldn't. He felt as if part of himself was missing now, taken away when the knife had pierced Ash's flesh. But he did it for Raj, for a friend, a friend who was his brother and Sai knew he would do the same thing for him.

Raj stirred in his sleep then as if sensing Sai's discomfort.

Raj opened his eyes and looked up at Sai. He looked pale and drawn, the loss of blood having taken its toll but Raj was strong. "How are you feeling," Sai asked softly.

It took Raj a moment to respond. "I feel weak. What happened?"

"You passed out."

"I figured as much," he said as he attempted to get up.

"Don't," Sai said reaching out to put a hand on Raj's shoulder, "you need to rest."

Raj smiled weakly and finally let himself drop back onto the mattress. "So I keep hearing."

"What exactly do you remember?" Sai asked, knowing the truth was close.

"Ash was there…he had a knife and I thought he was going to… – but he didn't because of you," Raj's voice trailed off as he realized something. "What happened?"

"He was going to kill you and – and he didn't get the chance to because I stopped him before he could."

"Is Ash dead?"

Sai nodded, unable to say the words. Raj nodded slowly and to Sai's surprise, there was no hint of shock or horror at what Sai had done. Instead, Raj reached up and placed a hand over Sai's, a thin lipped smile on his face.

"Thank you."

The door opened then and standing in the doorway was Krish and another man who looked somewhat similar to Raj but his hair was cut much shorter and he was not as muscular.

"Sai, could you please give us a moment?" Krish asked.

Raj watched Sai go, his savior and wished he could find a better way to thank him for saving his life. Perhaps in time such an opportunity might arise and when it did, he'd let Sai know that his deed did not go unnoticed.

"It's good to see you awake. We were concerned."

Raj barely acknowledged Krish. He was staring at the man by his side. There was something distinctly familiar about him. He looked very similar to Raj's mother with her soft features, but he also had the strong jaw of his father. There was no doubt – it was his brother. It was somewhat painful to be seeing their features on him – he remembered how much joy his life was filled with and he wondered if his brother resented him for being able to grow up with them.

"I'm fine," Raj was finally able to muster.

"Good. This is your brother Kavi and you'll be seeing a lot more of him. He'll be helping me out with the upcoming elections."

"What about Varun and Siya?"

"I sent them back home," he said slowly. "It's probably safer for them in America."

"And where is Priya?"

Krish smiled.

"She is safe somewhere that Chaudhry will never be able to find her and when this is all over I will reveal to you her location. Until then, heal and take it easy for once."

"I'm doing better than Sai it seems. He looks a little disturbed by the whole thing and I don't blame him. If you see him, could you ask him to come back? I still need to talk to my friend."

Krish nodded and turned to leave. Kavi was about to follow him when Krish motioned to Raj.

"You should stay here with your brother. Get acquainted. I'll return with Sai in due course."

When Krish had shut the door behind him Raj looked at his brother, their eyes meeting. He had so many questions but the words seemed stuck to his tongue as if glued there and instead he stared silently. He didn't know what to say or how to say it. He wanted to know about his brother's life and ask him why he had become a politician.

"You seem rather nervous," said Kavi.

"I'm not nervous," Raj said flatly.

Kavi shook his head and walked over to a chair at the opposite end of the room. Then after a moment of silence, Kavi began to speak.

"You don't know too much about me or what I really do."

"Krish said you're a politician."

"That's only half true. I'm mostly his bodyguard and I do what I'm told to do."

"You are no bodyguard. You don't look even the slightest bit dangerous."

Kavi smiled and seemed satisfied.

"Yes, exactly, people don't perceive me to be a threat, but truly I am. That's why I'm not his partner in this election, instead he's working with another politician and it's because that person is very influential in the slums and in the suburbs. Krish is very smart and he knows how to place people where they will suit him best, and truly everything is a façade."

"People don't think it's odd because you were raised by him and they think you aren't running with him because of your bond," Raj observed.

Kavi nodded.

"That's exactly it. So what of you Raj? What are you destined to become?"

"A businessman, as our father was."

He scoffed and Raj was immediately taken aback.

"He may have been *my* father, but he didn't raise me the way he did you. I was unimportant and he shipped us off to live in Mumbai. Both of them would send us letters but that meant nothing to me. I wanted my parents, not a bunch of letters."

"I was told they did that to protect you from Chaudhry and his men."

"That might have been the reason, but they kept you didn't they? One is to wonder why they only kept you."

"You don't think that's a question I've been asking myself?"

Kavi fell silent and after a pause, nodded.

"I suppose it's not logical for me to be upset at you for the decisions that they made all those years ago."

"No it isn't," Raj agreed. "We need to work together Kavi and if we do that we can end this mess sooner rather than later."

He nodded and that was when the door opened again and standing there was Sai. He stepped into the room and Kavi got up to leave. He turned to look at Raj. "I will help you," he said as he shut the door behind him.

When he had left, Sai stood there awkwardly.

"Is everything okay?" Raj asked.

"Not really, I don't know how to explain what I am feeling. I don't think this is normal."

"I appreciate what you did for me, and for the others as well. I'm in your debt Sai and if you ever need anything don't be afraid to ask."

Sai nodded and he wanted to tell Raj about the offer Krish had made him, but he was unable to do so. He couldn't tell him what he was being offered because he wasn't sure what his decision was yet. If he told Raj he might help him reach a decision and he wasn't even sure what he wanted yet.

"Could I go back to my room?" he finally asked. "I would really like to be alone right now."

"Of course, and if you need anything you know where to find me. I truly don't know when I'll be back on my feet again."

Raj watched as his friend left. He knew something was on Sai's mind and it definitely wasn't Ash.

Chapter 24

The sun was beginning to rise and the young man had yet to return from bringing back the information he needed in order to get Raj. It seemed something was wrong and he knew it would be wise to call it quits now before anything else occurred. He could no longer stay here and wait because remaining in one place too long was always dangerous, especially for someone like him.

Leaving the abandoned house discreetly he knew he would have to make the phone call. Things had changed now. Chaudhry was impossible to predict and he wondered if there was another task at hand for him. He was sure there was one.

He pulled out his phone and called Chaudhry.

Chaudhry answered immediately, his voice filled with expectation.

"I believe my informant has been discovered. How would you like me to proceed from here?"

"Come to me and we will figure out what our next step will be. I have a few ideas, but I'm not sure how to carry them out."

"Yes sir," he said and he hung up. He would now be catching the next flight out of India. No doubt there was much more bloodshed to come.

*****

There was something very wrong. Priya held her knees to her chest and felt the rocking of the ocean beneath them. At first it was beautiful to look at and the trip started off wonderful, but then the boat left the docks and now, in the open water, she was beginning to feel like she was in hell. Shaking and miserable, she thought of Raj. All she wanted was for Raj to be with her – he made everything better, seemed to know exactly what to say to reassure her but she was leaving him behind. She hoped to whatever God reigned over them that he was okay. She missed hearing his voice, feeling the strength that ran through it as he soothed her worries. When he held her, nothing in the world could touch her. Now, as the land faded against the horizon, she knew she wouldn't see him again for a long time, perhaps not ever.

Closing her eyes for a moment she heard someone knock on the door. Before she could ask who it was, the door opened. Siya entered the room and stood there silently appraising her as if it was normal to barge in on someone uninvited. Priya hated that Siya was completely unfazed by everything, hated that she seemed perfectly at ease with their being at sea, hated the fact that she was the one in control.

"You look awful," she said but there was no real concern in her voice.

"Thank you for noticing. What do I owe the pleasure?"

"I was checking in on you to see how you were doing. From the looks of it you aren't accustomed to this form of travel."

"No, not at all. How long will this take?"

"Generally a few weeks, but they'll be stopping in Porte de Santos in Brazil to drop off some of these artifacts," she said as she kicked one of the boxes lightly.

"Really? We're going to be making a stop in Central America when we know full well that there are people there that want Raj dead?"

"We won't be leaving the ship. We'll be fine."

Priya rolled her eyes as the boat rolled over another wave. She had no idea how people managed to virtually live at sea in these metal tombs. It was awful and made worse by the fact she had to wait several more weeks before they were on solid land.

"Is there something you want to talk about?"

She was unsure. Her mind was a mess of thoughts, each one fighting for control. She was afraid. She wanted this all to be over and she wanted Raj to be safe – to be together with her and safe. She was being left in the dark and now she was unsure about the true nature of the danger. Maybe now she was free of the danger, maybe now she could relax, but she couldn't. It seemed as if she'd never have a stable family of her own, because anyone she ever got close to was always taken away – Always.

"I'm just fearful about what the future has in store. I'm unaware if Raj is okay,"

She didn't know why she was telling Siya but one by one, she revealed her deepest fears.

"There is so much going on. One minute everything was fine and our future was set in stone, and then this."

She choked on her words as a wave of grief washed over her. She felt tears stream down her face in a relentless torrent and just when she was feeling more alone that ever, Siya wrapped her tightly in her arms and held her as she broke down.

"I know this must be hard for you but everything will work out the way it needs to, okay? You just need to stay strong – stay strong for yourself, for your child, and for Raj. He's going to be fighting monsters so he can be reunited with you. So please, just keep your faith and don't lose it because if you doubt it then you will have already lost this fight."

Shocked at Siya's sudden show of support, Priya met her eyes.

"I promise that I'll do everything in my power to protect my unborn child, Raj, and everyone I care for. No matter what the cost is to myself."

Priya began to feel tired then, her eyes fluttering. Leaning against the boxes, she watched as Siya stood up and grabbed a sheet. She reached out and placed the sheet over Priya, wrapping it around her gently as a mother tucks her children in.

"I trust you, and we will learn to work with one another. We're a family now."

Chapter 25

Raj was walking through the hallways of their new compound. It was so different from the place that had become his home. Everything was brighter – more open. Windows lined the walls and outside, the street, bustling with people was clearly visible. The people outside in the streets were relaxed and going about their business as if they felt safe. It was an alien scene to Raj. There was no sense of paranoia among these people the way it was in the slums.

It was shocking to see the difference in the way the classes lived and he began to wonder if this was how his siblings lived. Without fear of being gunned down because you crossed the wrong person, without constantly glancing over your shoulder to see if you were being followed. He briefly wondered what his life would have been like here, but then pushed the thought aside. He didn't wish to ponder things that never were. The future was more important now.

He a felt a little dizzy, but he was stronger now and was glad to be away from the confines of his bed. There was work that needed to be done and he knew he needed to move quickly. The sooner this storm passed the sooner everything would get back to normal.

He turned a corner and ran into Sai who jumped in shock before slipping away again, his eyes lowered. Raj had a nagging feeling that something wasn't right and he wanted to go speak with him to ensure he was okay, but then he thought better of it. Whatever was on his mind was something that he needed to deal with on his own.

He turned to watch Sai as he walked away. At that moment he felt like he was letting his friend down, but he needed to continue moving forward for now, and if Sai needed him he would come and Raj would be there for him.

He finally located the foyer of this magnificent home and he knew that this was the life only certain privileged people were entitled to. He had been told his entire life that everything a person endures is for their own benefit, and those challenges were for everyone, but always in different forms. Raj knew that not everyone endured the same thing, but it didn't matter because no one could walk a mile in another's shoes.

Stepping into the foyer he marveled at the chandelier and the light gleaming from every shard of glass, a mini rainbow on each surface. The paintings lining every wall oozed class and every surface, every item of furniture was spotless, the sunlight shining through the windows bouncing off the polished wood and glass. Nothing here was monotone. Everything was well cared for and meticulously arranged. This was the type of lifestyle he wanted to provide for Priya and their child, but first he had to make the best of what he had – just like everyone else.

Off the foyer was a large living space that flowed into the dining room and connected to a grand kitchen. He saw Rani sitting on the sofa, but instead of reading the way she always had, she was peering out of the window lost in her thoughts.

He approached her and sat down, waiting until she noticed his presence. She seemed to notice him then but her eyes remained fixed on the world outside the window.

"Sai refuses to speak to me. He doesn't even want to see me. He says it's safer if I leave him alone for now."

"Sai has gone through a lot these past few days and it's something I wish I could change, but you should let him come to you in his own time. It seems as though he's coming to terms with what has happened and that's only normal. Give him time and he'll be alright."

"You did this," she said turning on him. "If it wasn't for you none of this would have happened."

"Blame me if you want to because I too blame myself," said Raj with a shrug. "If I had been more capable of staying conscious I would have done the deed myself instead of Sai doing it for me. Do you think that seeing my friend like this is easy?"

"He's my brother, it's not the same."

"Don't think that just because I'm not related to Sai that I don't care. I'd do anything for him because he treated me like a brother. He's a loyal friend and I'll be the same for him," Raj promised.

Rani shook her head.

"You don't know anything about my brother and if you want to protect him stay away from him."

"And if I don't?"

"We'll cross that bridge when we come to it, but I mean it – stay away from him," she warned, her tone threatening.

He watched as she got up and walked away. He was unsure of what she meant. Of course he knew Sai. They were friends and they confided in one another all the time. Surely she was overreacting. Then again, he thought, trouble seemed to follow him wherever he went.

He heard voices from the kitchen and went to investigate. Krish and Kavi were deep in conversation. They both looked exhausted. As he approached them, Hari appeared behind them. Raj began to wonder what was happening and why he hadn't been informed of the meeting.

"You are looking better," Kavi said walking towards the refrigerator.

"I'm feeling more like myself," he said slowly. "Why do the three of you look as if you haven't slept? Is there something going on that I should know about?"

The three of them exchanged a look and Hari sighed before saying, "I'll tell you, but just give me a few minutes."

Raj watched as Kavi and Hari fished through the refrigerator and pulled out some leftovers which they devoured hungrily.

Hari gestured for Raj to follow him then and he did so. Hari led Raj down a hallway and down a set of steps. Finally, they emerged in another hallway and there were only two doors here. Hari went to the first one on the left and they stepped inside. Krish and Kavi were not too far behind.

"We were meeting with Mr. Raina, a very influential man who has agreed to fund us in the upcoming election," Hari said as he closed the door behind them.

"Alright," Raj said slowly. "So what does this have to do with you three looking like you haven't slept in days?"

"We met Mr. Raina in Dubai and he agreed to come out here to India for the elections. We only spoke with him for a few hours but we needed to make the trip quick and so we did," Hari said pulling up a chair.

"How come I feel as though you are withholding information from me?" Raj pressed, looking from one face to the other.

"You might not like it too much," Hari said as he gestured to Kavi. "But you will be interested in reading this."

Kavi provided him with a manila folder and Raj stared at it, wondering what else they had in store for him, how many more secrets.

Raj opened the folder and flicked through the contents.

The first document was about Mr. Mohit Raina, one of the most successful businessmen in India. He was the CEO of Raina Industries a firm specializing in high-tech gear, most of which was sold to the government. He had a major office in New York and another one in the District of Columbia and he was climbing the ladder of success rather quickly. In the file it stated he was only twenty-eight years old.

Raj finished reading the first of the documents and looked up at Hari. "How did he come into the business?"

"Rajesh Chaudhry," Krish said evenly. "However there is no documentation of Mohit Raina here in India. He doesn't even know who his parents are or *were*."

"Then why would you want someone like him to fund your campaign?"

"Because Mohit Raina was the one who terminated Rajesh Chaudhry and it was because he found out the truth about his parents – sound familiar?"

"There was nothing written about Rajesh Chaudhry being murdered."

"What did he teach Vik to do?" inquired Kavi. "And if he taught Vik to do that don't you think he taught all of the children he took under his wing how to do that?"

"I suppose, but there was never any information that Rajesh adopted another child."

"He didn't adopt Mohit and there is no documentation about him because he was born in that house to one of the sex slaves. His mother was an American girl of Indian descent who was traveling to India. Her name was Margaret Raina and she went missing. She was twenty years old and no one ever found her. After she gave birth to Mohit she was still being used as a sex slave. The entire time, she remained in the same house as him and he never knew. It was not until after he was officially groomed to take off with this business that he found out."

"How do you know all this?"

"Because I had someone on the inside all those years ago who knew what was happening. Margaret had endured all those years to watch her son grow up and when he was on the verge of becoming a monster, she escaped and somehow managed to find him before it was too late. She provided a sample of her DNA and tried to convince him that she was his mother, but he didn't believe her. She was killed that night, but he kept her DNA with him and he finally tested his own against it."

"That must have been years ago. How come he waited so long to take action?"

"Mohit is a very smart man and he bided his time before acting. Rajesh Chaudhry appeared to have died of natural causes, but that was simply a clever deception on Mohit's part. Mohit was raised with Vik and they still have a relationship. The reason I want him to help me with this election is because I know we'll win and I also know you can get Chaudhry."

"How long have you been planning this?"

Krish chuckled.

"For too long, but it's playing out rather nicely."

"This was supposed to be for my father – for Dev to carry-out wasn't it?"

"Dev Varma *is* your father and you have every right to call him as such. And to answer your question, yes. But he is no longer with us and this is now a task for you to carry out Raj. This is for you to end at long last."

Raj was silent for a long moment as he pondered what it meant. As attractive as the offer was and as much as he wanted Chaudhry dead, after everything that had happened he found it hard to believe that he'd be free once it was done.

"How do we know that by killing Chaudhry this will be over? How do we know that with him gone we'll be out of danger? What if someone close to him seeks revenge for his death?"

"There is only one person who would seek revenge and he is going to be taken care of."

"And who exactly is that?"

"An assassin named Sultan, the one who shot you."

Raj was confused.

"What kind of assassin misses his target like that? He's obviously not that good."

"That would be the only time he has never hit the target he was aiming at. Believe us he is not someone we can take lightly and his loyalty lies with Chaudhry. Before we even attempt to get to Chaudhry we have to get rid of Sultan. It is the only way and we are going to need to plan it very carefully."

"Hadn't you better get some rest first?"

It felt good to finally tell someone else to get some rest, after days of being cooped up and told off every time he tried to stretch his legs.

They were beginning to walk away when Raj stopped in front of Krish blocking his path. Sai was acting very strangely and something told Raj that Krish was responsible.

"I need to ask you something, Krish."

"What is it that you wish to ask me?"

"What did you tell Sai? He's been acting very peculiar of late. I'm worried about him."

"There's nothing you can do for Sai. This is his own war and it's something he'll have to get through on his own. He hasn't even accepted my offer, so it'd be best if you left him alone for now and waited for him to come to you."

Raj frowned. That wasn't enough.

"What did you offer him?"

"I offered him a position in my security."

"Why?"

"Sai won't make it through college and if you wish to believe the only reason he hasn't left for school yet is because of his sister you're wrong," Krish said. "He doesn't know what he wants to do or what he wants to end up as. The boy is confused, lost and needs guidance. I thought you of all people would have noticed that by now."

"Is there something about Sai that I don't know?"

"You should ask him yourself," Krish said as he walked out of the room.

Alone again, Raj looked at the glossy surface of the manila folder in his hand. The time for action was close, the time to end it all, finally and rid the world of Chaudhry so life could resume once more.

Chapter 26

The flight had been shorter than expected, still, he hadn't liked it one bit. Traveling by air left him feeling powerless as though it might all end at any moment. Sultan wasn't used to such weakness. He liked being in control. But, this was an exception he had been forced to make, his presence required.   He knew it wasn't going to be pretty and he'd more than likely be forced to listen to Chaudhry as he lectured him but it was a small price to pay for doing the job he loved most – killing people.

The airport heaved with people coming and going. Each one was in their own world and he began to wonder what ordinary people thought about. Mundane things, he mused. Picking the kids up from school, cooking dinner, watching T.V. None of it interested him in the slightest. Such things dulled the mind and body and before you knew it, you were aged and slow; your senses almost useless.

As he walked among them, he knew they had no idea they were walking side by side with a killer – they'd never know it.

He studied the way each person moved, working out their strengths and weaknesses just by examining the way they moved, the way they looked at the world. It was easy to get the measure of someone but one thing he hadn't quite mastered yet was working out *why* people did what they did. Maybe he was too cold, too detached from society to know what drove people to make the choices they did.

Making his way to the main streets he saw there were very few cars out at this hour. He had expected more people to be prowling the streets at night but it didn't bother him. He found a small neighborhood and there was one house among all of them that no one ever went near. The locals believed that the devil himself resided in that house and no one ever attempted to go inside – except Sultan.

As he made his way up to the entrance of the house one of the guards stopped him. He wasn't expecting that but it didn't worry him. No. Chaudhry would not do anything to him because he was his most valuable tool.

"What's wrong?" he asked, annoyed that the guard was wasting his time.

"Nothing, I just didn't recognize you at first. Chaudhry is waiting for you in his office."

Sultan nodded and walked past him. This residence was quainter than the other one they had. From the outside it looked like there could be a family inside, a son, a daughter doing their homework while their father, a doctor was working late, saving lives and mother was preparing dinner in the kitchen. Just a normal everyday household – but it was anything but normal. He was ushered inside, through the front door and much like the outside, the inside of the house was like any other, rich drapes hanging from the windows, a living room filled with cushions and a T.V. perched on a stand. It was well carpeted, no stains, the walls were pristine and Sultan began to wonder how it was kept so clean, considering what went on inside.

Making his way to the back room he saw two other guards standing there and they were silent as he opened the door to the office. He saw Chaudhry there and he was not alone. There were two busty women inside; their tight dresses leaving little to the imagination. One was sitting upon Chaudhry's lap and the other one looked Sultan up and down. He knew that these women were locals and wondered what they were doing there.

"It's nice seeing you here on time, as always. Girls," Chaudhry said as the woman on his lap turned to face him. "A moment please," he ordered with a flick of his hand.

They both nodded obediently and the woman who had been eyeing Sultan brushed her body against his as she left. Sultan watched her leave, an uncontrollable injection of desire leaving him momentarily distracted.

"What would you like for us to speak about?" he asked, when he finally regained his composure.

"Our business, you are very loyal to me Sultan and you have done wonders for me over the years. You have slain my enemies and you have helped me reach this level of success in my life and that is why I am not too upset with how things have transpired."

"I had her in my sights and that bloody bastard moved just at the wrong time," he said angrily.

"I understand. It seems as if we need to go about this a completely new way. You will be going to America for the next assignment. I know Raj's weakness, and we will use it to draw him out and into my web."

"How do you know she'll be in America?"

"Because Krish isn't as wise as he thinks he is. I haven't narrowed down her location there but when I do, I'll be sending you out there to retrieve her."

"Would I be bringing her back here?"

"No. Keep her there and call me when you have her. From there we will plan our next move."

"Are you still going to be running in the elections?"

"Yes." Chaudhry scowled. "Krish might have smeared my name negatively throughout the media, but I'll find a way to clean this up. Someone else will be taking the fall for me." His scowl became a smile then.

"And who will that be?"

"I haven't decided yet but rest assured I have several options."

Sultan nodded. He understood how Chaudhry operated and he knew he would be staying here in Rio for maybe a few weeks, but that was of no issue.

"Is there anything else that you'll need of me?"

"At this given time, no there is nothing you can do. However, one of those girls in the hallway is for you and I am sure you already know which one it is – go and enjoy yourself."

In the corridor he stopped to admire the girl who stood leaning against the wall, her curves fighting against the material of her dress, begging to be released. He sucked in a breath.

Brazil was a wonderful place.

Chapter 27

Raj had read through all the files and he wasn't too sure how well this plan was going to work. Chaudhry wasn't stupid. Fooling him would be no mean feat. It was possible that he already knew something was awry, but Krish and the others seemed confident that this would work so why was he having doubts?

Reading through the files he knew that Chaudhry hadn't withdrawn from the elections and he knew the man he was working with in this campaign. His name was Deepak Gupta and in the slums he was known as DeeGee or DG. He was notorious for his contempt for the poor. If he had his way, the entire slum district would be torn down and replaced with his real estate. It didn't matter to him that people would die and be left homeless. He wanted progress, progress for the rich, for those who served a purpose, and to him, the poor were a burden he could do without. Raj was not going to let that happen and he would ensure that everything was taken care of.

The other document was about Tapan Butala, once a business associate of Chaudhry, now his rival in the elections. He was unsure how that would work or even why they were running against one another. A knock at the door disturbed his thoughts then.

"Come in," he said and slipped the documents back into their folder.

It was Sai and he had that same troubled look on his face as before, only this time Raj saw intent, as if Sai had finally convinced himself to speak to Raj about what was bothering him.

"I need to talk to you," he said slowly. "I've been struggling with this for a while."

"You know you can tell me anything Sai. Is there something wrong?"

"Sort of," he said as he shut the door behind him. "You know how you were never interested in the girls at the compound?"

"Yes." Raj said, thinking back to the early days there.

"Well I sort of thought it was because you weren't attracted to girls, but then you got together with Priya and well, I know now you like girls."

Raj nodded slowly, still not quite sure what Sai was trying to say.

"Raj I care about you," Sai's voice trailed off into silence.

"I care about you too Sai."

"No, you don't care about me in the same way. I can assure you that."

"What're you talking about Sai?"

"I'm...I'm gay," he said. "I thought it was obvious but you never saw it."

Raj wasn't sure how to respond. He hadn't suspected anything, especially with Sai being so nonchalant about his relationship with Priya. Raj understood now why Rani had acted the way she did, why she was so adamant that Raj was hurting him. He looked down at his feet, unsure of what to say.

"Sai, I didn't know that and truthfully I don't know how to respond to that."

"Look, you don't have to respond to it. I just – I killed Ash because I didn't want him to hurt you. I still want to be friends and all, but you needed to know the truth about how I feel before we go any further."

Raj was silent for a moment.

"If you want to remain friends that would be wonderful, but if it bothers you being around me let me know, okay?"

"It does bother me but that's something I need to deal with," Sai said looking away. "Anyway, I have to go." Sai turned and left and Raj let him go.

He watched as Sai left his room, thinking about what had just happened. How could he have not seen it? He wondered how hurt he had been when he learned of his relationship with Priya. Raj remembered some of the conversations he had with Sai and he wondered how he had been able to bear their conversations about her. He felt as if he had been a horrible friend, but he couldn't worry about that now. He needed to go speak to the others and they needed to create an effective plan to take down Chaudhry.

Getting to his feet he walked across the room and made his way into the hallway. He made his way to the main living space and saw the three of them there. They were still not a hundred percent themselves, but once they were able to sleep more they would be back to normal.

"So do you have any questions?" Krish asked as he motioned to the manila folder he was holding.

"Why are Tapan Butala and Chaudhry running against one another?"

"What makes you think they are running *against* one another?"

"Because they are," he said slowly, confused by the response.

"They're making their odds more favorable. Think about it this way, you have five baskets in front of you and only in two of those baskets are the supplies you need to survive. Are you only going to choose one basket or are you going to choose all five to make your odds more favorable?"

"Since they both have the same goals and are partners in business they can achieve the same aim no matter who gets elected."

"That's a fine observation. However, what most of them don't realize is that they are also compulsive liars and excel in the art of manipulation. It's what has got them this far. That's why Chaudhry's reputation hasn't been smeared too badly by the discovery of that house of his. Whatever happens, they'll always come up with something to turn the tables in their favor."

"Are people really so blind that they can't see the truth even when it slaps them in the face?"

"It's not that. People choose to believe what they want."

"Are you worried about your chances in the election?" Raj asked.

Krish smiled and shook his head.

"Of course I'm not, I may not be able to talk people into giving me their soul but I stand by my word and I've never broken it before. Besides my strategy is to get everyone in the slums on my side."

"And how do you anticipate doing that?"

"With you Raj. You know the slums and the people there. You know how to communicate with them and you know what they need." He paused before asking, "So what do they need?"

Raj shrugged. "I believe the list would be shorter if we see what they don't need."

"If you got to choose how to rebuild the slums what would you do?"

"I'd provide them with infrastructure. Running water, reliable shelter, and food."

"And how would you go about doing that without funding?"

"Where are you going with this?"

"Get the people in the slums to vote for me and I promise you I *will* take care of them."

"They are most likely going to be pressured into voting for Chaudhry or Butala. They're afraid of them."

"Then maybe we should put their minds at ease."

"And how would you go about doing that?"

"You figure it out Raj. You know how to communicate with them. If someone who understands their hardships goes out there and works with them to help them better their lives will they not become loyal to that person?"

Raj nodded. He understood what Krish needed – a mouthpiece. Someone who knew how to communicate with them, but he hadn't been there in years. There would be so many questions, so much to explain.

"I assume you already have something in motion," Raj said searching Krish' intelligent eyes for the answer he knew already.

"Yes. They are going to destroy half of the Dongri Slum because of Chaudhry and Butala. They were able to buy their homes without their permission, but the people don't know that. They'll only be given two weeks to come up with an amount large enough to buy back their homes."

"How much do they need?"

Krish shook his head slowly. "They'd never get the money in time. It would take years for them to earn that amount."

"So you want me to save the day and reveal to them the situation?"

"Exactly."

"I'd be in the public's eye at that point. Won't that put my life in danger again?"

"Of course not. You'll be in the eye of the public with cameras following you everywhere. If anyone attempts to harm you it's on tape and believe me Chaudhry and Butala will never send out someone to execute another person while there is evidence that can be used against them."

"You're mad Krish, a mad genius!" Raj said shaking his head.

Krish smiled and nodded. "That I am, Raj that I am."

Raj sat on his own for a while once the discussion was over, pondering the plan. It was a good plan and for once Raj was filled with hope. Perhaps things were going to turn out better than expected, just this once.

Chapter 28

Raj looked himself over in the mirror. The person staring back at him was a stranger, one from another lifetime. He didn't like his new look, but he knew it was necessary. His hair had been cut, but it was still somewhat wild, at least wild enough to remind him of where he'd come from. He looked down at the Rolex on his wrist and wondered if this was the right approach. Suited, clean cut and sporting a Rolex didn't seem to be the way to win over the people of the slums. If anything, it might only make them distrust him more, being that they had been oppressed non-stop by people who looked very much as he did. Raj knew how it was for them though, he was them, and he was representing them. He was going to be their voice and he was going to win this for them. He refused to allow those people to lose the little they had so those with too much already could have even more.

There was a knock on his door and he turned as Hari opened it and leaned against the doorframe. He seemed a little nervous about the upcoming plan and Raj knew he wasn't used to being so powerless. Krish had made his decision about how to approach the situation and Raj was in agreement. Hari however, didn't quite seem comfortable with the idea of sending him into the slums like that. It seemed to go against everything they had worked to achieve, to throw Raj back out there in full view once again.

"Are you nervous?" Hari inquired.

He wanted to be truthful about how nervous he was and how skeptical he was becoming of their chances for success. The last time he had been in the slums someone had tried to kill Priya. Granted she was not there to be in danger but it still made him nervous. It didn't feel right going back there after everything that had happened. He'd run away hoping to escape it for good and now here he was returning in full view. He was born and raised in the slums. It was a part of him and would have remained that way had the man who raised him not angered a monster. He couldn't blame his father though – he did what he had to do to protect his family. He had to get even and he was also attempting to get others out of the way of danger.

"A little, but I'll be okay."

"We'll be hidden in the shadows if anything goes wrong," Hari said. "We'll be there if you need us."

"I don't think Chaudhry will know what we are planning. How could he? The mole he had is dead," Raj said, hoping it was true.

"Don't underestimate Chaudhry. He's a despicable man, but a very intelligent one too. For all we know he could be anticipating us doing something of this nature. He could be baiting us and that is something we can't deny as a possibility."

"That's true," Raj returned, "but I think he's probably preoccupied with other things, like his own plans. I mean the people in the slums are frightened of people like Chaudhry and they know if they are disloyal they'll die. Chaudhry will no doubt not even consider that they'll turn against him and face his wrath, besides I doubt they'll even trust me. Two families died in one day because of me."

"It wasn't because of you," Hari argued. "People die in that slum because that bastard barks orders. He does things to manipulate people and if they refuse to become his puppet he finds their weakness and exploits it – that's just how it is."

"Well there's no one here that he can use as leverage against me," Raj said, a trace of regret in his voice.

"Don't be too sure about that. You may be far from Priya but that doesn't exclude anyone else you care for. There are people in this building you are loyal to and you have a bond with."

Raj fell silent because he knew Hari was correct. He hadn't thought of that, but he knew if any one of them was in danger he would come out of hiding for them. No one here needed to die because they knew him. No, he would take care of them and he would take care of everyone in the slums. If he didn't, who else could?

*****

Sultan had been pacing back and forth all morning. He hadn't been able to find anything that could lead him to the location of Priya and it was beginning to irritate him. There was something he was missing because no one can just vanish into thin air, not unless they were powerful, with the resources and Priya was anything but, just a mere peasant girl. Then a thought occurred to him as his conscious fired a question at him. Maybe she was not alone…maybe there was someone with her helping to hide her from society.

He entered the house. Chaudhry was perched on the couch smoking, a detached look on his face. He didn't seem to have a worry in the world. Then again he was more detached than Sultan ever would be. He found and utilized every pleasure in life whereas Sultan spent his days watching people and plotting their death. That was what made Sultan believe Chaudhry was a sociopath, but he would never make a comment like that to his face.

"If you were to hide someone from society where would you put them?" he asked Chaudhry, seating himself on the opposite couch.

Chaudhry snorted. "I have never hid a living person, only their lifeless bodies. Why are you asking me anyway?"

"Because Krish hid Priya away so we couldn't find her. Either she's somewhere in a remote location, or someone with the resources to keep her hidden in plain sight is assisting her."

Chaudhry stubbed his cigarette out and sat up, rubbing his chin as he thought about it. "You're on to something there. If I were Krish I wouldn't put her somewhere remote, no...I would not have that much control over what could happen to her. No, he would surely leave her with someone he trusted. That person would need to be discreet."

Chaudhry mumbled something and became a little more animated as if he knew the answer. He stood and made his way over to his laptop. He opened it and tapped the desk impatiently with a finger as it loaded. He typed in the password and Sultan watched him for a few moments, his face lighting up as his fingers flew over the keys. It took several minutes, though it felt like longer. Finally, Chaudhry stepped aside and motioned for Sultan to look at what was on the screen.

Sultan scanned the five faces on the screen. "Is there a way we can narrow it down?"

"I doubt it. Let's go one by one."

Sultan nodded. It could take a while, but at least it was better than nothing. They were spread out across America. He turned to leave, to ready himself for the journey but Chaudhry stopped him with a hand on his arm.

"Leave no survivors but when you find her, keep her alive and call me. We'll find a way to bring her home to her beloved Raj and in time we'll have ourselves a bloody reunion."

Chapter 29

Raj was overflowing with anxiety as he approached the slums. The spaces around him seemed to grow smaller, closing in on him, the edges dark and fuzzy and he could feel his heart doing its best to beat its way out of his chest. It was a panic attack, he knew, he knew them well after everything he'd been through. They never got easier. He couldn't forget, he realized, what had happened to the people he cared about. He would never forget the fact that he was the reason the Banik family had been killed after his own family. He would never forget how Mahi had taken a bullet for him, and he most certainly would never forget how he watched the life drain out of his friend, how his eyes had lost that last glimmer of life. By going back it was possible he was putting more people in danger. He didn't know how to deal with it because he realized that by going there to save lives he was possibly putting more at risk too.

Sai and Kavi were sitting across from him as the sedan rolled along and they seemed oblivious to the risks. However, Sai kept looking at him like he knew what was happening inside Raj's mind. He knew there was something on his mind – something upsetting him. No one knew about the horrors of what had happened other than Hari and Krish. Kavi had only been told a few details, but did he truly care? He never truly knew them so was it safe to assume that he also didn't feel much of a loss at the news of their passing? That was something Raj had never wanted to ask and would never ask.

"What's the matter?" Sai finally asked.

"Nothing," Raj lied. He'd already spoken to Hari about his feelings so why did he still feel like he had unresolved issues bloating his mind? Why did he want to talk over something that had already been discussed and dealt with?

"You're not a very good liar Raj, so please tell me what's on your mind."

Raj shifted uncomfortably when he saw that Kavi too was staring at him, waiting for him to explain himself. He felt a little silly if he was honest, wanting to revisit feelings he'd already dealt with, but it clearly wasn't done, he still felt like there was more to say.

"I'm not too sure how to describe how I'm feeling." He sighed.

"This has something to do with what happened in the slums, doesn't it?" inquired Kavi.

Raj nodded slowly.

"You're not responsible for anything that happened," Kavi said firmly. "You didn't ask for that to happen."

"I should have been home," Raj said, the words exploding from him soaked in anger. He felt as if he was breaking down inside. "I was supposed to be there and I wasn't! I left because I was angry and upset. Maybe if I'd listened to Mom that day she'd still be here. Maybe they'd all still be here."

Kavi stared at him, his gaze unblinking. "You would most likely be dead if that were the case. I have no idea what it would feel like to love someone so much and then see them like *that*. That was out of your control Raj and for whatever reason it was supposed to happen. We all have a destiny and not everyone likes their ending, but we have to deal with it."

"Has anyone ever sacrificed their life for you?" argued Raj, fighting Kavi, wanting to place further blame on himself. "Did you leave that person to bleed out in the rain while you fled to safety?" Raj fought the tears pushing their way to the corners of his eyes as the memory set off a wave of emotion inside him, emotion that hadn't been sufficiently explored. "Did you run for your life...while...while your friend lay dying?"

"Everything led you right here," Kavi said sharply. "You have a beautiful girl and soon you'll have a child. You're about to make a difference to the lives of everyone in the slum, hundreds, thousands will benefit from this. Fate sucks sometimes, I know, but the truth is," explained Kavi. "If it hadn't happened where would you be right now? Nowhere... This was meant to be, regardless of how twisted it is, this is the road you were meant to go down. Whether or not you like the outcome is something for you to contend with, but there is nothing else that can be done."

There was nothing else Raj could say. Kavi was right, this was right, despite all the strife that had come before. He had vowed to get revenge for everything that had happened and this was a way he could do it. He would be able to honor them.

His head dropped for a moment as he wished his family could see him at that moment, wished that they could reassure him they were okay and that it was alright, he was doing the right thing. He wondered if they were proud of him or if they were furious, especially because of what was at the end of this road. His family had always believed that killing someone would sever your soul and he wondered if souls even existed. Raj had no answers to that question but if there was, at least that meant his family may still be able to see what he was doing in their absence, to see that he was making a difference. He had to admit that this was the most likely road he needed to go down.

The car came to a gentle stop then and outside the window, a familiar sight materialized. He was home. He remembered everything in an instant as if it had been thrown into his mind in a jumble of images and emotions, none of having any order but still so familiar. If it was bad before, it was even worse now. He wondered if everything was deteriorating because the factory was no longer standing. How many people were reliant on that place? How many people were living in a worse state than they were a year ago when all of this took place? Raj could not believe that it had *only* been a year. He never fathomed he could change this much in such a short amount of time.

Finally he took a deep breath and got out of the car. There were workers from the city here doing inspections of the quality of living. They never helped out, even if they found that someone was dying due to malnourishment. All they did was document how many people were in a home and how much the income per household was. Depending on the income would determine whether or not they got to stay in their small dank, rat infested homes. Raj had seen people removed from their premises. He'd heard stories about people being murdered because they refused to leave. Out here no one knew what luxuries were and the small things that people took for granted in the city were things they didn't have here. Only a few residents had running water and very few people had shoes or more than two sets of clothes.

He stood and watched as people began to notice him standing there. The car drove off leaving him there to face these people, these people who he had once called neighbors. He knew they wouldn't trust him, even if they knew who he was. It was in their nature, mistrust, sown into the very fabric of their existence. Besides, they no doubt thought he was dead – yet here he was.

He froze when he saw someone familiar walking among the city workers. This was someone who had informed Raj that *they* would be watching; Inspector Kumar. He didn't appear any different than he did a year ago and he was still wearing his uniform. Most likely in that year he had been fabricating more lies about how and why people were being murdered. Raj remembered his statement about how his family had been murdered. He was a dirty cop and a man with no morals. Raj would have to keep an eye on him as he no doubt would be watching Raj very carefully.

Inspector Kumar glanced in his direction then, and stopped, his eyes narrowing. He remembered. "Well, Raj Varma is it not? I'm surprised you had the guts to show your face back here."

"What do you mean?" Raj asked, trying not to show any emotion.

"You disappeared after the death of the Banik family. Everyone here believes you are the one behind their death."

A fire erupted inside of him, but he refused to show any emotion. He couldn't give this worm of a man the satisfaction of knowing he still held power over Raj. "I'm sure you made up a story. You're actually better at that than your day job," Raj said, hoping for a reaction.

He watched with satisfaction as inspector Kumar frowned, a flicker of emotion crossing his previously smug face. "Do you honestly care what "my kind" think Inspector Kumar? About a year ago you told me we didn't matter and here you are still flaunting whatever superiority you believe you have." Raj smirked just to add a little more flavor to the comments, knowing it would cut his pride to the core.

Inspector Kumar stepped towards him then and the city workers retreated. They knew better than to interfere. He was sure this man was only where he was in the world because someone put him here. He was a pawn in this game Raj realized. He was here to sow lies and because of his position he had the power to do it as often as he liked and no one would ever dare question his motives.

"Why are you here Mr. Varma?" Inspector Kumar asked through gritted teeth.

"I'm here to find out what *you* are doing here. I presume you've already begun to force them from their homes whilst reminding them just how powerless they are to stop you." Raj remembered that day well.

"They have no other choice but to leave," a balding man said suddenly.

Raj looked away from Inspector Kumar for a moment and smirked at the newcomer. "No choice? Really? Why would they not have a choice?"

"They cannot afford to be here any longer. This land is about to be sold."

"I suppose you're right," Raj said his eyes moving from one set of eyes to the next. "This land is being bought by men running for Prime Minister. Do you honestly think you people can force them to leave? Do you even care about them?"

"We care about the greater good and by using this land we can get these people jobs! With jobs, they'll be able to make a better life for themselves."

"Really, so if I took your home away from you right this second, you'd merely say 'oh well, never mind I have a job so all is not lost?' and then proceed to climb out of the gutter and go to work each day? Is that what you're saying?"

Everyone was silent, but Raj knew Inspector Kumar was thinking about his options. "Who do you represent then? Who would want an uneducated piece of crap representing them?" Inspector Kumar almost spat the words at Raj's feet.

"You would know, now wouldn't you Inspector? You seem to have connections to higher places so just ask them."

Inspector Kumar scoffed but Raj knew he was uncomfortable. People were now paying them more attention, hanging out of their windows, and standing in front of their homes, watching and listening to the exchange. They were curious as to what was going on.

"Have you evicted anyone from their own homes today?" Raj asked casually.

"That's none of your damn business," Inspector Kumar said venomously.

"Actually it is," Raj said as he pulled out a checkbook. "You see this place made me who I am today. Whether or not you believe me is up to you. And I'm writing a check to the people who believe they have any power over us. You'll have to develop elsewhere because you're not going to take anyone else from their homes."

Inspector Kumar laughed and prodded the checkbook in Raj's hand. "This'll be a bad check, you can be sure of that. Someone like you would never have the sort of money that would save the slime that dwell here."

Raj finished filling out the check and did it the way Krish had taught him to. He pulled it from the book and handed it to the balding man whose brow glistened with sweat. He was nervous and the hand that reached for the check visibly trembled. "You should not pass judgment on anyone Inspector Kumar," Raj said, meeting the eyes of the officer with his most venomous stare. "Now, do me a favor and get the hell out of my slum. We don't care for people like *you* hanging around where you don't belong."

Inspector Kumar hesitated, unsure of how to act. He was clearly furious with Raj but also afraid of stepping out of line. Raj had played his hand perfectly and he watched as they left, dragging their feet after them. Everyone in the slum stood there as if they had been frozen in time. They most likely didn't understand what had happened and Raj had not fully processed it yet. He had won – it was a small victory and but he knew a war was coming. There was always a war where Inspector Kumar's kind were involved.

Chapter 30

Raj had made the decision to remain in the slums instead of returning to the city. He couldn't deny the emotions that stirred within him at being back in the slums. Here he was, walking among the people who had started their lives here and were stuck here, but they were people nonetheless. Everything about them was different to what he'd seen in the suburbs and he so dearly wanted to help them. They deserved more than what they were being given and Raj began to wonder where he would be if life had panned out differently. He most likely would never have met Priya. Was it truly possible that everything happened for reasons that were beyond their knowledge or did they simply cling to the hope that it did? Even if your circumstances seem hopeless, is it not possible to reach inwards and find the strength to push forward onto better things? Despite that thought, he knew he was no philosopher and that he shouldn't dwell on such things. He was here now and he was going to make a difference.

"You're that Varma boy," an older woman said.

Raj examined her weather-beaten face and recognized her as Mrs. Doshi. He remembered how she would keep his mother and his aunt company. She was widowed and Raj remembered how it had happened. Her husband had been yet another victim of the corrupt forces he was now battling.

"Yes," he finally said. "And you're Mrs. Doshi. You would come over on occasion to speak with my mother and aunt."

She nodded and seemed pleased that he remembered. "We heard awful stories about you, but we don't believe a word of it. Everyone here knows that *they* lie about everything. So could you tell us the truth? What really happened?"

She wasn't the only one waiting to hear the truth. A small crowd had now gathered around him and on their faces he saw expectation. They wanted the truth but Raj knew he would have to withhold some of it, for his and their sake.

Raj took a deep breath and began to tell them his version of the events. "We all know my family was murdered and that night the Banik family took me in. Then whoever was after me found me there. He killed Mr. and Mrs. Banik and Mahi and I…" he clammed up as the memory resurfaced as clear as a full moon on a cloudless night, but fought through the rising panic to continue. "We…we snuck out the window and tried to escape but he had a gun and shot at us. The bullet that was meant for me struck Mahi instead – he saved me. We ran through the night and we tried to keep going, but Mahi was too badly hurt. He died and I left him there…in the rain."

There was silence for a moment and then something occurred to Raj. They wanted to *kill* him but then something changed and they decided they wanted him alive. He was unsure why he didn't question it before but now it was consuming his thoughts. The crowd of people had swelled and now as he looked at them, he could see the questions on their lips. They wanted answers and he would give them but first he needed answers of his own.

"What's wrong?" Mrs. Doshi inquired.

"I'm not sure yet," he said as he ran through the crowd. "There is something I have to do real quickly. I won't be too far."

He walked into the overgrown edge of the slum where he knew they would be waiting, watching. He wanted Hari; he was the one who could answer his question. He saw Hari leant against a tree, a puzzled frown on his face.

"Is something wrong?"

"You told me you would tell me everything," Raj said trying to contain his frustration.

"I haven't hidden anything from you."

"Then explain to me why one moment Chaudhry wanted me dead and now he wants me alive? Why did that change?"

He saw the expression on Hari's face and knew at once that Hari had withheld some information from him. He felt a surge of anger as he clenched his fists. All he wanted were the answers. Surely, he was entitled to them after everything they'd been through. Without knowing the full truth he was vulnerable.

Hari sighed then and said, "Raj, I don't know the full story but Krish does. When you get back to the city you should ask him for the truth."

"Tell me what you know," Raj demanded.

Hari was torn and Raj knew that. Something wasn't right. Raj was tired of the secrets. The anger welled up inside him then until it simmered on the surface, turning his face into a mask of rage.

"Chaudhry wanted me dead so I couldn't blow the whistle on him," Raj said slowly. "He thought I could connect him to what my father had been investigating. There were more files – more evidence that I hadn't yet seen. You made it so I didn't have everything," Raj said, his anger straining to be released. "Since I didn't use the file he assumed it was indeed destroyed and his motives changed."

"Everything in that file will help get Vik Chaudhry and it'll destroy him! I made a judgment call and you found out the truth about everything anyway," Hari said.

"No thanks to you. I was tracking articles trying to figure out who was responsible. If I'd known the truth from the start maybe I'd be in a better position than I am now."

"Raj! Everything in that damn file is still safe but we're not going to release it until we know that we can get to Chaudhry without him manipulating any of it. We will get him."

"That's not good enough," Raj shouted, his anger bubbling over.

"It'll have to be."

Raj glared at Hari. "No, I want the truth. No matter what you do. I'll make my own decisions from now on. I'll be going after Chaudhry and I'll do it my way. Pinning these horrific deeds on him will never be enough to bring him down."

"I'm not disagreeing with you. You told me you want to kill him so do it. I'm just making sure we can weaken him first. It has to be this way Raj and you'll realize that soon enough."

Raj looked up at the sky, at the clouds like grey sacks of rain floating above them waiting to pour more misery down on him. He knew the information might not have any bearing on the future but he couldn't help it. He had asked Hari to tell him everything and he had, at least everything usual to their efforts at the time. Why would he want to tell him something that occurred before that? Despite that he was still angry. He couldn't look at him.

"I'll be staying here for a few days."

"When did you make that decision?"

"The moment I sent Inspector Kumar away," Raj said simply. "Plus this is where I'm from. This place made me and if we want to gain popularity I'm going to have to stay here and prove to these people that this doesn't bother me."

"They'll ask you a million questions."

"Good, because I have answers. These people don't trust the police and they know me. They knew my family and they knew all the good they contributed here. With them gone it seems this place is dying and I'll be giving them something to put their faith in."

"That's noble of you, but you should come back to the city. This place is not safe for you."

"Then let Kavi and Sai stay if they want to."

Raj walked away before anything else could be said. He began to feel a little better as he approached the slums but he was still upset because he hadn't seen the entire file, but that was something he was going to see in a few days. There was information in there that he was sure he needed.

*****

Night had finally come and Raj felt as if the people were on his side now, though he was under no illusions. They'd just as easily abandon their loyalty to him should Inspector Kumar gain the upper hand again. The people of the slums were full of questions that needed answering, questions about the past, questions about the future and what it held for them. Many were still afraid that the killing wouldn't stop, especially if they fought back against the forces attempting to drive them from their homes. Raj was tired though, he needed rest.

He promised them that all their questions would be answered in the morning and retreated to his family home, apprehensive and afraid of the truth it held.

He walked through the gate and stood looking at the front door – the last obstacle between him and the reality beyond. He hesitated, his hand reaching for the doorknob but then falling to his side again as the cold chill of fear blanketed his heart.

He finally mustered the courage to push the door open and take command of his body. He stepped into the hallway and was at once struck by a flood of sensation, the smell of his mother's cooking, the laughter from the living room, the smiles as they greeted him upon his return – all just memories now, but still so vivid. For a few moments he let his memories paint the now dust covered walls with life, bringing back his mother and father, his aunt and the days they spent together.

He saw his mother step into the hallway, a smile on her face, "Come on Raj, you can help me in the kitchen."

"Yes, Mother," he said, following the ghost of her memory to the kitchen, now barren and devoid of life and joy. They'd shared many a conversation there as she rolled the dough in her hands and moved smoothly throughout the kitchen, talking all the while. The warmth of the oven was gone, the steam rising from pots and scents of cumin and turmeric all a mere wisp in his mind now, but the pain was real, the one that felt like a needle had pierced his heart.

He wiped his eyes with his arm when he heard a noise behind him and turned to see Kavi standing in the doorway, his face solemn as he ran his eyes over their surroundings. He looked at Raj then and nodded softly before looking away again, his eyes falling on the blank space where the oven had been. Kavi would never truly know his parents. He would hear stories about them, but he would never know how it felt to be loved by them. Then again he was raised by a loving couple and Raj wondered if he even considered their parents his actual parents. In the same way, Raj considered Dev his father instead of Vik.

"Is everything alright?" Kavi asked his voice soft.

Raj shrugged. Things could be better, much better but he wasn't going to complain. "You know I can still feel them, *see* them here as they were before…"

"I've heard good things about them," Kavi said. "I wonder what our lives would have been like if we'd all grown up together. The way it should have been."

"If not for people like Rajesh Chaudhry there's a strong possibility that things would now be completely different. Maybe you three wouldn't have grown up in the suburbs the way you did, because then dad would never have lost his money," he paused for a moment. "I would never have been born."

"You don't know that for certain," Raj said. "For all we know you could still have been born, but not under the same circumstances, we can never know for sure. But we probably shouldn't dwell on the possibilities of how things could have been. We should probably deal with reality as it stands now."

"When did you find out that Krish and his wife were not your parents?"

"We always knew. Krish never hid that from us and he made sure to tell us everything he knew about them – everything that he knew about you. I'll admit we were all jealous because you got to see them every single day. Even though you grew up here in the slums you still got to know them. We always wanted to meet you and them, but we were always told it was too dangerous. Krish tried to hide everything but not everyone you bring into the fold can be trusted."

Raj nodded in agreement. "After I found out I wasn't the only child I wanted to know you. I felt like I'd be able to get some closure because my family wasn't completely gone."

"So they never talked about us?" Kavi asked a trace of regret in his voice.

"I'm sure they did," Raj said trying to make the best of it, "they never told me certain things and I wonder if it was because they felt the less I knew the safer I'd be."

Kavi nodded but said nothing. Raj wasn't finished with his journey into the past just yet and with Kavi behind him, he made his way into the living room.

He couldn't help but stare at the space on the floor where their bodies had lain, covered by bloodstained sheets. The feelings of that day were there again, in his heart but this time he held them, controlled them, and kept them in their place – a reminder, not a reason to lose control. He gritted his teeth as he remembered the intense rage he'd felt at their loss, his desire to murder the man who had taken their lives. That desire still burned within but now it was tempered by patience, by the knowledge that it wasn't just him involved anymore, the lives of others were at stake too. Chaudhry needed to die.

Granted he was sure someone just as despicable would rise to take his place but that was a battle for another day.

"Do you still consider the slums to be your home?"

"Yes, but I know I can never come back. I've grown as a person and I need to go down this new path. Not just for myself but for the future I want to have with Priya and our unborn child."

As Raj looked around the room he knew he was never going to change this part of himself because this was his foundation. Closing his eyes, he felt the peace of the moment and drew it inwards. All was calm now, but it wouldn't be long until the storm broke.

Chapter 31

They had not yet docked. Priya felt as if the voyage was never going to end. However, she no longer hid herself away below deck. She had finally found her courage and she was now looking at the beautiful sunrise where the wisps of pink dusty cloud met the mottled surface of the ocean as the sun began to creep over the horizon. As long as she looked at the horizon and ignored the rocking motion of the boat beneath her feet, everything was better. She heard a sound and turned to see Siya standing next to her.

"Are you feeling better now?"

"Somewhat, but I couldn't miss this sunrise. It's helped me put things in perspective," Priya explained, still watching the sunrise. "This is what I have to do in order to be safe. Hopefully when this is all over I can travel by air. There'll be less stress - hopefully."

"It is less stressful, and it takes a lot less time. We should be on land in nine days though so it'll soon be over."

"Sure we can't leave the boat?"

"We can, but we cannot go far. Brazil is not somewhere I've been before and I'm not sure how the people are. We'd better stay close to the boat though, anyway, just in case," Siya said, turning to leave.

Priya nodded and continued to focus on the horizon. It was heavenly and the only thing that could possibly make it better was if Raj was next to her. She stared down into the ocean, watching the white surf as the boat cut through the water. She prayed that Raj was okay and that things had died down. She hoped he was resting and not being his usual self, running about trying to save the world. She laughed gently at the thought and nodded to herself. Yes, no doubt he was, in fact she was sure of it.

*****

Raj was restless that night and he was unsure if it was because of where he was or if it was because something was wrong. He got to his feet and walked towards the window and as he looked outside he could have sworn he saw a shadow briefly skip out of view. It could easily have been nothing, but he felt as if it was something. If he'd learned anything from the last year, it was that if something looked wrong – it was wrong.

Moving away from the window he shook Kavi awake. "What...what is it?"

"I think someone's watching us. There was movement out there. I'm sure something's not right, I think we better check it out."

Kavi was on his feet in a heartbeat, quickly pulling on some jeans and a t-shirt. Raj saw him slip a small gun from within his boot. Good, he thought. They'd need it. They heard footfalls in the hallway.

Kavi moved without sound, creeping along the hallway, gun held against his chest and Raj began to see why he was a bodyguard. He was slick rather than robust, stealthy rather than direct and didn't hesitate in his movements, even when the footfalls grew in volume.

He turned a corner and a second later, there was a thud as someone fell to the ground, followed by a grunt.

He rounded the corner quickly and saw Inspector Kumar on his back on the floor. Kavi moved forward with intent and easily lifted Inspector Kumar from the ground, surprising both Raj and the Inspector with his strength.

"Why are you here?" Raj demanded.

"You seem rather intelligent so maybe you should tell me." The inspector wiped a trickle of blood from his lip with the back of his hand. "You just assaulted a police officer," he said, an evil grin spreading across his face.

Kavi was unfazed by the comment and shoved the inspector against the wall. "Yes, that's kind of what happens when you find someone *illegally* prowling around inside your house, inspector." Kavi, however, didn't smile. He was all business.

Raj remembered what Mahi had said. There had been three of them. Three killers had been in his home waiting to kill them and even though he didn't have proof he knew, deep down, that Inspector Kumar was one of them.

"You were one of the three people that Mahi saw that night weren't you? Raj asked. "It was you, Chaudhry and Sultan, no doubt."

The inspector said nothing but the look in his eyes told Raj all he needed to know. Raj was infuriated and wanted to kill him then and there, but he knew they needed him for something else.

"We should take him elsewhere."

Kavi seemed to know exactly where Raj had in mind. He turned to Raj. "Call Hari and let him know what's going on."

"You're a coward, Raj. I was here to help you be reunited with your family, that's what you want isn't it?" Inspector Kumar sneered, his teeth coated with his blood making it look even worse and Raj wanted to reach out then and throttle the corrupted inspector until he was dead.

Every fiber in him wanted to lash out but instead he reigned in his emotions and left the room. He picked up the phone and dialed Hari, the phone shaking in his hand. It took Hari a few rings to answer and once he did he sounded groggy. Raj explained to him everything that had occurred. Hari sounded breathless. "I'll be right over."

Chapter 32

Upon arriving at the compound Raj noticed that everything seemed different. There was a chill in the air and the place no longer seemed familiar, as if he were arriving for the first time, despite the memories he had of his year spent there.

Raj watched as Sai and Kavi tied Inspector Kumar to a metal chair and he watched in fascination as they attached spark plugs from the car to the chair. Raj would never have suspected they'd be able to fit a car in the bottom level. Something about the way they moved told him this wasn't the first time they'd done this.

"You won't get any information from me," he snarled.

That was when Kavi got in his face. "I know how to break people and I will break you. I don't care how long it takes, but eventually, you *will* talk."

Inspector Kumar fell silent then and Raj watched them finishing preparing their means of torture. He was not completely comfortable with how they were handling everything. Sai, on the other hand, didn't seem bothered at all. He was placid – detached. This didn't mean anything to him and Raj wondered how that was possible. When he killed Ash it seemed as if something inside of him broke. He no longer smiled as much and there was a sterile quality to his behavior. Raj wondered if everyone who killed ended up that way.

He pushed the thoughts away before they could take root.

"You need to leave right now Raj." Hari stood before him, his face grim.

"Why? Don't you think I can handle this?"

"No," Hari said. "Go up the stairs and to my office. The file is there on the desk and it would probably be best if you read that. I'd rather you didn't see this."

"I thought you had given up on violence," Raj said, frowning.

Hari flashed a wry smile. "I'm a flawed human and I only became this person because of the wrong I've committed. I'm realizing that I can't be both things and right now this is more important than the values I've tried so hard to take on. So, go and read. We'll come and retrieve you when we're finished here."

Raj nodded and left without a word. He wasn't too sure what was going to happen from here on out, but he'd take it one step at a time. Despite the nagging urgency in him to act quickly and finish this thing once and for all, he knew it was best to take his time. There was more to come and he knew he'd do well to take each step with caution. Taking a deep breath he took another step forward.

Chapter 33

Chaudhry picked up the phone. "What do you want, Tapan?"

"I've done what you asked of me. Inspector Kumar is now wanted by the police. They believed the story you fed to the media and are now hunting him. It's only a matter of time before he's arrested for the trafficking of innocent women."

"Good. Now is there anything else you would like to share with me?" Chaudhry was pleased. Things were proceeding as planned and he knew it was only a matter of time before Priya was in his grasp too.

"There's been a recent development in the slums, I'm afraid. Raj Varma was able to pay off the city workers so the people in the slums can stay there. How would you like me to proceed?"

"Find a way to get that land. I don't care if you have to massacre them. You know exactly why I want that land."

"I understand and I'll be in touch if there're any more developments."

"Excellent," Chaudhry said as he hung up.

There was a knock at the door then and he turned, surprised at the sound. No one ever came unless summoned and he hadn't summoned anyone this night.

He gestured for one of his guards to answer the door. It took a minute and that was when he saw an envelope being carried towards him with a handwritten note attached to it.

Getting to his feet he took it to the desk across the room and removed the knife from his pocket. He cut the envelope open and froze as his eyes fell on the contents. Photos of Inspector Kumar's bloody head stared up at him, the burn marks on his scalp and face a clear indication of how he'd died.

He snatched at the note, fury burning his insides. The handwriting was familiar but the message was something new to him. No one ever crossed Chaudhry, they certainly didn't threaten him.

You're next.

The threat was nothing to him, but he realized they were becoming bolder and that was dangerous. They were getting in his way and he needed to eliminate them before they could ruin everything. His hands shook with the fury coursing through his veins as he jabbed at the phone, dialing Sultan's number. The search for Priya would have to be cut short. There were more pressing matters to deal with.

Sultan answered immediately. "Yes sir?"

"I need you to go to Mumbai for me," he said through gritted teeth. "I need you to get rid of that meddling little worm, Krish. I'll let Tapan know you're on your way. He'll meet you."

"Are you sure it's wise to cut short the search for Priya?"

"For now. Krish is getting in my way and he's proving to be a real threat. In fact get rid of as many of them as possible and if you are able to get to Raj let me know."

"Yes sir," he said just as the line went dead. He didn't know how long it would take Sultan to fulfill this task, but he would be waiting in the shadows until he knew it was safe to come out. He didn't want anyone to attempt to tie anything back to him.

Picking up another cigarette he lit it and walked away from the envelope that held graphic photos of the decapitated head.

Chapter 34

September 2nd, 2008

Priya stared at the woodland surrounding her new home. They were isolated and it seemed, far from civilization. She looked down at her abdomen and she saw how much it had grown in the past few weeks. She only wished Raj was here to experience this alongside her – Raj. He was always on her mind and she wanted to be there with him. She wanted this all to be over and she wasn't even sure how much longer she had to wait.

Not knowing was one of the worst parts of it. Not knowing how long, not knowing if he'd make it to see his child, not knowing if they would ever be a family.

She turned towards the bedroom they had set up for her. It felt more like a prison cell than a place she could call her own. She hadn't been allowed to leave and the only time she'd seen anything remotely interesting had been a couple of weeks earlier. Siya's husband Navin Patel came from a very successful family. He was a second generation American and was beginning to take over his father's business. Priya had no desire to socialize with them because they had made it obvious they were more interested in each other. Most days she felt like a prisoner, but the storm would soon pass. She had to keep telling herself that just to get by these days.

Getting to her feet she felt the cool hardwood floor on the soles of her feet and was deciding what to do next when there was a knock at the door.

"Come in," she said softly.

Siya opened the door and entered. She was wearing colorful scrubs and a golden name badge. Her hair was tied back and she seemed as if she had lost several hours of sleep.

"I was just coming in to check in with you. Is everything okay?" she asked.

The answer was a simple no, but Priya couldn't tell her that. She couldn't confess how miserable she was feeling because that could somehow come across as being ungrateful and Priya was anything but ungrateful. "Everything's perfectly fine. I'm just anxious. All I can think about is Raj, and the baby. Will we ever see each other again? Will we ever be a family and if so…how long do I have to wait? Not knowing anything is driving me mad; I don't know how much longer I can take it!" Priya bit her lip as a single tear rolled down her cheek.

Siya stepped into the room and shut the door behind her. She took a seat in the desk chair that was across from Priya and was silent for a moment. It was as if she didn't have a response for her, but she finally spoke. "Everything is going to work itself out. I know this situation is not ideal. We're keeping you locked up like a wild animal and you've no idea what's going on outside these walls, but don't lose your faith, Priya. You're a strong young woman and I know you'll get through this somehow because I've seen the fire in you."

Somewhere inside her, there was a ray of hope but she didn't know how long she could hold on. No one knew what had happened to her – to her family. How could anyone else understand her, except Raj? She'd lost everything and it seemed as if she was never meant to have that – a family. She felt as if she was losing everything she'd thought she was about to gain, a family, a life, a fresh start. Everything she wanted was there with him and now she didn't even know if he was okay. All she wanted was for him to be okay and to hear his voice, just once so she knew there was still a chance. She wondered if he even thought of their child; something that was going to forever bind them together or if he was so intent on revenge that even that eluded him.

Priya curled up on her bed and began to cry.

Chapter 35

Raj understood why Hari and Krish had decided to wait to reveal the file to the public, but he was sick and tired of waiting. He'd seen how easy it had been for Chaudhry to pin the blame on a dead man and it made him paranoid about what was coming next. He wondered if they had an insider but part of him wanted to believe that he could now trust those working to aid him. He was tired of the mistrust, of the constant worrying. He regarded those at the table with him; those he hoped would help him to put right the wrongs that Chaudhry had so selfishly committed.

Dinner was a silent affair, each person seemingly lost in thought and Raj found himself thinking once more about Priya. He wondered if she was dealing with the pregnancy okay without him. He wondered if she could feel the baby kicking but he mostly wondered how often she was thinking about him.

At last, someone broke the silence.

"It seems that you've gained the trust of the locals in the slums, Raj," Krish said.

"I've not given them a reason not to trust me. You can sense the difference out there now. They aren't as paranoid as they once were."

"I think it's mostly because those city workers won't be going out there anytime soon. Especially with Inspector Kumar out of the picture."

Raj was a little apprehensive. "And what of that?" he asked. "What if someone blames me for his disappearance? After all, I wasn't exactly his greatest fan, was I?"

"I'm sure he had more than one person who wanted him gone. Come to think of it, I'm sure there were more than a few who would have loved to have done what we had to."

Raj was eager to learn what they had found out from him before he died. He was certain they would have learned he was working for Chaudhry. It was as plain as day but surely that wasn't all they learned.

"So far everything seems to be going well. I'm very pleased with our progress though I am required to make a statement tomorrow afternoon," Krish continued.

"I thought Raina was supposed to be your spokesperson."

"He's helping to support my campaign, but he doesn't have the same people skills I do. He's good at what he does, don't get me wrong, but I'd rather speak for myself in this case."

"Who will you be taking with you?" inquired Sai.

"I only wish for you and Kavi to accompany me. There's no need to be traveling with too many guards. Leave that kind of thing to Chaudhry as the showman he pretends to be. I prefer to work with as few people as possible; besides, they might take that as a show of guilt when I'm far from guilty."

The dinner ended and Krish rose as the plates were cleared away.

"Raj, come. We have much to discuss," Krish asked, nodding in Raj's direction.

Raj rose from his seat without hesitation and took up a place at Krish's side. He wasn't sure what they were about to discuss, but he hoped Krish perhaps had some news about Priya. Was she okay? Was something wrong? One question led to another in his mind and he began to feel hopeless but before it could bring him down, he forced himself to stop. It would do him no good to fret about something he had no control over.

"Please take a seat," Krish said as he took his own. "I'd like to thank you for the help you've given me, Raj. If it were not for you I don't think I'd be as popular as I am currently. Now I want you to name your price."

"All I want is to be with Priya again," Raj said, and he meant it.

"Is that all?"

"Krish that is all I need. I want to go to school and find a job, especially since we are expecting. I'm fearful I am going to make a mess of it all."

"I'm sure you'll be fine. Everything is going to be okay. You just need to believe that."

Raj didn't want to admit his doubts. Everything he'd worked for seemed to be in vain. All he wanted was to be able to get back what he felt he had lost. He had lost his ability to feel like he was in control. He could no longer think of anything else other than all the chaos going on around him, and they were going to bring a baby into this world, a world of running and risk, killing and lies.

"Tell me what you're thinking." Krish looked him in the eye as if urging him, pleading to know the contents of his mind.

"I don't know...it's all a mess. Priya's gone with our baby, Chaudhry's still alive," he paused trying to make sense of the chaos. It's going to be alright though, isn't it?"

"We have to believe it will, Raj. Do whatever you need to do because I can assure you it's far from over. You must be prepared to suffer a little. Are you prepared to be brought to your knees?"

"No."

"At least you're honest. – Raj if your parents were here now they would be so proud of you. You have a good head on your shoulders and the courage to fight."

Raj was silent for only a moment. "Do you think, when it comes down to it, that I can actually kill Chaudhry?"

"I don't think you can," Krish answered quickly as though he were certain.

"Then why am I going to be the one in charge of pulling the trigger?"

"You don't need to plan it, believe me, but killing is something we are all capable of and when it comes down to it – it would be better to kill him. Imagine the fear that would end when he is gone. Everything will work itself out, and even if you think you cannot do it, that doesn't mean you'll fail to do it when the time comes."

Raj nodded and said nothing.

"You're free to go Raj. If you need anything let me know, and could you please have Sai and Kavi come here? I'd like to speak to them about tomorrow."

Nodding he got to his feet and he walked out of the office. His mind was spinning, lost in a confusing miasma of possible futures. He needed to lie down.

*****

Krish was reading over the local paper. He couldn't shake the feeling that something was going to go wrong. He would have put it down to paranoia but he knew better than that. Theirs was a precarious situation. He heard a knock on his door and turned to welcome the newcomer but was surprised to see it wasn't Sai or Kavi. Instead he saw his wife standing there. She too seemed to know something was wrong. She was highly intuitive, preferring peace to conversation but he knew she was far wiser than him. Everything he had accomplished was because of her insight. She was invaluable to him, he loved her.

"What's the matter, love?"

She shut the door behind her and took a step towards him. She looked awkward as she stood there hugging herself.

"I've been thinking about everything that Chaudhry knows about us. How do you know he isn't going to be able to figure out anything more? Siya's in danger, she needs to know," she ordered, her voice trembling.

"We took precautions with Siya, there's nothing more we can do. She's more than capable of taking care of herself," Krish said reassuringly. "Why, is something wrong?"

"Call Varun," she nearly whispered.

A chill went down his spine. No, it wasn't possible. None of this was possible. Varun was safe. He had to be. He picked up his phone and dialed Varun's number. To his shock, the call went straight to Varun's voicemail.

"It's possible his phone died or he has it off while he is working," he reassured himself, not quite convinced. "We shouldn't worry," he said, but he knew he was only saying it to reassure himself. "I mean he *is* working odd hours at the hospital and you know that." Somehow, his words seemed empty.

His wife shook her head, the look of fear on her face like a portent to bad news. "You know I don't worry about things needlessly. Something's wrong and you need to do something," she turned and left him sitting there, a growing feeling of horror freezing his insides.

She slipped out of the room and Krish sat there frozen for a moment. He didn't want to believe it. He knew he couldn't deny the possibility though, he needed to look into it and he needed to be sure. He grabbed for his tablet, almost dropping it in the process. With shaking hands, he searched for anything, something that might give him a clue as to what was happening. Then he found it – the truth.

This afternoon police officers were sent out to a local Hollywood address. Upon their arrival they found an unidentifiable body and police are making the assumption that the deceased is the homeowner, Varun Wasimrao. Police are now furthering their investigation to find the truth about what happened and who is responsible.

Krish didn't know what to feel. It was like it wasn't real, it was a cruel prank. His door opened then and he looked up to see Kavi and Sai. He wondered briefly if he should tell Kavi what had happened to his brother but he still couldn't believe it. Kavi saw the look on his face and frowned. He knew something was wrong but Krish didn't know how to tell him. The two of them had been inseparable until they parted ways. Varun went into the medical field to save people and Kavi was a trained assassin. Despite that, they looked past their differences and now Kavi had lost yet another part of his family.

"What's the matter?" asked Kavi.

He couldn't hide this from him, but maybe he needed to do that for now. He needed Kavi to be completely focused, but he might lose his trust if he kept this from him. There couldn't be any more secrets.

"Your brother..." Krish started to tell him but the words felt glued to his tongue.

The expression on Kavi's face changed immediately. "What happened to Varun?"

"Sultan most likely happened," Krish said slowly.

"How did they find him? How were they able to track him? We made sure there was no paper trail and now he's – he's gone!" Kavi said, his voice cracking, tearing into fragments as his emotions took over. "What happened, Krish?"

Krish didn't say anything. He'd already said too much, already torn enough of Kavi's world down around him.

"Krish you need to tell me how bad it is," Kavi begged.

"The body at the scene, it couldn't be identified."

"Then how do you know it's even him?"

"You can't live in denial Kavi."

"Does Raj know?"

"No, I just found out. Kavi if you need to leave you can. I know this is hard."

Kavi fell silent and a look Krish recognized all too well appeared on his face, the look of a man who had made up his mind to throw it all away on one last roll of the dice. He was going to get even and Krish knew there was nothing he could do to stop him. It was his brother after all. What right did he have?

Chapter 36

He was going to get even. He was going to make sure Varun hadn't died in vain, then and only then would he allow himself to mourn. That was all he needed. He needed to avenge his brother. He was a good man, a man who had chosen to serve others and now he was gone, cruelly taken away. Kavi had no choice, and even if he did it wouldn't matter. This was his decision and he would make every single one of them pay.

He was like a ghost as he moved in and out of the shadows. He was a natural killer. He remembered how everyone would talk about them as if they were the moon. Varun was the light side, the one that shone brightly through the darkest of the nights; Kavi was the dark side – cold and unexplored, a mystery. Growing up together, it had been Kavi who kept them safe. No one touched his brother and escaped his fury and this was no different except now, he meant to kill. If only Varun had remained here it would have been easy to take care of him.

Slinking through the alley he knew where he was heading. There was only one way to get to the people he wanted and they were comfortable in their own home. No one ever crossed their path and no one even dared look them in the eye for fear of what would happen.

They claimed Chaudhry had nothing to do with them. He knew that to be utter bullshit.

He approached the gates confidently, sure of what was about to happen but already shorn of any fear that might have stunted his progress.

"Get the hell out of here!" A voice warned from the shadows.

"I want to speak to your boss."

"Well, I assure you, he doesn't want to speak to you, now get lost before I—"

"If I were you, I'd ask him because my patience is wearing thin. You don't have much time, now move." He pressed his face against the bars and watched the guard wilt under his stare.

The guard faltered and finally gave in to his demands. Kavi waited for a few minutes and soon the leader of the Silas Gang appeared. His name was Asim Raju and he grew up in the suburbs yet he wanted nothing to do with that life. Instead he took the money he inherited and kept his gang in his deceased mother's home.

"What do you want Kavi?" he asked, glowering at him through the gate. "Are you here to accuse me of being involved with someone I don't even know?"

"Drop the act. You know who Chaudhry is because you've helped him out before and he has helped you just as much."

"Even if you were correct why would I help you?"

"Asim, if you help me I will help you, it goes both ways, you know that."

"I'm insulted that you think I need your help. I've all I need right here," he said motioning to the land around him, the virtual palace at his back. "What could I possibly need from you?"

"I know you're lying. I promise you, you're treading on thin ice with Chaudhry. You're moving into territory you have no business being in. That is exactly why your daughters are growing up without a mother. Help me and I will help you to ensure that nothing happens to your children."

It took longer than Kavi thought it would for him to respond. "What did Chaudhry do to you that makes you want to offer something of this nature to me?"

"Sultan killed my brother and he did such a thorough job they couldn't even identify his body. Help me get to Sultan or even Chaudhry so I can get my revenge."

"Bloodlust," he snickered. "It's in all of us. I suppose I can help you. You just need to promise me that I can get my hands on Sultan before you finish him. He took something away from me as well."

Kavi nodded, letting himself relax a little. He'd figured that getting Asim on his side would be more difficult. Satisfied, he began to walk away.

"Wait," Asim said. "I have one final question for you."

"And what is that?"

"Are you planning to get to Tapan Butala?"

Kavi didn't know what they had planned for Tapan Butala. He knew they should be trying to do something to him but when Raj won the slums over from them he felt they had done enough.

"Why is Butala a concern of yours?"

"I may not be a good man because of the things I've done, but I have only killed those who truly deserved death. I've gotten rid of murderers and rapists and that is why Chaudhry and I don't have a good relationship. I eliminated his own men without even knowing, but it was because they deserved it. I know what Butala is and what he's done. I also know what he's planning to do."

"And what exactly is he planning?"

"He wants to kill everyone in that slum and it's because they've sided with Krish."

"Do you know how he plans to do it?"

"I only know some vague details," he said slowly. "But we know it will be a biological attack of some kind. I don't know how to prevent it."

Kavi nodded. He was still not able to think clearly, but he knew who he needed to talk to. He knew what he needed to do. With his mind set on his next action, he approached the gate once more and said "I'll be in touch. If you ever need to speak to me, you know where to find me."

Asim nodded and they parted ways. Kavi wondered how it was possible that two criminals who walked on different sides were able to make a truce. Asim had never been a horrible criminal and it was true, he only killed off those who deserved it. Kavi wondered how he had even managed to become something of an ally to Chaudhry. Kavi's mind was like a computer now, skimming over the possibilities and it didn't take him long to find the answers he needed.

He needed to tell the others.

*****

Raj was restless and as soon as he heard the knock on the door he jumped up and opened it to see Kavi standing there. He knew something was wrong because he'd never seen that look in Kavi's eyes before. Kavi silently motioned for Raj to follow and knowing something was very wrong, he did so without hesitation.

"What's going on?" Raj finally asked as they walked down the hallway.

Kavi refused to look at him and Raj knew something serious had happened. Did this have something to do with Priya? He quickly pushed the thought away because he knew that if this was something to do with Priya he'd have known by now. Raj knew this was something more personal. Someone he was close to was in trouble of some kind. He wondered if it had something to do with Siya or Varun.

When they reached Krish's office they walked inside and Hari and Krish were waiting for them. Hari looked weary; a shadow of his former self and Raj wondered if he'd been up with the baby again. He had barely seen Hema around the house. The women here knew how to disappear.

"What is it this time?" Hari muttered, stifling a yawn.

"I spoke with Asim and he's given me some information I needed to talk to you all about."

"What can Asim know that we don't?"

"Butala is planning to attack the slums."

"You should start from the beginning," Krish said as he noticed the puzzled looks on all of their faces.

Kavi let out a sigh and nodded wearily. "Asim is the leader of Silas," he started. He knew Hari already knew some of this information. "He and Chaudhry had been partners of sorts. How their relationship started we don't know. All we know is that Asim only ever killed those who deserved to die and most of those people were

Chaudhry's men. Because of that, their relationship went downhill and Chaudhry sent Sultan to kill Asim's wife."

"Alright," Raj said. "How do we know we can trust him?"

"We follow a code Raj. Plus Sultan made a video documenting everything he did."

"Wouldn't that be used against him?"

"Maybe if there was evidence that it was Sultan in the video. Even though we know it doesn't mean we can prove it to anyone else. For now we have the same goals."

"Why do *you* want Sultan dead?" Krish said, a puzzled look on his face.

Kavi said nothing. He simply stared at Krish, unsure of what to do.

"What are you keeping to yourself," Krish finally asked.

"Varun was killed," Kavi said his voice shaking. It was painful putting into words what he still didn't want to admit to himself. "He was most likely tortured first."

"Why would Sultan, or even Chaudhry, want Varun dead?" Raj asked.

No one had any answers but finally Krish spoke up. "There are only five people that I would trust to keep Priya safe and Varun was one of those five. They're looking for a way to get to you Raj."

"This is all my fault," Raj said as he thought about the brother he never got to know. Varun was the brother that Kavi and Siya got to know. Someone they loved and now he was gone, and all for what? Raj felt sick.

Raj stood then, eager to escape. He walked out into the hall and headed for the front door. There was somewhere he needed to go. He needed to think, he needed to find himself again, to see through all the chaos in his mind. He knew where he was going, a place from the past.

Chapter 37

Raj was on his knees. He looked up to the sky above him. The heavens opened up once more, just as they had that day when his world had been torn from him and tossed into the gutter of the slums. The rain pounded against his scalp and he relished the sensation as it pounded away all the misery and imbued him with an inner strength he'd lacked for several days now. It was time for him to stand up and take responsibility, to do everything in his power to stop the suffering.

He couldn't afford to mope about, worrying and fretting about what the future might hold.

Lightening ripped through the darkness before his eyes like the flash of a camera, blinding him but giving him strength at the same time. He felt as if the elements were speaking to him, shouting at him, telling him to do something.

"Mother Universe," he screamed to the heavens. "Guide me on this path!"

As if in answer to his cry for help, the heavens shook with a crash of thunder that shook the ground and seemed to stretch off into the distance, an echo fading across the sky. When the sound faded completely, Raj let out a long breath and straightened his soaking body.

He had the answer he needed.

*****

Morning had come but he still hadn't slept. He was lost in thought. A voice pulled him away from his train of thought and he looked up. "Tapan," Katherine said as she stood there on the balcony. She was stunning and she was all his. She was naïve and it worked to his advantage. Everything he asked of her was done perfectly and without question. Even if someone attempted to tell her of his vindictiveness she wouldn't believe them. He controlled her and he loved the power he felt.

"Yes my dear, is something wrong?"

She shook her head. "I see you've been restless. I didn't know if there was something I could do to help you sleep."

"Everything is perfectly fine. I'm just a little on edge because of the campaigns coming up. You also know that I'm losing out on the deal I was supposed to be making out in the slums of Pune and Mumbai."

"Yes, I heard that. I know you'll come out on top. No one else in this election is as innovative as you are. I'm sure you'll do perfectly fine."

Tapan smiled. Katherine knew nothing of his past or of the hell he was about to unleash upon the slums. He knew his plan against Krish and his loyal supporter Raj. Tapan knew what they were playing out, but he was going to be playing this game better than them. No one suspected what he was going to do.

"Thank you for believing in me sweetheart. I don't know where I'd be without you," he said and kissed her forehead.

He took a step away from her as they heard the doorbell ring. He peered over his shoulder. "It's most likely DeeGee. He said he'd be over today so we could discuss our plans in the campaign. I'm sorry I didn't tell you about this earlier."

Katherine embraced him and kissed his face. "There's no need to apologize. Go and do whatever you need to."

Katherine waited until he was gone before quickly hurrying into the bedroom. She pulled out a device from her pocket and walked over to her dresser. From behind a hidden drawer she pulled out her laptop and booted it up. Within seconds, wearing a headset, she was listening to Tapan's conversation.

"It's good to see you Tapan," she heard Deepak Gupta say to her husband. "I just wanted to bring you the virus you asked so kindly for."

"Is there anything else I should know about how you got this?"

Katherine heard a laugh. She knew DeeGee was a man who trusted few people, but even he couldn't see through her façade. She heard him speak. "I have my connections but I'm not about to reveal them to you. That would not be wise on my part, because then you'd have no use for me now, would you?"

"That's true," Tapan agreed. "So what's the best way to transmit this to everyone in the slums?"

"Put it in the water and their food supply. Everything will work out, plus I'll ensure that you are able to present them with a cure. They'll put their faith in you again."

"And there's no way that this could be traced back to me?"

"Of course not Tapan. Do you honestly think I would put you in jeopardy? We have the same goals after all and right now it doesn't look like Chaudhry will be able to join us in the elections. He's staying in Rio for now and even though he managed to escape any blame in the recent troubles that still doesn't guarantee success in the elections."

"And you think I have a chance? You know they think I had something to do with the death of my family."

"They could never prove it and you played your part very well in that matter. Plus we both know they'll never be able to put you anywhere near them at the time of their death."

There was silence for a moment and Katherine waited patiently.

"Is there anything else that you need me to do?" Tapan asked.

"Yes. Sultan will be here this afternoon and we need place him somewhere."

"Why is he back here?"

"Why else? Chaudhry is going to terminate Krish once and for all. He's been messing up our plans and it can't go on any longer, he has to go."

"That's very true. Sultan is more than welcome here. Also, there is no need to tell Katherine anything about him coming here. She's going to travel to New York to visit her grandmother. I guess she's having complications and wants to see her before she passes. It's pathetic but I'd rather she wasn't here anyway. She gets in the way."

"I do hope she's taking that disgusting toddler with her?"

"Yes, she is, thankfully. We'll be able to get more accomplished here with her gone."

Katherine smiled to herself and ended the recording. She packed the laptop into her suitcase along with her clothes and stepped back, a smile on her face. It was almost over. She wouldn't be coming back.

She ensured that Tapan had helped in digging his own grave, only he didn't suspect anything. He'd been an easy target.

As she was zipping the suitcase she heard Tapan walk into the room. "Do you need me to drive you to the airport?"

She shook her head and smiled. "That's fine Hun; I already made arrangements with the car service. I'll be fine. I'll call you once I arrive."

She grabbed her suitcase and walked down the hall to Emery's room. He was playing with his dinosaurs and she smiled at him knowing it was over for him too, they'd be leaving this hellhole for good. She'd played her cards perfectly.

"Are you ready to go see grandma?"

He looked up at her and nodded. "Yes mommy," he said as he got to his feet and walked over to his small suitcase. She took him by his free hand and they started their journey to freedom.

Chapter 38

Raj had returned and now they were all together. They needed to figure out how to protect the people in the slums, but how could they protect them if they didn't know where the strike was coming from?

Sai looked up from the computer. "Who is Dr. Rohan Mysore?"

Krish straightened immediately. "He's a biomedical engineer. He's been trying to find cures for certain illnesses. Why, what's going on with Dr. Mysore?"

"He reported a break in at his laboratory but nothing was found missing."

"Then that's a lead we need to follow up. I suspect there is something missing, but for some reason he's not saying anything. I think that's a place to start."

Kavi and Sai exchanged looks and nodded to one another. "We'll look into it. We'll call you when we know something."

"Good, and Raj I think you should head back to the slums with Hari. We need to keep an eye out because there's something not right here."

"Do you think we should bring Asim with us?" Hari inquired. He knows more about what we are looking for."

"Yes," Krish said and it was obvious he was deep in thought. "You should go and speak with him and figure out how he knows this."

Raj got to his feet and left the room, his own mind going over the details of their plan with a fine tooth comb. Raj felt as if they were missing something but he couldn't quite figure out what. He knew it was something obvious and yet it eluded him.

They walked outside to the car and Raj was deep in thought the entire way. He was curious to know how someone like Asim was able to get all of this information.

As they pulled away from Krish's home he noticed that Hari was watching him carefully. "Is everything alright with you Raj?"

"I'm doing better than Kavi," he said simply knowing that for once he was right about his feelings.

"You seem troubled. You want to talk about it?"

"What do you know about Asim and his gang?"

"I know they're vigilantes more than thugs. They do more good in this community than people realize," Hari said. "A lot of them feel that they are the reason people in the slums are being killed off, but that's just what Chaudhry wants."

"None of this makes sense," Raj said, irritation tainting his words. "I can't figure it out. It's one big shit storm if you ask me."

"It makes perfect sense Raj, but you are new to this information and that's why it doesn't make sense to you – but it will," Hari assured Raj.

"Kavi was anticipating killing someone last night," Raj said. "I saw the look in his eyes, but for some reason, he didn't do it."

"Your brother knows how to get information out of people and that was what he was trying to do. Perhaps he thought he may

222

have to use violence to get what he needed but it turns out he didn't –
luckily for them."

"How do you know you can trust them? Kavi said something
about a code, but surely that's not true is it?"

"I assure you Raj, the code is very real and is the very reason
I know we can trust these people. You can call us crazy all you want
but this is just how we operate."

Raj nodded and they were silent for several minutes as they
made their way to Asim's residence. From the outside you'd never be
able to tell that something dark resided inside, but that was something
about appearances. They were deceiving and not everyone was keen
to see past initial appearances.

They parked up the road from the residence and made their
way towards the house, watching for any signs of trouble. He didn't
see anyone outside, all appeared to be quiet and Raj wasn't sure if he
liked that – it usually meant trouble. As they were walking up to the
door a heavyset man appeared from the shadows. "Names," the man
said in a voice you wouldn't want to hear in a dark alley way.

"Hari Singh Sidhu and Raj Varma."

"Follow me."

Doing as he said, Raj stepped inside. He had been expecting it
to be cold and uninviting, but it was welcoming more than anything.
This was a family home, or at least that was how it felt. Raj saw that
there was a playpen set up and children's toys all throughout the area.
He saw that there was a child no older than three sleeping on the
couch. She was sucking her thumb and Raj thought it was a strange
thing to see considering where they were. Raj saw a man standing not
too far away. He was watching the child fondly and when he saw
them, his face lost its friendly expression.

He gestured for them to follow and they did so. They made their way to a small office that was just off the living room.

"I presume you've come to question me?"

Hari was the first to speak. "How were you able to get the information about what Tapan Butala was planning?"

"First off, Butala had the idea, but it was Deepak Gupta who actually followed through. How I know is through one of the people I work with. He works in the same lab as Dr. Mysore. He knew what went missing and he knew exactly what it was for."

"In that report Dr. Mysore said that nothing had gone missing. We sent someone out to go ask him a few questions."

"Your friends will not get any answers," Asim said simply. "Why would they keep the only person who knows the cure alive? They'd allow him to make the report and state nothing was taken. They'd also tell him that by lying, his life would be spared, but that's not the case. No, instead they'd kill the only person who knew how to make the antidote."

"What went missing?"

"It's a poison known as ricin and they had no cure for it, but that was what Dr. Mysore was working on - the cure."

"Ricin," Hari repeated, thinking it over. He knew that poison; he'd heard the name before. "If I'm not mistaken, ricin is a very rare poison is it not? Why would he be looking into curing something that rare?"

"Because it's not as rare as people think it is. This poison is being used in biological warfare and he's attempting to cure those who have suffered its effects. This poison can kill quickly and right now it's in the process of being tested in small concentrations across the African continent."

"Why, what's the point of testing in another country?"

"Why else would someone do something of that nature?"

Raj thought on it for a moment and nodded when the answer came to him. "Money."

"Yes. And who better to get that money from than those who work with the blood diamonds. They kill off anyone deemed a threat and soon that entire tribe dies out if they're poisoned with the right dose. How else do you think certain people have unlimited resources?"

Raj didn't like it one bit. It was yet another twist in the corrupt mess they were trying to unravel. Hari's phone began to ring then.

"Hello," he said.

There was silence as he listened and then after a moment, he hung up and looked at Raj.

"That was Kavi. You were right Asim, Dr. Mysore is dead."

"How do we protect everyone if this is what we're up against?"

"We need to be smarter than our opponent, that's how," Asim said.

Raj was silent for a moment as he thought about it. He wondered if the plan was a sick way of winning back the loyalty of the people in the slums – what else could they possibly gain from doing it? "This may sound crazy," he began. "But what if they have the cure? What if their plan is to make it *look* like the people are suffering from some kind of illness? It would make sense then for them to come charging in, the saviors of the slum. It would make sense, especially if they need to win back the trust of the people, which they do."

"That's a good theory," Asim said. "I'll be addressing it shortly."

"Why you? I'm sure the two of us," he motioned to himself and Hari, "are perfectly capable of taking care of it."

Asim nodded, "You care for those people because you were one of them once, but now you are not. You might have been able to win their trust but if you get involved in this situation they're going to become suspicious and you know full well that would play right into Butala's hands."

"I can help though, I want to help," Raj insisted.

"Your presence would do more harm than good," Asim snapped. "You have good intentions, but I know what I'm doing and this is not for the glory I can assure you that. I'm doing this because it's the right thing to do and anyway, I'm a monster, you're not. Let the monsters deal with monsters."

Raj wanted to argue but he knew Asim was right. Asim made sense and there was no denying that.

"So I guess that means we're heading back to Krish's," Raj said, turning to Hari.

Hari nodded and got up to leave. Raj knew there was nothing more they could do, but still, something bugged him.

"Why are you doing this?" he asked Asim, pausing at the door.

"Doing what?" he asked simply.

"Helping us catch the monsters. Why would you put yourself in that position?"

"I have two children that are being raised without their mother. They may not live in the slums, but they deserve better. Hell, every single person here deserves better. There's so much bloodshed and not enough people care to do anything about it and the longer we let this continue, the worse it'll get," he explained and Raj could see he was passionate about it. "If we stop it now it could mean we would have a better future. I don't want my children to have to go through the same suffering I went through and thousands more are going through because of scum like them. I want them to live peacefully and without any worry and without having to take extra precautions to be safe. That is the life they and every other person out there deserves and I'll help to make it possible."

"Then why have a gang?"

"We are *labeled* as a "gang", but people don't really know what we're trying to do here. They'd rather put a label on something than attempt to understand it."

Raj nodded. "I'd like to help you if I can."

"I'm sure you would, but we both know this is not the lifestyle for you. Right now you are stuck in it, but you're not bound to it. You are meant to be something different and deep down you know that's true."

There was no way Raj could explain how he knew that was true. Hell, he couldn't even explain how Asim knew that, but there was no use arguing about it. They left the house then, Hari and Raj and as they walked to the car there was a clap of thunder overhead. What other news was on the horizon, he wondered.

Chapter 39

Katherine walked slowly through the doors of Raina Industries alone and unafraid, she'd done her job and now it was time to put the final touches together. Everything seemed to be going the way it needed to and as she walked to the front desk she saw Jeanine sitting there, focused on her computer screen.

"Kat," she said as she looked up. "Are you here to see Mohit?"

She nodded and Jeanine picked up her desk phone and made the phone call to her boss. "Mr. Raina," she said. "I know you're busy but you have a visitor."

Jeanine put down the phone and smiled politely. "He'll meet you in his office. He's just finishing up his meeting."

"That's perfect," Katherine said with a smile. She was so close.

She walked to the elevator stepped inside. She and Emery would soon be free from that horrible man. The two of them had spent more than enough time in his presence to know he was sick and she was glad to be helping with his demise. This had been a plan of theirs for years and it finally worked itself out. Everything was good, but the thought of it all being so made her a little paranoid. She felt as if it was too easy, but maybe this was the way it was supposed to feel when you played your part perfectly.

Stepping out of the elevator she walked down the carpeted hallway and she found Mohit's office. She opened the door and saw Mohit standing at his desk, a smile on his face.

"How was your flight?"

"It was long, but Emery was good the entire time."

"Tapan is not suspicious?"

"Are you kidding." she laughed lightly. "He thinks I'm smitten with him."

"I'm sure it must have been hard for you to keep up the act."

"Not really. Tapan never speaks to me because he felt we shared nothing intellectually and that was fine by me."

"So you have all the information I need?"

"Yes I do, but before I give it to you are you sure this'll bury him?"

"Of course I'm sure and I'd never put you in any sort of danger. You'll be like a ghost. I'll make sure you disappear from his radar for good."

Katherine nodded and got out what she had spent the past two years retrieving. She knew her job had been done and now it was time for her to live the life she wanted and the life her son deserved.

She handed everything over to Mohit he nodded his thanks. "A mere thank you will never be enough, so I hope you enjoy your life from here on out Katherine. Everything you need will be at your hotel and if you have any questions you know how to get in touch."

She nodded and got up to leave. It was finally over. She was finally free.

*****

Krish was sitting at his desk when he heard his phone ring. The number was blocked, but he took the chance and answered it anyway. For the first few seconds he heard nothing but then he heard Mohit's voice, "We have the location of Vik Chaudhry."

"You were able to play your hand rather well it sounds like," Krish said. "Is there any other information that I should know?"

"Sultan is in Mumbai. He's been ordered to eliminate you. Take care and watch your back. I'll be monitoring everything on my side."

"Good, and Mohit thank you for everything."

"Of course," he said. "So how are you going to get your hands on Chaudhry?"

"That's not for me to decide but for the person going after him."

"What's your proposal?"

"You'll soon see. Be sure to be watching the news because that's where you'll see my next inquiry."

"Is there anything in particular I should look out for?"

"I trust you will know when you see it."

"Alright," he said slowly. "Do you not want to know where Chaudhry is located?"

"No, I have a plan that should get him back here."

Mohit was silent for a moment. "Then I'll leave you to it, Krish, until next time."

He got to his feet and couldn't help but feel numb. Everything was moving much quicker than he thought it would, but now he had the upper hand and that meant everything to him. He left his room and headed down the hallway to find Raj.

He knew where to find Raj and when he saw him he immediately knew what he was reading. Krish had never known what it felt like to lose someone. He wondered if Raj felt any form of connection to his brother, and Krish knew there was one person he had not informed about all of this and that was Siya. He wasn't ready to tell her because the moment he attempted to call her it could compromise hers and Priya's safety. He couldn't put her in danger. When this was all over he knew he would have no choice but to break the news to her.

He approached Raj and stopped behind him, waiting for him to notice his presence. Raj looked up a moment later. He seemed to know something was on his mind.

Krish began, "Everything's beginning to play out better than I hoped."

"What do you need from me?" Raj asked, knowing that it was almost time to take action.

"I need you to allow Sultan to capture you."

"Why would I let that maniac capture me?" Raj said, taken aback by the request.

"Because if he's able to get his hands on you, Chaudhry might very well make an appearance. When he does, we'll be waiting."

"I'm confused," Raj said slowly as he tried to work out the plan, "Why would I want to sabotage Kavi and Asim's plan to capture Sultan? If he gets me…how could they possibly get him?"

"Because you know that we can do both, but only if we go about this properly."

Raj pondered the thought. He wasn't sure he liked it. It seemed risky to give himself up after everything, after all the effort they'd made to make sure Chaudhry couldn't touch him. Now, to just walk into his web voluntarily seemed like a waste. Still, he trusted Krish and if Krish thought it was a good idea, then Raj would put his faith in him.

"Are you sure we should kill him instead of destroying him with the contents of that file?"

"Don't tell me you're getting cold feet."

"I am getting cold feet, Krish. There are too many variables and even you cannot calculate them all. The chances of me getting out of there alive are slim to none. Plus how do we know that once I'm captured Chaudhry won't just kill me? How do we know he hasn't changed his mind again? How do we know for sure that giving myself up is the right thing to do?"

"Then do what you want," Krish said. "If being captured doesn't bode well with you then we can come up with another plan to get Chaudhry out in the open."

Raj hesitated for a moment and Krish sighed. "Think about Priya. Think about Hema and all the other women that have been victimized because of Chaudhry. Do you think presenting that file will do anything, Raj? Yes, it's a risk but it's also our safest bet and if it works, we'll all be able to get on with our lives. Releasing the contents of that file alone might only make things worse. He's a powerful man."

He couldn't deny that was true the more he thought about it. "What's your plan?"

"We'll go over it once everyone else is here."

"Are you sure they'll accept your plan?"

"Like I said," explained Krish, "if they don't, then I'm open to better suggestions."

Raj wanted to feel optimistic about the plan but it was difficult. Succeed and he'd be where he belonged, at Priya's side. Fail and he'd be dead.

Chapter 40

Night had fallen. Sultan was in position just outside the residence he knew Raj to be hiding in. He crouched low and glided across the lawn, silently gun in hand. He was at home with the darkness; it was his ally and had covered him during many similar missions. He was a master of disguise, a creature of stealth and even in full view of the public nobody recognized him to be the cold blooded killer he was. He was too good to get caught and most people were too stupid to catch him – including Raj and his cronies.

Everything was proceeding flawlessly.

The water had been poisoned along with the food that Tapan would be bringing to the slums the following day. Each threat would be eliminated and everything would be right again. They'd regain control and in the process, Sultan might get to do what he loved best – killing.

He cradled his gun in one hand as he jogged along the hedge and peered over the top towards the light in the window. There was someone there, a silhouette framed against the orange glow.

Sultan smiled. Raj was standing there staring into the darkness, as if inviting Sultan to take him. Stupid boy, he'd played right into his hands. This was easier than he thought. Sultan crept towards Raj silent and confident, a cat stalking its prey.

When he was close enough, he stopped and reached for his gun. He placed the tranquilizer into it and aimed it at Raj. He watched as Raj looked up at the stars, his lips moving as if he were praying. Prayers wouldn't help him, not now.

Sultan pulled the trigger and the dart embedded itself in Raj's neck. He looked surprised, that wide-eyed stare fixed right on Sultan's location, almost as satisfying as the look of a man about to die.

Perhaps next time, the gun would be loaded with a bullet and not a tranquilizer.

*****

Kavi didn't like it at all. He knew his brother was outside somewhere waiting to become a target, an easy target. He couldn't help but think about what had happened to Varun. The same thing was on the verge of happening to Raj. He knew the plan was good but it wasn't perfect and in that little window of imperfection, there was a chance that Raj could die. They didn't know where Sultan would take Raj nor if Chaudhry was even interested in keeping him alive.

He turned to watch Sai in conversation with his sister, anything to take his mind off what was happening. Kavi knew their relationship was strained because of what Sai was committed to doing. It was something she didn't believe in and he knew how hard it was to continue a relationship with someone who fought your decisions every step of the way. There was hope though; if he had managed to work things out with Varun...surely they could too.

Time seemed frozen as he watched them, not really seeing them, more in his mind than with them. There was so much happening at once, so many plans, so much balancing on a knife edge. They were close to victory but they were also close to miserable failure, failure that would cost more lives. Raj, Siya, Hari, they were all at risk and not just from one angle, but several.

He glanced at Krish and saw that he was calm, nothing of the storm raging within Kavi present on his face. Then again, Krish was as good at hiding his emotions as Kavi was at drawing them out of his enemies.

He was a good man though and Kavi was glad Krish had taken him under his wing and brought him up. He couldn't have asked for a better teacher.

Yes, there was still hope.

After what seemed an eternity his phone rang and he answered immediately.

"Kavi," Hari said. "Sultan took Raj and it looks like he's heading to the Butala residence."

"Is Raj okay?"

"For an unconscious person, yes he does. It looks like he used a tranquilizer on him. All we can do at this point is watch from a safe distance."

"Did Asim intercept the ricin?"

"I don't know. He hasn't called to check in with me so I'm assuming nothing has happened yet."

Kavi nodded to himself. "It's going to be a long night."

"It sure is, but stay on the line no matter what. I'm going to tap into the phone cables and see if we can hear what's happening."

There was nothing but static for a moment but then through the fog of static he heard Chaudhry speaking to Sultan.

"Are you sure you were not followed."

"Of course I'm sure," Sultan said angrily. "I'm not an idiot."

"I know that. Just hold on and I should be there in a few hours. I'm just waiting for my plane to come in."

"What would you like me to do in the meantime?"

"Babysit Raj until I get there. Afterwards I am going to send you out on another task for me."

"To find that woman?"

"No, I already have someone going out there," he said. "Krish thinks he's able to hide people from me, but I have a good feeling I know where she is."

"Will there be any survivors?"

"No. Everyone will be dead and Raj will no longer have any weaknesses. I'll make him become one of us."

"Where do you think she is?"

"I know she's in Virginia. Krish is a simple man, easy to predict. I know she's with his daughter. Krish only trusts a few people so it's more than likely he would trust Siya to keep her safe."

The line went dead and Kavi glanced at Krish, panic in his eyes. They both knew – the wild goose chase was over. Chaudhry had her at last. Somehow Chaudhry was able to find a way to get to them – to get their information. As to how Chaudhry knew, there were a few theories buzzing in Kavi's mind.

Chapter 41

Priya couldn't shake the feeling that she was being watched. She felt eyes on her, watching her every movement. It was paranoia, she knew but it wouldn't go away. It remained in her mind, scratching at the walls like a caged rat.

Getting to her feet she walked to the window and as she looked outside she heard a crash from downstairs. She heard Navin and Siya in the other room, screaming something but she couldn't understand what they were saying.

There was nothing she could do but to hold her breath she watched as the door of her room opened quickly. She couldn't breathe, her lungs refused to work, but then he appeared and it was like a bucket of cold water had been thrown over her. The look on his face was one of glee, and she flinched away from him retreating until her back was against the wall. They had found her at last. He raised his gun and everything changed.

Barely in control of herself, fueled by instinct alone, she stooped low and she launched herself at him. They grappled; each of them trying to wrestle the gun away but neither succeeding, then she heard running footsteps approaching fast. She ignored them, intent on grabbing the gun. The world around her was a blur of color and noise but then something else broke through – a gun shot. She fell, her senses fading out like a light retreating into dark and at once, she knew she was losing her grip on consciousness. Her eyes closed, her lungs turned to stone and her world was plunged into a vacuum, black and void of life.

Chapter 42

He stood there silently, and it seemed as if he had crossed over into an alternate universe. Everything was falling apart before him and there was nothing he could do about it. That was when he peered over at Krish. Kavi did not see any sign of emotion on his face. It was as if those words did not affect him in the slightest! He felt his blood begin to boil and took a deep breath. Kavi was attempting to keep an open and level mind, but it was proving to be rather difficult.

Kavi glared at the door. He needed to get out but Krish stood in his path. He was ready to burst, and he barely restrained himself from punching the man in the face. Containing his anger, he met Krish's eyes searching for something, anything that would show him that Krish wasn't a sociopath. Kavi glowered. Didn't he realize what was going on? And if he did, then why, by all the gods in the skies, was he acting this way? Kavi had thought he cared about them as if they were his own; surely Krish wouldn't dare harm him if it came to a fight. Kavi took a step forward.

Krish remained where he stood, steadfast and determined. He would not let Kavi pass. After all, it was for his own good. Kavi wanted to yell at him, and he wanted to knock him out of the way. He had lost the parents he never knew, a brother he loved, and now his sister and his remaining brother were in danger. Everything was spiraling out of control, and he wanted to balance the scale. He wanted to fix everything – he wanted to protect everyone he cared about. They would not suffer the fate his parents had. He wanted to reverse all of this, but he knew he could not. For now, though, he was focused on Siya. He needed to go to her. Needed to be there for her. Needed to protect her. He owed her that.

Krish blocked him when he went to take another step. Kavi did not want to analyze why he was not allowing him to leave or argue his way out of this predicament. All he knew was that Krish was prohibiting him from doing something he needed to do. Something he had every right to do. Kavi narrowed his eyes.

"Get out of my way," he said evenly.

"Why? So you can run amuck? Kavi, you need to think clearly!"

"You were supposed to make sure Siya was safe! Yet you're here blocking me from protecting her. You were supposed to make sure Varun was safe and he is dead," he roared. "If you can't do that, then at least let me do it."

Krish did not lower his gaze, but Kavi finally saw the emotions there, if only for a moment. Krish had raised the three siblings – he loved the three of them, and now it seemed there was no longer a "three of them". Everything Kavi had ever loved was being ripped from him and he could no longer take it. He was going to finish this battle. There was no other option at this point; he could not wait for a plan to unfold. Who knew, maybe he would be the one to kill Raj.

"I need to leave Krish, but I swear on my brother's grave that I will not do anything rash. I just need to get away from everything," Kavi pleaded.

Krish did not step aside. Fueled by anger and hurt, Kavi shoved his way past and strode into the main hallway. Krish did not stop him. A shiver ran up his spine; Rani was nowhere to be found and Sai was leaning against the wall. He knew something was wrong, but he did not care. He could not care – he felt numb, and nothing mattered at this point. His legs moved on their own accord and he slipped past Sai.

Making his way outside, Kavi stopped for a moment to look at the night sky. The moon had been devoured by the clouds that loomed overhead. He walked into the darkness alone.

* * *

Siya was shaking as she kneeled over Priya's body. All she could see was the blood that dyed everything a ghastly red. It was everywhere. Priya's black hair was soaked, and her face was stained as well. Siya knew that she had to calm down, to detach herself from Priya, to push away the rising panic. She was not going to let her die – she could not let Priya go. She sucked in a deep breath. It wasn't Priya's time to go.

Siya's hands shook as she touched Priya's neck, feeling for a pulse. There was nothing there. Involuntarily, she felt tears sting at her eyes, and she knew then that she could not, would not, give up on Priya. She carefully lowered her lips to Priya's, breathing her life's breath into her mouth, pumping her chest to help her breath. Siya spoke between breaths. One. Two. "Don't give up, Priya." A third breath. A forth. Where were the medics? "You need to stay with us." Five. Six. "There are so many things you've yet to experience!"

Sirens pierced the night, and Siya drew in a shuddering breath. She did not know how much time had elapsed and she didn't really care. And then someone was behind her, pulling her away from Priya. She struggled against the invisible arms and reluctantly moved away.

She turned. Behind her was her husband, Navin. He gently pulled her into his arms, turning her face towards his chest, but she was not comforted, and she could not help but watch as the EMT's worked on Priya. Siya watched as they loaded her on the stretcher, and she watched as they quickly made their way to the ambulance. She could see and hear everything through the broken glass, and she could smell the strong scent of rain in the air. Siya saw several police officers, saw that most of them were analyzing the scene with notebooks in hand. She knew what they were looking for, knew they were not going to find the information they sought.

"Are the two of you all right?" an officer inquired.

"We are shaken," Navin said. "But we are not hurt physically."

The officer nodded slightly. His thumbs were in the loops of his pants, and it was obvious he had questions. "Well, we are going to take you out of this room so our team can process the scene," he began, awkwardly clearing his throat. "We will be asking you questions separately."

Siya nodded, and they got to their feet. She turned towards her husband, and shuddered when she saw the swelling of his eyes and the blood that had run down his face, leaving a gory trail. She did not even remember him getting struck in the face, but he did not seem to notice. Siya smiled at him, and he took her hand in his. They walked into the hallway together, and they made their way to the living room. He squeezed her hand reassuringly and then let go as another officer gestured for him to leave the room.

Taking a deep breath, she sat down on the couch, unable to meet the eyes of the officer sitting across from her. Questions she had not asked herself were finally coming to mind. She wondered how they had been found, and she wondered if Priya was okay. She wondered what was going on in Mumbai, and she hoped everything was fine even if everything that had happened proved nothing was fine.

"Could you tell me your name?" the officer asked.

She looked up to him, and she watched as he took out a pen and paper. "My name is Siya Wasimrao Patel."

"And is this your residence?"

"Yes, well actually it is my father's home. He bought it for me when I moved to this country for schooling."

"All right," he said and he finally met her gaze. "And who was the girl who was here earlier?"

"Her name is Priya. She is my brother's girlfriend, and she was here because she wanted to see what America was like. She wanted to become a nurse, like me, and she wanted to experience what it was like here."

"Does Priya have a last name?"

Siya blanched. "I honestly don't know it. I only ever address her by her first name."

"Was she involved in any illegal activity?"

"Absolutely not," Siya said sharply. "What type of question is that? She is in the hospital right now, fighting for her life, and you imply that she is the criminal?"

"It is one I have to ask. It seemed that whoever was here wanted her dead. Now is there anything else you wish to tell me concerning this issue?"

"Priya was not involved in anything illegal. She was better than that, and whoever was here could have easily been after me or my husband. Maybe he went into the wrong room and Priya was in the way, at the wrong place at the wrong time."

"Is Priya a legal citizen?"

"No, she is here visiting, but she has all the proper documentation."

"So she was not here to give birth to her child?"

"Of course not," Siya spat. "Do you honestly think your country is that appealing? You American cops are just as arrogant as those in our own country. Besides, these questions should not be about an injured girl. You should be asking questions about what I saw and who was in my home." She emphasized the words, fighting to control her temper.

The officer smirked. "All right then, what did you see?"

Siya wanted to slug this man. How dare he speak to her like that, as if she were some common criminal? She could not believe his arrogance. She knew, however, that she could do nothing. Police officers were protected. They could get away with just about anything they wanted to and even if they engaged in gross misconduct, she suspected they could play their hand and claim they acted in self-defense. No, she needed to calm down.

"You obviously don't care what I saw. You will not do anything with that information anyway." The words came out anyways.

"You are mistaken. I would do anything to protect the people of this city – the people that belong here. Now tell me what you saw!"

She took a deep breath, fighting the urge to slap him. Racist bastard, she thought to herself. "I don't need to tell you anything," Siya said haughtily.

"I could arrest you for withholding evidence. I don't think someone like you would like for that to be on your record." She bristled at his condescending tone.

"If you keep up that tone," she began. She knew she could not say anything like that to him because he could find something fictitious to get her arrested. She held her tongue with great difficulty.

"Yes, it is best if you remain silent. We will analyze everything in your home, and it would be best if you do not get in our way."

Siya stood up and she shook her head. "Of course, as long as you stay out of mine," she snorted venomously.

The officer got up, and she saw his golden name tag: Officer Fitzpatrick. She filed the name away as she watched him walk away. A few moments later, Navin returned to her side and laced his fingers through hers. She glanced over at Navin and the officer who had questioned him looked at her.

"You should pack what you can. We will be looking over your home for any evidence as to who was here."

Siya nodded, and the officer gestured for them to lead the way to their room. Of course they were being escorted, she thought. She jumped when her phone rang. Siya entered the room, ignoring the officer and her husband. Without looking at the caller ID, she answered.

"Siya," she heard Krish say. She knew he was attempting to stay calm, but traces of panic leaked into his voice anyway. "Siya," he said again. "Are you all right?"

"Somewhat. I will call you in several hours, and I will explain everything to you then." She cast a surreptitious look at the officer stationed by the door and at Navin, hastily shoving clothes into a bag.

"Was – was he already there?"

"Yes," she said lightly. "I will tell you everything later."

Hanging up, she paused for a moment before turning back to Navin. Siya supposed she shouldn't be surprised that Krish already knew what was going on. He was always in the loop.

Chapter 43

Raj was engulfed by darkness for a moment, but that didn't stop him from sitting up. His head was pounding, and he felt as if his skull was going to explode. It took him a few minutes to come to his senses. He looked around, realized he was not tied down, and observed the small room around him. There was a blue door with a small window, but no real windows adorned the walls.

He got to his feet, swaying slightly. He peered out through the glass, pounded on the glass. No matter how hard he tried, he was not getting out. He was a prisoner, and he did not even know where he had been taken.

He could not see anyone outside of his cell; there were no guards, or other prisoners. He did notice a window higher up, however. It was narrow and barred, and he realized he must be in a basement somewhere. He wondered where Sultan had taken him, and he wondered when the weariness from the tranquilizer would wear off.

That was when he heard a door creak open, and he could hear footsteps coming towards him. It wasn't long after that before he could see Sultan – or at least a person whom he assumed was Sultan. He barely remembered what Sultan looked like before he shot him. Whoever he was, he looked weary. Despite that, he could see the venom he carried with him. Raj wondered what it was about him that made him want to kill – he wondered if killing someone gave him pleasure.

"It is good to see that you are awake. Most people wake up after maybe two days, and you were only out for several hours."

"Are you Sultan?" He rasped.

He smiled and nodded. "Yes. There is no one else out there like me." The smile was a mocking one.

Raj said nothing. He remembered Kavi wanted to kill Sultan and he knew Asim wanted to as well. This man had single handedly ruined so many lives, and he walked around so nonchalantly as if he were untouchable. This man had killed the brother he never knew and he had killed the parents he loved. This monster had killed the Banik family. Although he didn't have the evidence to send Sultan to jail, he knew in his heart the man before him was a murderer.

"There is no one else out there like you, you say? I am sure we don't want too many people as twisted as you out there. You are nothing more than an obedient dog that kills when told." Raj spat scornfully.

He knew he had hit a nerve when Sultan hit the blue door with his fist and Raj saw the naked fury in his eyes. A duffle bag, previously unnoticed, fell to the floor. "I do what I want when I want to do it. There is nothing more to it than that. I am not a dog!"

"Somehow," Raj mused, "I don't believe you. Anything Chaudhry tells you to do, you do it, and you never question it. The moment Chaudhry is out of your life, you will be wandering the streets clueless about what to do with the remainder of your life. You will go insane."

"I do not rely on him!" Sultan roared.

Raj smirked. "You should never deny the truth. Hasn't your father taught you that?"

Sultan glared at him hatefully, and Raj knew he wanted to kill him, but could not. He had orders to leave Raj alive.

"You are definitely your father's son. He will be pleased."

"I am nothing like Chaudhry," Raj spat.

"You should never deny the truth," Sultan mocked as he began to walk away. "You will meet your father in a matter of hours."

"My father is dead," Raj said evenly, refusing to take the bait.

Sultan shook his head almost sadly. "When you meet Chaudhry, you will see how similar the two of you truly are. I will be here when he arrives. What a touching reunion it will be."

Raj watched as he grabbed the duffle bag and stalked away. The door slammed and he heard the lock turn. He had the feeling the ricin was in there. He only hoped they were able to protect the people in the slums. This plan had to work. It simply had to.

•

Chaudhry had just arrived back in India and now he stood before his old home. He walked to the room that he had spent so much of his life in and opened the door. He knew no one else had been here since they learned about what he did here to innocent women and children. He thought back to how everything had been done here. He knew that any man would do what he did if it meant that they had endless money and an endless amount of women at his beck and call. Chaudhry had bedded many women, and every single one was willing. He knew what they wanted, and how they wanted it, and that was why so many of them remained loyal to him.

As he was placing everything in its place, Chaudhry felt oddly alone. He had never been without security before, but he did not need it. No one expected him to return. He was safe, and he was where he needed to be. This was where he belonged, and he was not going to flee again.

He sat at the foot of his unmade bed and savored the silence. Too soon, his phone began to ring. It was not a number he recognized, but he picked up anyways. Chaudhry waited. He said nothing.

"Chaudhry, this is Vinay. I needed to talk to you, sir. I am at the meeting place."

There must be something wrong, Chaudhry thought – there was something in Vinay's tone that disturbed him.

He headed out to the atrium where his assassins always met, disconnecting the line on the way. He wondered if he would need to kill Vinay. Most of his assassins were unable to follow through with a task or they were killed first, leaving him with only a few dependable servants. The only one who had stayed with him throughout all these years was Sultan. He had never failed him, and that was why Chaudhry had given him the most important mission of all. Sultan was to terminate Krish.

Chaudhry strode down the hall and into the atrium. Vinay was obviously nursing an injury and he was disgusted by the weakness written all over Vinay's body.

"Were you successful?" he demanded.

"Yes sir. They reported her dead," the assassin replied, bowing his head.

"What happened?" he inquired.

"I was at the home and I got to her easily, but she fought back. Then I was attacked from behind, but I managed to shake them off and get away. The ambulance took her away, but she was dead on arrival. I came straight here after hearing the medics, sir."

Chaudhry nodded, and he looked at Vinay. He no longer had a use for the injured assassin, and he took out the knife he always had concealed. His movements were quick and calculated; Vinay was not quick enough to deflect the body. Chaudhry stood over him, watching as the life fled from his eyes.

Pulling his knife out of his chest, he left the corpse behind as he returned to his chambers.

•

Tapan adjusted the tie he was wearing and smiled at his own reflection. Only weak people let life unfold on its own; the strong fought for what they wanted. Tapan was sure he was going to be strong. He was sure he wanted to be this man, and he was going to make sure that he was going to come out on top.

He turned as someone walked into the room, and he smiled as he looked at Shanta. A white shirt of his clung to her damp body, and he could not help but want to undress her. Katherine didn't know of his mistress, and as he looked at her tanned body, it seemed to glow. How he wanted her right then and there, but he needed to go to the slums and finish what he had started.

"You look stunning," he said as he walked towards her. He watched as she fiddled with the buttons, and he knew what she was hinting at.

Inches from her, he was trapped by her brown eyes, and she took a teasing step back. She was taunting him, and he loved her games. He wanted to grab her and throw her down on the bed. He wanted to hear her scream out, and he wanted to feel that rush of adrenaline and pure power. She would let him do anything he wanted, and he watched as she began to unbutton the only three buttons that were done.

"Do you want to have some fun before you go?" she purred.

His eyes were transfixed on her magnificent body, and he tore his gaze away from her. "Not right now, my dear. But trust me, when I come back I will be sure to finish where we left off."

He watched as she bit her lower lip and thrust her chest out towards him, and he pulled her close to him. He kissed her roughly, and they fell onto the bed. It would only take a few minutes, Tapan reasoned, and lowered his lips to her neck. Just then, his door swung open.

Looking up, he saw DeeGee standing there, and he too looked lustfully at Shanta's beautiful body. Tapan quickly got to his feet and covered her naked body with the sheet. "What?" he demanded, fighting to keep his voice even.

"Your car is here. I did not realize you were in the middle of something," DeeGee apologized.

Letting out a sigh, he fixed his tie and walked over to the door. "I guess I will be leaving then," he replied. He turned to the pouting woman and smiled at her. As he walked into the hallway, he did not realize that DeeGee was not behind him, but he had other things on his mind.

Stepping outside, he got into the car. Sultan was already seated, carrying the duffle bag. Generally, Tapan would make a comment about how his duffle bag would stick out, but he had quickly learned to never question Sultan. He looked down to his left hand, and saw the missing pinky that Sultan had taken.

Neither man spoke as they headed into the slums. They were not heading to the Dongri slums. No. They were heading to the Bandra slums. They were about half an hour away, and he knew he had probably lost their vote as well. Everyone in the slums had spoken about how Raj had saved their homes and they had sided with Krish. But today, he was going to talk to them, change their minds. He knew there was something that would make them vote for him. Something that DeeGee had so kindly retrieved for him. Tapan wondered how many people should suffer before he gave them the cure. As he adjusted in his seat, he smiled at himself in the rearview mirror. His plan was working fabulously.

Chapter 44

Hari walked silently beside Asim. He had already told Asim what was happening, and neither of them knew what to do. It seemed as if everything they had been working for up to this point was going to waste. As they walked up to the door, they saw Krish waiting on the porch. He was deep in thought and barely seemed to notice them.

"Did you hear from Siya?" Hari asked worriedly.

"I only know that she is okay. She told me she would call back in a few hours, and I am still waiting," Krish replied, worry and impatience evident in his voice.

There were no words of comfort Hari could give. He was not sure if there was even a way to comfort someone who was under a cloud of despair. He had just lost Varun and he had almost lost Siya. It seemed that everyone he knew was being picked off, one by one, and there was nothing being done about it. Hari was itching to do something, and the more he was here, the more he felt like reverting back to his old ways. He wanted to make his enemies suffer, but he knew he couldn't.

"If she says she is okay, then just believe that. She is a strong woman who knows how to take care of herself," Hari said, wanting to believe in his own words.

"She is not the only one I am worried for. We do not know if that assassin is still in the area. We are completely blind, and I need to be several steps ahead of our opponent."

They were silent. Of course they had touched on the theory of having a mole in their midst, but they had no suspects. Everyone they had talked to was loyal to Krish, and there was no one else who could be leaking information. It seemed Chaudhry had more resources than they were aware of and they were losing this fight.

"We should go inside and plan," Asim pointed out.

Krish did not even look at them. His eyes were focused somewhere in the distance, on something they could not see. It seemed as if he was unsure of what to do next, as if he was already admitting defeat, but had found that he could not, would not, give up. You have to earn what you get, Krish told himself. That's what I told Hari all those years ago.

"Let us go then," he said as he stood up. "The storm is just beginning, it seems."

•

Kavi was sitting by their tombstones, and he wondered what his life would have been like if he had been raised by his parents and not Krish. He had seen them before, had seen Raj as well. All he wanted was for them to feel his presence and invite him inside. He wanted to be part of their family, and he knew he was not alone. He knew Varun and Siya both wanted to know what they were like, and they wanted to know why they had kept Raj and not any of them. It wasn't fair.

Kavi knew it was absurd to speak to a tombstone in the hopes that they could hear him and send him a sign as to what to do next. Everything he was going through was because of those decisions made by his father all of those years ago. Krish had told him his father had become obsessed with getting even, and he wanted to dispose of men like Chaudhry because the world would be a better place without such monsters. Still, didn't destroying others make you a monster as well, regardless of your intentions?

There was nothing here, Kavi finally deduced. There was nothing else that could be done to get the answers he so desperately sought. The night he had found out about their deaths, he had been ready to go and exact revenge. He had wanted to find Chaudhry and he had wanted to kill him slowly. Yet monsters like him were elusive and hard to corner. That was the only reason his brother was acting as bait – so they could get Chaudhry and Sultan. There was supposed to be another plan, but this was the one they had all agreed on. They had agreed to let his brother go out alone, and now Siya was in danger as well.

He got to his feet and gazed at the Dongri slums, a mere five hundred yards away. The Dongri slums were obvious, and people as intelligent as Chaudhry would not attack the slums everyone was focused on. He would go to another slum. One with more people and one that was relatively close by.

Kavi broke into a run, his surrounding blurring as his feet carried him home. He did not know how long it had taken him to return; it didn't matter. He quickly made his way into the house, and froze for a moment as he saw them sitting there. Hari, Asim, and Krish. They had been talking about something, and they were obviously startled by his barging in.

"Kavi, is everything alright?" someone asked. He waved the question away.

Catching his breath, he looked at them. "Bandra slums is where they will go," he gasped. "They would not go to Dongri because they know we will be watching it. Besides, the Bandra slums have more residences with running water, and there are more people there."

Kavi waited for someone to say something. Instead, Asim stood up. "I will gather two of my own, and we will go into the

Bandra slums to intercept the enemy, should they show their slimy faces."

"Why you?" Kavi asked.

"Because I know the Bandra slums, and the two men that will be joining me were from those slums. This is all about trust and trusting in the knowledge that we can get the job done. If you wish to come along, Kavi, you are more than welcome to join us."

"I will come," Sai announced as he walked into the room. He was dressed in ratty clothing and it was obvious he had been waiting for an opportunity to present itself. "I know someone in those slums too. His name is Kalyan, but he goes by Kyle."

"How do you know him?"

Sai looked around the room as if looking for a spy. "He is my uncle."

Sai was the first one out the door; Asim and Kavi followed behind him. Krish wanted to speak to Kavi, to let him know that he had talked to Siya, but he knew time was of the essence and he was not going to be the one to distract him. The good news could wait.

Chapter 45

Kavi knew both the men Asim picked, and he could trust them with anything. Kumar and Madhav had been with Asim since they were both nineteen years old. They had been brought to him by a man named Mukesh Khanna, commonly referred to as MK. He was a somewhat successful man who, despite being able to afford living in the suburbs, remained in the Bandra slums. He felt as if it was his responsibility to care for the people in his slums, and he continued to do charitable work for them. However, he had only dedicated everything he had because he had lost everyone he had loved. His family had been killed in a house fire, and he had inherited their money. He then married a beautiful woman who died of cancer, but not before giving him a daughter they named Esther. She was taken from his custody when she was five, and now lived with her grandparents. MK was not allowed to communicate with her.

As they drove, Kavi felt anxious. He wanted all of this to be over, and he wanted it to be over soon. He felt as if everything was taking too long, and he had a feeling they might be too late.

"Where is the best place to find Kyle?" Kavi asked, breaking the tense silence that enveloped them.

"In the bar," Sai said. "The only bar the slums now have."

"Why didn't he take you in after everything that had happened?" Kumar asked curiously.

"He does not like me," he said slowly.

"And why is that?"

"Rani's mother is not my birth mother. My father had married another woman before, and she died in childbirth. When I was maybe a year old, he remarried and she took me in like I was her own. That was when she got pregnant with Rani. In Kyle's eyes, I was a troublemaker, and I am the reason they died." There was a tinge of sorrow in his words.

"He was just looking for someone to blame," Kavi said. "It wasn't your fault."

Sai shrugged, and they came to a stop. Everyone, except Hari, got out of the car. As they made their way to the dilapidated bar, Hari hid the car.

As Sai walked up to the bar, he saw Kyle cleaning glasses. He knew Kyle would most likely avoid any conversation, and hesitantly approached him.

"What the hell are you doing here punk?"

"I need your help."

"Who do you owe money to?" he spat as he placed the glass down on the bar.

"I don't owe anyone anything," Sai said evenly. "This is about protecting the people here, and I know you make it your business to know the up and up."

Kyle slung the dish rag over his shoulder, clenching his jaw. It was obvious he was debating whether or not to give in, and he finally did.

"What the hell is going on, kid?"

"Could we talk somewhere private?"

Nodding, Kyle gestured for him to follow. Sai nodded to Kavi, and they all followed.

Kyle lead them to the back room, shutting the door and taking a seat after they had all filed in. "So what brought you back here?" he asked.

"Everyone in the slums is in danger."

"Oh really? Living in poverty and being malnourished isn't dangerous enough?"

"Do you know who Tapan Batala and Vik Chaudhry are?" Sai retorted.

"Who doesn't? They're thugs who are politicians and they are running in the elections. Well," Kyle paused for a moment, "at least Tapan is, since Vik dropped out. Why?"

"Tapan and Vik were working together, and they wanted to flatten the Dongri slums, and now they are planning to do something – we don't know what – to this one."

"To my slum? If they were planning anything, I would know."

"Would you?" Sai challenged. "I brought you this," he added, handing him the printed article about the death of Dr. Mycroft.

Kyle opened it, and skimmed the page. "Ricin is not that dangerous if you think about it. Everyone here is more likely to get dysentery and that is worse than this."

"Do you honestly not see the significance of poisoning the slums with ricin? If enough people are getting sick and they start dying and suddenly Tapan comes along with a cure, don't you think that will make them want to vote for him? The only reason people in the slums are on Krishnaji Wasimrao's side is because he gave the bank a giant check so they would not lose their homes."

"I know that," he snapped. "So what do you want me to do with this information?"

"Help me find where they will most likely put the poison. If we make it so they cannot introduce it to the water supply, we can protect the people. We don't need anyone else to die."

"You are one to talk," he growled. A long silence ensued and nobody dared breathe, much less speak. "I will help you." Kyle announced at long last.

Sai nodded firmly and stood up. Together, they walked back to the counter. Kyle pulled a man over. "I will be gone for a few minutes. You are in charge until I get back." The man nodded.

Finally, they made their way outside, and Sai noticed the luxurious SUV parked by the curb. He watched as people began to crowd around it. Tapan was the only one who got out, which meant that he was the diversion while Sultan went to plant the poison. Sai felt his blood begin to boil.

•

Raj sat in the room with the blue door alone, wondering what was going to happen. His mind was spinning, and he only wondered how everyone else was doing. He wondered if Priya was all right and if she was thinking of him the way he was thinking of her. He wondered when his bastard of a father would come and see him. Suddenly, the door swung open to reveal him.

"Hello my son," he smirked. "It is nice actually being able to meet you in person."

"I wish I could say the same."

"Really, Raj, you should lose that attitude. I am your father after all."

"My father is dead," Raj snarled.

"I can understand why you think he was your father, but trust me when I tell you that he never loved you. He only took care of you because he did not want to lose your mother. Besides, every time he looked at you, I am sure he did not see you as his own. I am very certain he despised you because of who your real father was."

"I doubt it," Raj spat. "He was a better man than you would ever know.

Chaudhry chuckled and shook his head. "I am sure you are old enough to know the real truth about everything and not the doctored documents you were most likely shown."

"I am sure you don't know how to tell the truth," was his weak reply.

Chaudhry snickered and Raj heard the harsh jangle of keys. His door was being opened, and this was his chance to kill him. But he could not do it. He was intrigued by what Chaudhry was saying, and he wanted to know. Surely there was no harm in waiting.

"You are not attacking me," he commented. "I am not surprised. What do you know about your mother?"

"I did not know much about her. Even when I would ask, she would only tell me bits and pieces of her past."

"Your mother grew up in the suburbs, and her father's name was Naveen Jani. She was his only child. She grew up rather wealthy, and she grew up going to school with me," he said, as he took out a faded picture from a manila folder. Raj saw his mother in the front row, and he saw Chaudhry standing in the back.

"When we were teenagers, we became even closer," he stated as he took out another picture. It was a picture of an older version of the same girl. Chaudhry had his arms around her. "Your mother and I were lovers Raj, and we were meant to be together. When she went to university, it was not for schooling. She was supposed to meet Dev, and she was supposed to get information out of him. See, my father wanted his money and ideas. Your mother was used as a pawn. Dev was a very intelligent man, and he had ideas for inventions no one else had. He finally invested with my father and my father took everything Krish and Dev had."

"Why would my mother marry him then if she did not love him?"

"Because he had pertinent information we needed to get back, and she was also pregnant with his children. The answer to why she gave up Varun, Kavi, and Siya was because they were not the children she wanted – they were not mine. But you are."

"You raped her! That is how she got pregnant with me, and that is the only reason she had one of your children!"

"No! We made it look like a rape," Chaudhry spat. "Your father was getting too close and I had to do something. It was her idea, and it surely wasn't the first time we were together. She had been sneaking behind his back for years!"

"You killed her!" Raj roared, stalking towards Chaudhry.

The door swung open to admit a slender woman. It was his mother. Raj felt his heart beating like a drum in his chest at the sight of her.

Raj couldn't breathe. He did not know what to make of this. Everything he had known about Chaudhry was quickly unraveling. Everything he had known was a lie, and he could not believe it. He did not want to believe it, and yet there she was in front of him. He thought he had lost her. Despite his relief, he was angry. She was alive and she had betrayed her husband. And he could not forget Chaudhry wanted to kill Priya. There were still too many things that did not add up.

"You look as if you have seen a ghost," she commented as she walked over to Chaudhry. Raj watched as she kissed him lightly on the lips.

"You wanted dad to die," Raj said. His voice was shaking. "You let this all happen? What, did you want me dead as well? Am I expendable?"

"You weren't going to die," she said slowly. "We made arrangements to make sure you would be brought to me."

"Oh really? That is exactly why you sent a hit man to the Banik's? That is why they had to die?"

"Rita knew too much as it was," his mother chided.

"The boy is right. Sultan was supposed to kill him."

Raj watched as several emotions covered her face. "You were going to kill him?"

"Yes, originally, but I did think better of it."

Raj stared as she nodded as if it was okay. She acted as if Raj had not almost died several times because of her. He was furious. She seemed so warm and loving, and now he realized it was all just a façade. She was just as cold and heartless as Chaudhry himself. They were both heartless monsters.

"Why do you want me alive? I can destroy you."

"But you won't," Chaudhry said with certainty. "You know now that Krish was only giving you bits and pieces of the story."

"Krish gave me the information he knew."

"So your loyalty remains with people who have no blood connection to you?"

"Yes. They, at least, do not attempt to kill the people I love."

Chaudhry stepped closer to him. "That girl is not worth your time, and you should know that. I sent someone to take care of her, and she is dead and so is your child."

Fury overcame him, and he lunged at Chaudhry. His mother grabbed him by the neck of his shirt and held him back. Raj was shaking, and he felt as if he was about to cry. He hadn't cried since he was a child.

"She was everything to me," he said. "She was not a threat to you, and neither was our child."

"Whoever that girl was, she is no longer part of the equation. She is dead, and you will soon see that I did you a favor Raj."

Raj could not move and it seemed as if he was paralyzed. He did not want to believe that Priya was gone. He could not believe he would never meet the child she carried. He should have been there to protect her. Raj fell to his knees, a broken man.

Chapter 46

Siya had made her decision about how to handle the situation at hand and as she had ended her phone call with Krish, she knew she had done the right thing. Setting her phone down on the table, she saw Navin watching her. His chin rested on his hand, and he was in deep thought. He was probably trying to make sense as to why she had just lied, and she was waiting for that question to pass over his lips. She would not answer until he had asked.

Finally, he sighed, and he sat down beside her. This part of the hospital was mostly silent because these rooms were only for those who were at the end of their rope. Navin grabbed Siya's hand, and he looked at her with thousands of questions lurking in his eyes. "Why did you lie and say that Priya is dead?"

She looked away, avoiding his gaze. All of this time that she had been with Navin, and she had never allowed him to see this side of her. The side that knew how to lie – the side that knew how to plot and make things go her way.

"If she is reported dead by the papers and by the news, the assassin who was sent to kill her will leave. He will report back to the man who sent him, and we can take Priya somewhere else. Somewhere safer."

"I understand why we lied to the media," he said slowly. "But why did you lie to Krish and say that she was dead?"

"We are keeping Priya safe. I don't know if there is a mole in there with Krish. I never know what conversations are truly private. All I do know is that by saying what I did, I managed to make them all focus on getting Chaudhry. The moment he is eliminated-" Siya stopped talking. She saw the expression that passed over Navin's face. He never knew this side of her. And now he would never love her as he did before.

"I never knew you could think that way," he finally said.

"Navin, this part of me is not who I wanted you to see."

"That is probably for good reason, because this side of you scares the hell out of me." Siya looked away, holding back her tears. "Siya, I understand it. This world is not safe, and that was proven to us several hours ago in our own home. I just wish you were more honest with me about everything going on in your life."

Siya was silent, and she looked at the bed. Priya was in a coma and she had been bleeding heavily when they arrived. She had been on the verge of losing the baby she carried, but the doctors had managed to save the child. The only question remaining was if Priya would ever wake up.

"I never thought it would get this far. I never imagined they would find me, find us, and they did." Siya whispered.

She felt Navin squeeze her hand and he smiled slightly. "We survived it, didn't we? Everything is fine right now. All of us are still here, and you should know you can trust me Siya. You can tell me what is going on because if you leave me completely in the dark, I am not going to be able to help you."

"I suppose you are right," she said with her hand on her own bulging stomach. She still did not know the gender of her child, and she wanted that to remain a secret. Siya got to her feet, and walked over to the door. She locked it, and then settled beside Navin. "I will start from the beginning."

•

Krish looked at his phone. He did not want to believe what he had just heard. It could not be true. He had made sure he left no paper trail leading to any of his children – the children he took into his home – the children he had vowed to take care of. He could not breathe and he could not come to terms with the fact that everything was falling apart right before him.

As he sat there, he knew he could not stay in this trance-like state. He needed to fix everything. He needed to get back into the fight, and he knew they needed to regroup. That was when he got to his feet. After all, Krish was never a man to dawdle and waste precious time.

Walking over to his desk, he took out one of his phones. Dialing the number he knew by heart, he waited impatiently for the phone to be picked up, "This is Mohit Raina speaking."

"Mohit, this is Krish. I know that Katherine gave you what you needed to end Tapan Batala. Would you mind terribly if I had you fly out here and we put this plan in motion?"

"Actually I was going wait until the elections drew closer. Why, what is wrong?"

"Fly here, and meet me at Four Seasons. I will make a reservation for you and we will talk then."

Mohit was silent on the other end of the line, but he finally spoke. "I will be there sir. Give me until tomorrow afternoon."

"I will see you then," Krish said as he disconnected the line. They needed to have the upper hand now. Krish was not going to lose this fight. It was time to bring in reinforcements.

•

They had separated into groups of two in order to cover more ground. Sai was walking alongside Kyle, and he could not help but feel the tension. No matter what Kyle said to him, he would never believe his story. He was not the one responsible for their deaths.

As they continued to walk through the narrow alleys, Kyle stopped suddenly and pointed out a lone man standing by the main water supply. Sai went to make a move, but Kyle stopped him. He shook his head and spoke softly, "He is most likely armed."

"So what? He is going to poison your people."

Sai moved past him, but Kyle grabbed his forearm and pushed him backwards. Sai could see the gun he had in his hand, and he saw that sinister smile on his face. It took Sai a moment to process everything, but he did not understand why his uncle was betraying him now.

"Why are you doing this?" Sai asked. He could hear his own voice shaking.

"You are just like your father. Getting into business you don't belong in."

"How does the death of hundreds of people benefit you?"

"Once more people with bigger paychecks come around, I will be making more money. Batala and Chaudhry have a great plan; you were going to screw it up, and I won't let you."

It was as if Sai could not move, but it only took him a moment to recover. Lunging out at Kyle, he grabbed at the gun, and the gun went off. He knew Sultan had probably heard that shot and hoped desperately that it wasn't too late.

268

Sai made a quick decision, and he smacked the barrel of the gun against Kyle's temple. Looking over his shoulder, he saw Kumar and Asim – there was no sight of Sultan.

"What the hell is going on?" Asim barked.

"He is working with them," Sai said. "C'mon, help me move his body before anyone gets out here."

Without any further questions, they did. Heading down the alley, Sai wordlessly indicated the forest at the end. The three of them kept their heads down, after setting down Kyle's body, unsure of what was going to happen next.

Chapter 47

Raj was not sure what he was supposed to do. As he looked at his mother, he could not believe she had deceived him for all these years. He thought she was dead – he remembered the dream he had. The one when he was told not to give up on living. He was told not to pursue Chaudhry – he was told not to make the same mistakes. Yet here he was in the lion's den, and he knew this was not what the plan had been.

"Stop looking at me as if I have hit you," she chided. Her words used to be so sweet and endearing and now they were hurtful. She was not the woman he thought she was.

"You betrayed me and our family. How could you live with yourself?"

"Raj this is your family. This is your home. I did this so we could all be back together. You, me, and your father."

"You had my father killed! Chaudhry wanted me dead and even with him admitting that fact, you are not fazed. You fooled everyone! You don't even care that the woman I loved, the woman carrying your grandchild, is dead."

"Why would I care? That person was never supposed to be part of your life. She had to be eliminated."

He wanted to hurt her – he wanted to make her feel the pain he felt. He wanted to destroy her, but he knew nothing good would come of it. He would take Chaudhry from her, and he would make her feel this way.

"You are not a God, and you have absolutely no right tampering with the lives of others."

"You should know by now that there is no God. There is only man, and we make our own decisions. We make things unfold the way we want them to. If we did not do that, then nothing would ever get done."

"The reason the world is out of balance is because people like you think you can do whatever you want," he said darkly. "You are the reason why civilization is in ruins. You are the reason people are afraid to leave their children unattended."

She rolled her eyes, and he remained sitting. He was too weak to do anything more. There was nothing he could do yet, but he knew what he needed to do. Chaudhry had left the two alone after Raj's attempt at throttling his father.

That was when they heard Chaudhry come back downstairs, and he was not alone. Following behind him was Sultan and Tapan Batala. Raj felt sick as he began to wonder what was going on out there – he had a feeling there was nothing good to be seen above ground.

"Raj, I am sure you already know who these men are, though I doubt you have had any formal introductions."

"Sultan," Raj said. "You killed the Banik family and you chased me into the woods. My friend died after taking a bullet for me. You tried to kill Priya several months ago and missed, and you were most likely responsible for the death of my brother Varun."

"It is good to know that someone is familiar with my work." Raj shook his head at the response and shifted his gaze to Tapan.

"You killed your own family to gain their riches. They knew you were a monster. Now you are trying to gain power, and you don't give a damn who has to die for you to get what you want."

Tapan nodded, and he nonchalantly fixed his sleeves.

"This is where you belong," Chaudhry said. "You know that, don't you Raj?"

He thought on that for a moment. "I don't belong to this. You of all people should know that. I was raised by a decent man who taught me values. He was a man who taught me to work hard for everything I earn, and I do not have to do anything illegal to get there."

"You will become one of us," Chaudhry said confidently.

"I will never become one of you. You should terminate me the way you had wanted to in the beginning. I will not conform."

Raj saw the anger in Chaudhry's eyes, and he knew he wanted to lash out, and so he stood there waiting. He did not want to give the first blow, and Chaudhry finally took a step back.

"Then your fate is sealed Raj."

"Kill me then," he snarled.

Chaudhry shook his head. "No, you do not die yet. Your time is coming and you will serve your purpose soon enough."

He motioned for Sultan, and Raj watched as he quickly came towards him. Raj ducked out of the way. Tapan tackled Raj to the ground, and he watched as his fist came towards him. He felt it as it made contact with his face. He felt as if everything around him was blurring. He felt more blows landing on his body. It took a few more hits until he finally fell unconscious.

Chapter 48

They went to the closest and most secure place within distance – the compound. Sai remembered his first night here. He had cradled Rani in his arms, and he had stayed with her until she had fallen asleep. She was restless and her dirty face was tear-stained. He knew there was nothing more he could do than stay there. He had promised to protect her, and always be there for her. Thus far, he had never broken his promise, but he was no longer the same person who had once brought her here. He was someone different now, and he was not sure if that was a good thing or a bad thing.

Placing Kyle on the bed, Asim bound him to the bed with rope they had found in the closet. They all watched him, waiting for him to stir. Sai wanted answers – he wanted to know what he meant when Kyle had spoken of his father. He had never known his father to stick his nose in places it did not belong. Sai himself barely remembered Kyle muttering those traitorous words as he tried to shoot Sai in the head.

Sitting there in silence, Sai reflected on what had happened up until the death of his parents. He had always thought they were in the wrong place at the wrong time but they hadn't been, had they? He shoved the thoughts away when he saw Kavi. Kavi's face was filled with turmoil, despite his best efforts to conceal it.

"What is going on?" Sai asked.

Kavi sat down on the floor and shrugged. "Everyone in these slums will soon be living in hell. We do not even know what is going on with Raj. We have no idea what is going to happen to him – hell, we do not even know if he is still alive."

"Did you get in touch with Krish?"

"Yes. I called him on the way here. He spoke with Siya. She is fine."

"You don't seem to be reassured."

"There are too many unknown variables, and now the Bandra slums are poisoned and the only ones with the cure are the very ones who are poisoning them."

"We will figure all of this out."

Kavi shook his head. "We need to be one step ahead of everyone, and right now we are not. I know we can weasel information out of him, but who is to say that is enough?"

Sai understood. It was possible he did not even know anything, and even if Kyle did, who was to say that he would actually speak out about what was going on? Sai knew what they needed to do, and he was worried because the thought of putting Kyle through pain did not bother him whatsoever. What kind of monster was he?

"We will figure everything out, Kavi. Keep thinking positive thoughts."

He snorted. "I don't think positive in situations like this, Sai. Right now, the odds are against us. We sent Raj in there to get Chaudhry and I am sure they were expecting that. I am more than certain they know more about our plans than we do theirs."

"I don't think so," Sai said. "We have so few people in the fold that I doubt any of them are leaking our information."

They were silent for a while, and then Kavi shook his head. "I don't think anyone has the ability to betray us, but do we really know everyone?"

"I think we can trust everyone. Maybe Chaudhry is just better at doing this than we are. It is possible he is smarter. I am sure he is able to predict our moves because we act like one unit instead of as separate ones. Maybe we need split up, communicate efficiently, but act separately."

"It is possible," Kavi began. And then they heard Kyle begin to stir and they shared a look. They both knew what needed to be done now.

•

Katherine was walking home with her son. Things were going just the way they should and she finally felt like she could breath. She was free and her son would now be able to live the life he rightfully deserved. A life he would never have received in India.

As they approached the stairs to her building, she picked him up in her arms, and swung around, savoring the sound of his laugh. It was her favorite sound in the world, and she smiled brightly at him. Emery was still fatherless, and he had never once asked about Tapan. He had never asked about a father in general, but she knew he needed one. Every child needed a loving father.

The doorman tilted his hat at the pair as they entered the lobby and she smiled and nodded as they passed. She watched as Emery ran as quickly as he could towards the elevator and pressed the button. The smallest of things made him so excited and so happy, she mused as she quickly made her way towards him. It took several seconds, but the golden elevator doors finally slid open, and they stepped inside.

"What do you want for dinner, sweetie?"

She watched as Emery thought about it. "I like grilled cheese," he said finally. "And chicken nuggets and I love ice cream."

Laughing softly, she nodded. "It sounds like a good dinner. And do you want to watch a movie?"

He shook his head. "I don't like watching movies. They are boring."

There was nothing she could do about that. He was a typical four year old boy. He was always running around wanting to do something. She was constantly chasing after him to make sure he was okay. In a city like New York, you always needed to be alert. Katherine was still unsure as to whether she was completely safe yet. She was still paranoid. What if not everything had been worked out?

Finally, they came to their floor and Emery quickly darted out of the elevator and set off down the hall. Katherine froze for a moment when she saw Mohit standing outside of her door and she wondered what was going on.

Emery stopped in front of him and she shook her head. Why was her son so trusting of a complete stranger? He could get hurt so easily, she fretted. She quickly made her way towards them, and Mohit put his hands up. She knew he needed to be here. There was no danger. Not yet, at least. Unlocking the door, they all walked inside her unit and she heard Emery ask, "Who are you?"

"I am a friend."

Katherine peered over her shoulder and she watched as Emery was thinking on it. She saw the resemblance between the two of them. It was not obvious and Mohit did not even know he was the father. It was only one night – one night before she had left everything behind in the states. Still, they were long overdue for a talk.

"Emery sweetie, could you please go to your room for a moment."

He nodded and he slowly walked away. She walked into the kitchen, nodding for him to follow. She needed a bottle of wine.

"To what do I owe this pleasure, Mohit?" She asked, eyeing him warily.

"I am meeting Krish in Mumbai tomorrow, and I will be giving him the information on Tapan. I wanted you to have all the back-up files – just in case something was to go wrong."

Katherine looked to the briefcase he was holding, and she shook her head. "I did my part. I no longer want to be part of any of this. You of all people should know that."

"I know, but you are the only person I trust Kat. We have history and I know that if anything were to go wrong I could trust you. I am not asking you to come forward if something does go wrong. Just keep this information safe. There is no one I would ask to do this."

She saw that look of desperation in his eyes. Mohit had been there for her all along. She knew him – she trusted him – she loved him, and that was why she was going to do this.

"I will do it, Mohit. But only because you asked so nicely."

He sighed with relief, and she watched as he put the briefcase on the table. She watched as he slowly walked away. She did not want him to go. Mohit opened the door and he turned to say good-bye. She stepped into the hall with him.

"Be safe," she said.

"I always am."

"No," she said, as she took a step closer to him. She fixed his collar, struggling with the words that needed to be said. She knew what she wanted to say, but she was not sure how to say it. "You are reckless; you can't plan what is going to happen when you set the mountain in motion."

He grabbed her hands gently and lowered them. He looked amused. "Once I plan something it goes south. I would rather go with the flow than think about what I will be doing tomorrow."

A chill ran down her spine, and she felt his forefinger run down her jaw. "You will be in Mumbai tomorrow."

He stepped closer to her and kissed her softly. "True, but I have no idea what happens after tomorrow."

Katherine pouted as he moved away from her, and she felt light headed. "Mohit, you are welcome here. And I am sure Emery would love to have you here."

A smile lit up his features and he nodded. "I know Kat. Take care of yourself."

She watched as he got inside the elevator, and reluctantly headed back inside. She saw Emery standing there, and he seemed upset.

"Where is he going, Mommy?" He asked.

"He needed to go to work," Kat whispered.

Stepping inside her home, she locked the door behind her.

"Will he come back?"

"Yes Emery, he will come back." Katherine promised, hoping against hope that she spoke the truth.

Chapter 49

Raj's unconscious body lay on the floor, and Chaudhry shook his head. "What a waste," he murmured. Chaudhry looked to Sultan. "You know what to do from here."

Sultan nodded and he headed upstairs. Chaudhry knew no one would ever find Raj because no one had ever found any of the other people he had disposed of. He turned towards Alka. Why was the woman upset?

"What is the matter my dear?"

"You said you were just going to use him. And now you are going to kill him?"

He stepped closer towards her, and he backed her into the corner. "He did not want to conform, you heard him say that. I should have killed him from the beginning."

"You told me you would not touch my son," she growled.

"Do not grow a conscience now. It does not flatter you. This is now my decision, and there is nothing you can do about it Alka."

She bowed her head and gave up. Looking at her son's unconscious body, she wondered, for the first time, if she had made the right decisions. After all, if she had, then why was her son lying on the floor hurt and condemned to death? Alka looked at Chaudhry. He was powerful – untouchable. He knew what he wanted and he got what he wanted. He was not afraid to pursue anything, and he did not care what the consequences were. Now as she wondered at how vulnerable Raj was, she was not sure if she could allow him to die.

She was shoved aside, and she forced herself to watch as Sultan opened the coffin. The wood appeared to be strong, and she knew it would be nearly impossible for him to get out. She could no longer watch the gruesome scene and turned to walk away. She took one last glance at Raj and fled from the basement.

Alka shook her head. This is what needed to be done, and there was no point in arguing that fact. She needed some fresh air to clear her mind. Looking at the sky above, she prayed that Raj remained unconscious the entire time.

•

Hari had been keeping a watchful eye on the Batala residence. It was luxurious, even compared to most other houses here in the suburbs. He knew that it was a fortress inside. The Batala family had all been paranoid people and they knew how to hide what mattered to them most. There was most likely a bunker with plenty of supplies and more than a dozen exits for them to escape through.

With that thought in mind, Hari knew he needed to watch more than the main entrance to the residence. He had to think strategically. If he was paranoid and he needed an escape route, where would he keep it? Somewhere secluded and where no one ever travels, Hari decided.

As he moved, he felt his phone vibrate and reluctantly answered.

"I'm actually kind of busy at the moment Krish. What is going on?"

He listened for a moment and then nodded. "Alright," Hari finally said. "I will call you the moment we know something for sure."

Hanging up, Hari took a moment to pray to any God or Gods out there. They needed this to work. He knew they needed to expel the darkness from here and this could be their last chance. He silently moved forward, knowing he needed to stay hidden – undetected. As he stalked around the house, he felt a sense of relief wash over him and he was unsure why. There could hardly be a more dangerous situation than this.

•

His eyes opened and he realized that he was trapped in complete and utter darkness. He felt the walls around him and he could smell the moist dirt that surrounded him. Everything around him suddenly got smaller and he felt his heart begin to race inside his chest. He wanted to break free from this moist prison. He needed to escape – he was terrified. Raj forced himself to take a deep breath and close his eyes.

There was no reason to panic, he told himself. Everything was perfectly fine. He was still unconscious and everything he had been experiencing was a horrible dream. He was still in the compound – he was recovering from being shot and Priya was sitting next to his bed. Her small hand was in his, and when he woke she would be there with that beautiful smile. She would be okay – everything would be okay, because all of this was a dream.

As he attempted to focus on Priya's beautiful face, he remembered what he had been told. She was gone. Priya was dead, and so was the child she carried. The woman he loved was no longer living, and the future he thought he had with her had vanished. He was going to die. Yet if he died, he would be with her again. Or would he? He had never thought too hard before on what happened to someone after their death.

He began to tremble, and then he screamed. He did not know how to get this raw grief out of his system and he felt tears falling from his eyes. He could not just give up. He could get out of this, but why would he want to? What was there to live for now? The only person who had brought light to his darkness was gone – she was gone because he could not protect her.

Raj had never wanted to give up so badly, but there was part of him that could not do it. There was something that told him to keep fighting. He was still needed in this fight. He needed to plan, get out of this box. Raj froze when he heard a sound above him. What was going to happen now?

Chapter 50

Mohit peered out at the Arabian Sea, a glass of wine in his hand. He glanced at it once, before draining the rest of the drink. He yawned, set the glass down, grabbed the remote, and turned the television on. He saw that the media was talking about Chaudhry. Suddenly, Mohit was wide awake.

"We are here right outside the Bandra slums, and as you can see behind me, we are unearthing several coffins," a reporter said, gesturing to the overturned soil behind her. "This is not your typical cemetery either. There was a brutally beaten gentleman inside one of those coffins. He is still unidentified but medics say he will survive." The scene cut to the ambulance driving away. "Stay tuned for more information. This is CCTV-" Mohit turned off the TV. Lost in his thoughts, he barely noticed that someone was knocking on the door. He sleepily trudged over and let Krish – what was he doing here? – inside. Mohit noted how pleased Krish seemed with himself.

"What is going on, Krish?"

"Everything is shifting in our favor, don't you feel it?"

He shrugged. As of lately, he was too preoccupied to take a good look at anything. "You could tell me what just happened to make you sense the shift."

"We are burning Tapan Batala at the stake. Chaudhry and Batala made a mistake, and now we have evidence of their criminal activity."

"Oh, so not just the two years of undercover that Katherine did," he said cynically. "A woman who has Batala admitting to several dozen misdeeds."

"I am not saying her work is not important. Everything she gathered for us will bury him. Right now, this particular misdeed of his will make it impossible for him to run. However, he did something I will not be able to undo."

"And what is that?" Mohit demanded irritably.

"They poisoned the Bandra slums with a toxin known as ricin. We attempted to stop it, but we were unable to do so. Dr. Mycroft was the only one who had the cure, and he is dead. From what we know, Batala and Chaudhry are the ones who currently hold the cure."

"How smart," Mohit said, as he sat down and motioned for Krish to do the same. "Well, there should be a way for you to get that in your hands."

"There is," he said. "I have a plan in motion."

"Please tell me what is going on, Krish," Mohit sighed.

Krish glanced over at the television. Grabbing the remote, he turned it on. "The land this man had been buried alive on belongs to Tapan Batala. As of now, Mr. Batala is in custody. So far, we have twelve coffins dug up, and we are expecting to find more," the reporter recited.

Mohit looked at Krish, and he smiled at him.

"Who was the gentleman buried alive?"

"Raj Varma. We had a plan to get him close to Chaudhry, but it obviously did not work."

"That was not a well calculated decision," Mohit muttered.

"I do not disagree with that statement, but he is safe now," Krish's voice trailed off. He realized how selfish he was becoming, and how emotionless he was feeling. "Anyways, all I need is a date Katherine collected for us, and you can leave."

"I know that much Krish, but I want to stay and see this out with you."

"If you don't mind my asking, why would you want to stay here?"

"You are going to bury Chaudhry. I will help you, stand by you until the very end.

Krish nodded solemnly. "And I with you, my friend."

Chapter 51

Siya had not left the hospital yet; she did not want to. Even though she knew she should leave, didn't know what Priya would remember, she needed to be there to comfort her when she finally woke. She didn't turn when Navin walked in. He sat down beside her, weary from work and the stress of the past few days.

"How are you doing love?" he asked.

"I'm fine," she said. "How are you?"

"Tired. I wish you would leave with me tonight. I miss you, Siya."

"I miss you as well, but I do not want to leave."

"Siya, you are going to have our child in just a few weeks. You should come with me and relax. You need a good night's sleep."

He was correct, but the moment she left, she knew no one else would be here for Priya. She would be completely alone. "I will stay here until she wakes up."

"You know there is a chance she will not wake up. She suffered a blow to the head that should have killed her."

"Priya is able to breathe on her own," she retorted. "She is still there and fighting."

"But you don't know how much of her is still there, Siya. Why are you not thinking about this clearly?" Navin sighed. "She might not wake up."

"I don't know what to do if she were gone Navin. I do not want to be the one to tell my brother she died because we were not cautious enough."

Navin was silent, and he nodded. "I suppose I understand where you are coming from. I'll get you some fresh clothes and some food."

She watched as Navin left, and there was no denying that he was upset. She wanted to get up and run after him. She wanted to fix their relationship. After she told him everything about the situation, he had pulled away from her, if only slightly. Why couldn't he see she was still the same person he had married?

She took Priya's hand. It didn't feel like her hand. Siya usually spoke to her – told her stories, but tonight, tonight, she was silent. She did not know what to say, and she was almost glad when her phone rang. It was Kavi.

"Hello," she said.

"Hey Siya, is everything okay?"

"Yes. Did Krish tell you anything?"

"Of course he did. But there are a few things you need to know."

"What do I need to know?"

"Did Krish tell you about Varun?"

Siya felt as if all the life had been drained from her in that moment. "What happened to Varun?"

"He is gone, and we almost lost Raj. He is in critical care right now," Kavi's voice was empty.

She felt sick, and a sudden surge of pain raced through her body. She gasped.

"Siya, is everything alright? Siya!"

She looked at the bloody floor and shook her head. "My water broke," she finally said. "I need to call Navin." Even to her, she sounded hysterical.

"Siya, everything will be okay," Kavi said, but she did not believe him. Everything around her was spinning, and she felt faint.

•

Raj was beginning to recover and he was not surprised to find many people surrounding him. Kavi walked in, face creased with worry. "What's wrong?" Raj wondered.

"Siya just went into labor."

"And what else is going on?"

"We were not successful in stopping the ricin from getting into the water supply."

Raj attempted to sit up, and he felt a hand on his shoulder. It was Sai, and he seemed to be just as weary as Kavi. "We need to go and do something," Raj said. He could not believe they were not doing anything.

"There is nothing we can do, Raj. You, of all people, should understand that."

"There is always something that can be done. Why aren't you warning them?"

"Think about how that would look. We know they are getting poisoned. We cannot say how we know, or why we know, or what the cure is."

"People are going to die," Raj snarled. "Do you not care about that?"

Kavi clenched his jaw. "I do care, Raj. I feel helpless, and so does everyone else in this room. If there was something we could do we would do it, but there is nothing that can be done. You need to accept that."

"I can't accept that," he replied and he attempted to get up again. Raj was furious and aggravated. They needed to gain the upper hand, and so far they were unable to do even that. He hated being behind a man like Chaudhry. A monster – someone who could manipulate everything. Raj had a question he had not asked.

"Who found me?"

"Hari did. He got a call from some woman. She was hysterical. He called in anonymously, and they listened. They dug you up, and right now Batala is in for questioning. The land he was burying people on is owned by him."

"How many others were buried alive?"

"We aren't exactly sure. So far, they've found twenty-eight bodies. I doubt that Batala will be able to wiggle his way out of this."

"Did they bring anyone else in for questioning?"

"No. There was no one else on his property when they went there."

"How convenient," Raj said. "How long do they want me to stay here?"

"Your frontal lobes are swelling and you might have a concussion. They want you here until the swelling subsides."

"I don't see why I have to be so careful. Everything I love is gone, and now I am going to take Chaudhry out of the picture."

Kavi watched him carefully and Raj wondered if he could sense that he was hiding something from him. The only thing Kavi did was nod. "We will leave you alone now. One of us will be here at all times if you need anything."

Raj said nothing; he could not help but feel anger pulsing through him. If he did proceed forward to kill Chaudhry, would it mean that he, Raj, would finally be at peace? And even after the task was done, where would he be? The only thing allowing him to push forward was Chaudhry and once he was dead where would Raj go? What would he accomplish? All of these questions flowed through his mind and he felt his eyelids droop. He drifted off into a dreamless sleep.

Chapter 52

It was quiet that night, and Alka could not help but feel repulsed. She knew that she was in love with Vik. The history they had together was just that, history. He had promised her that Raj would be all right and that he would not harm him. Yet he had done the opposite. He wanted him to die, and she had a feeling there was a reason Vik had kept him alive for so long. This was a mind game, and he was playing his hand. She knew she could not stay here – especially not after what they had done to her son.

She got to her feet, unsure of where she should go. It could not be a place that was obvious. It had to be somewhere she had no connection to. She could not be found. As she walked around, she heard Sultan muttering under his breath. She saw his duffle bag, and she knew he had been given another assignment. Everyone here was a monster, and she was probably the worst of them all.

She made her way into the hallway. Sultan had disappeared and it was silent. She knew staying would be the wisest thing for her to do. Vik would not suspect her of conspiring against him, but at the same time, she did not want to betray him. Then again, he did betray her. He disposed of his son as if he was garbage. Raj had a bright future ahead of him – a path to greater things had opened up to him when she had disappeared from his life. He was going to have a family, and he was going to become something, but he was gone now. She still did not want to believe he was gone. All those thoughts swirled around her mind as she made her way into the living room.

Sitting down on the couch, she knew what this place used to be. She had been here several times before when the women and children were here. Of course she knew of all the despicable things

Vik did – they were the same deeds her father had carried out. For all those years, she always believed this was normal – that these women and children deserved it – everything happened for a reason. But now, as she let her mind wander, she knew there was something very wrong about all of this. She needed to stop everything. Calling anonymously in the hopes that her son might live was one thing. Actually running away was another.

Her mind began to spin. There were so many things she could do. Her thoughts were interrupted when she saw Vik standing before her. She looked into his eyes, and she saw nothing. No emotions. He was a cold and cruel man, and she used to think that made him stronger, that it made him better. Dev had worn his heart on his sleeve and she had thought he was weak. But he cared for her and for Raj. She remembered the day they had staged her death. She remembered Dev's reaction, and she wondered if Vik would be consumed by grief if she were to die. As her eyes met his, she knew he would never mourn for her.

"You know it had to be done."

"You only kept him alive because you thought you could brainwash him, didn't you?"

Vik was silent for a moment, and he finally nodded. "He would have been a wonderful asset. But as we found out, he is nothing like me. You should have given him to me when he was a child. Had you done that, he would have grown up to be just like me! But instead you wanted to raise him, and look at what happened. He was soft."

Alka knew Vik had wanted Raj. She had already lost three of her other children. Children that Dev wanted to keep safe – children she never knew. All of her children were targets – one of her sons was already dead – Varun. She remembered sneaking glimpses of

Kavi, Varun, and Siya as they grew up. Varun was always the softest of all of his siblings. He was much more logical and withdrawn from the rest of the world. He was introverted, and she wondered why Sultan was given orders to kill him. Varun was hardly a threat.

"Why did Sultan kill Varun?"

Vik smiled, and took several steps closer to her. "Why do you care?"

"I want to know what Varun did to deserve death."

"Sultan tortured him for information. Varun lasted several hours of torture, and he finally died of shock. Sultan found information he needed that Varun had tucked away, and then we went after Siya. She was the one hiding your son's pregnant girlfriend, and we needed to eliminate her."

"Did you hurt Siya?"

"No."

Alka broke his gaze, and she shook her head. His cold hand latched onto her chin and forced her to meet his eyes. She could see the familiar anger. The anger that emerged without reason. She had always been terrified by him, but she was never allowed to show her fear.

"You need to understand that everything we are doing is for the greater good. Everything! These are not selfish acts. People must die for our new way of life to begin. Those who are weak will die off and the strong will live."

"You are poisoning people, assassinating people. You just sent Sultan on his way to go kill someone else!"

"This is what needs to be done, and if you can no longer stomach that, then you should be gone too. You have a choice. Either you stay by my side or you die."

"I will always stand by your side," she said without hesitation. "I am unsure of why I am getting upset over this."

"Most likely because women are not as strong minded as men," he said. "Now I will be heading to my chambers and you can join me if you like. If not, I know where I can find another companion."

"I doubt I will get any sleep tonight. I will stay out here, and I will see you in the morning."

He nodded, and she watched as he disappeared. She used to think that men as powerful as him were supposed to have other women – her father did. But Dev never treated her this poorly. He always treated her like a queen, and he was always trying to make her smile. She had destroyed the one thing that made her the most happy – it was a happiness she thought was fake, but she knew now that it was real. It was a sort of happiness she doubted she would ever feel again.

•

Siya woke up to a bright light shining overhead. All she remembered was talking to Kavi, but she did not remember what it was about. She glanced beside her and saw Navin standing there, looking worried. She remembered her water breaking, and her heart dropped. As she sat up, she felt soreness and pain all along her abdomen, and she immediately felt nauseous. However, she could not see her child. Where was her child?

"What happened?" she asked. She could hear the panic in her own voice.

"Our son is fine," he finally said. "They had to take you for an emergency C-section. He was in distress, but it was most likely because you had preeclampsia."

"But we have been monitoring everything."

"Not for the past six weeks we haven't," Navin said softly. "You had more issues than our son did. I was worried you were never going to wake up."

Siya held his hand in her own, and she felt as if everything was going to be okay. "Would I be able to see him?"

"Of course you can, but you should wait a little while. In the meantime, you should be thinking about names for our son."

"Who is looking over Priya?"

"My mother is at the moment. If you would like, I can go in and check on her and let you know how she is doing."

"I would like that very much."

Navin knew he should tell her about Priya and her new condition. Siya had only been found in Priya's room because Priya had coded. It would break Siya apart if she knew Priya was now on life support. He knew Siya would ask him what had happened to make her need it. What had changed in her health? That was something none of the doctors or nurses could explain, but Navin seemed to know the answer. Had Priya not coded, he would have arrived back at the hospital forty minutes too late. He would have lost his wife and his son. God works in mysterious ways, and he knew

Priya would have done whatever she could have to get help for Siya, even if it meant her life would be compromised.

He walked into the private room and saw Priya laying there. The tubes were in her mouth, and he knew she was gone. However, that child inside of her was still very much alive. He took a seat next to her, and held her limp hand. He felt the tears stinging at his own eyes, and he could not explain or even express his gratitude.

Thank you, Priya.

Chapter 53

Raj finally stirred from his sleep, and he knew it was now night. There were fewer staff, and he knew it would be rather easy to escape. He could go back to Krish's, but everyone there would most likely want him to come back here. He did not want to wait in here and do absolutely nothing. He swung his feet over his bed, ignoring the dizziness that threatened to send him toppling over. It took him several seconds to focus on his surroundings. When he had, he wished he hadn't. She was standing there. Raj could not believe she had the nerve to show up here.

"How did you find me?" he growled.

Alka looked at her son. "I called your friend, Hari. I wasn't sure you had survived until he mentioned it. He's going to send someone here to finish you off."

He said nothing. She had not flinched when she learned Varun was dead. She did not even attempt to help him when he was being beaten. She had killed his father and his aunt. She was a cruel manipulative monster, but as he looked at her now he was not too sure that was the case. Maybe she had come to her senses, and maybe she had always been the caring woman he remembered. Maybe she had simply lost herself along the way.

"Why should I believe you?" he inquired. "You do not seem to care for anyone other than yourself or your love Chaudhry."

"Vik was not always a monster," she said tersely. "I am not here to defend him. I am here to right all the wrongs I have made in my life. I know what Vik planned to do in the slums, and I know where he kept the antidote. Now it is yours, and you can protect those people. I do not want anyone else to die."

Raj did not know what to say. Kavi silently entered the room, and the tension in the room was palpable. Raj did not know what his reaction would be to this stranger. He looked at Raj, silently inquired who this person was. He watched as his mother turned towards Kavi, and he saw a look of shock on his face. It was as if he knew her. Raj wondered if she had ever met them or seen them on occasion. He wondered why she would. She admitted to not loving them, but maybe, just maybe, she was lying.

"Kavi, this is Alka Varma, and she is our mother."

He watched as a look of pure anger passed over his face, and he shook his head. "You are dead."

"She staged it," Raj said. He did not want to go into the details. He just wanted to leave and do something productive. "Kavi, can we please leave? On our way, I will explain everything to you."

Kavi shot him a look, and Raj figured he wanted to know if they could trust her. All he could do was shrug. He finally gestured for her to take a step in front of him. Raj knew that Kavi knew something was awry, but he kept everything concealed and got to his feet.

"I brought you a change of clothes," he said as he tossed them over. "Be quick about it."

He attempted to dress as quickly as he could, but he felt as though he was becoming disoriented. It probably wasn't the best idea to leave. Still, he knew there was nothing the hospital would be able to do anyways, other than monitor him.

Finally, he was dressed and they were beginning to walk out. Raj saw the corridor was vacant and he wondered where all the nurses were. He looked to Kavi, and he wondered if he was able to make them all leave so Raj could walk out of here without any issues.

As they walked, Raj felt fatigued, but he knew he could make it to the car. He saw his mother glance over her shoulder at him. He wondered what made her change her mind and come here to betray the man she loved. Raj wondered if she was mentally impaired, because most people remained loyal to the one they loved.

When they were finally outside, he saw Hari standing patiently. Raj seemed to understand this had been their plan all along, to get him out of the hospital, and he was beginning to wonder why. He knew his mother was not lying. Chaudhry knew he was alive, and somehow they knew Chaudhry's plan.

He got in his car and closed his eyes for a moment. His head was pounding and he was beginning to feel sick to his stomach. He now understood why he was on bed rest. He knew that, even though he was leaving the hospital, he was still going to have a short leash.

"Now start explaining," Kavi said. Raj could hear the harshness in his voice despite the fact that he was trying to conceal it.

"Yes, please do," Hari said from the front seat.

Raj looked to her; he wanted her to explain everything. He was too tired.

"I grew up knowing Vik Chaudhry," she began. "We were lovers, and I was told I needed to get close to Dev," she said, looking straight at Kavi. "I needed to know everything your father knew, and it was to protect Chaudhry from being exposed."

Raj listened as she explained, and continued to watch Kavi. Kavi appeared to be emotionless the entire time, but Raj knew he was containing the anger and pain he was feeling.

•

Tapan was not being held for anything, but the media was having a field day with his story. He wondered who had stumbled upon what he was doing, and his mind immediately went to Alka. She was a wild card, even if Chaudhry would deny it. He was blinded by her, and she was going to be the reason they fell.

As he walked into Chaudhry's home, he knew where to find Chaudhry. He did not think to knock on the bedroom door and simply barged in, only to slam it shut when he saw Chaudhry with a woman who was not Alka. Shutting the door, he waited several minutes. Then the door opened to reveal Chaudhry his robes.

"What the hell Tapan! Do I ever walk in when you are with a woman?"

"No, but I did not think you would have someone in your bed. Especially since Alka is here. Are you not concerned about her loyalties?"

"I have never questioned her loyalties because she has never betrayed me, and I doubt she will start now. What is making you question my judgment?"

"How do you explain someone locating Raj Varma? How do you explain them finding the others we have buried in that area? She knew we were going to bury him."

"Yes, but she did not know where. Besides she was with me ever since we left. She has not given any information to anyone, and she would not sink to that level. I trust her."

Tapan shook his head. "She makes you weak and blind. She is what that girl was to Raj."

"She is not a weakness of mine, nor does she make me blind. I could live without her. If she were to die tomorrow, I would not care."

"Then let me get rid of her. I sense she is not to be trusted."

Chaudhry was beginning to get angry, and Tapan knew it was true that he loved her. He finally smiled. "Get rid of her then. She should still be around here somewhere. Hell, do what you would like to her. I truly do not give a damn!"

"Great," Tapan said evenly. "I will leave you now."

He watched as Chaudhry nodded and walked away. He wondered where Alka would be, but he was certain she would not be here.

Chapter 54

They had been talking for hours, only belatedly realizing it was mid-afternoon. Krish and Mohit had finally finished listening to all of the recorded sessions Katherine had compiled. There had been so many other things Tapan was responsible for that Krish had not known of. He needed to get this out in the open. Tapan had been able to shrug off the dozens of questions the press had about the mass grave in his backyard. Despite the fact that he was trying to play it off as a mistake, the people no longer trusted him. However, he had already poisoned the slums, and soon people would be lining up to report their symptoms. Tapan could still win this, and Krish could not let that happen.

"How would you like to proceed?"

Mohit shrugged his shoulders. "I am unsure of the best way to actually proceed."

"I agree with you. Maybe we should just wait until an opportunity presents itself," Krish said as he grabbed his water. As he was taking a sip, he heard his phone ring. He had told everyone not to bother him today, but he knew they would not be calling if it was not important.

"What is the matter, Kavi?"

"Sultan is looking for you."

Krish was not too surprised by that. He knew Chaudhry and Batala would want to eliminate him. "That is not shocking. How do you know?"

"Because," he said slowly. Krish knew something was wrong. "Alka Varma is not dead. She staged her death, and she came forward. It is a crazy story Krish, and it would be easier to explain when you are here. Will you be coming back soon?"

"Yes. Should I leave right away?"

"No, do not break your routine. Sultan most likely knows when you plan on leaving, so do not do anything out of the ordinary. Trust us."

"I do trust you Kavi, and I shall see you in a few hours."

He disconnected the line and turned towards Mohit. "So will you still want to join me at my residence until this is all over and done with?"

"Yes," Mohit said, and he seemed slightly taken aback.

"Then get everything together and please follow me. And do not seem too paranoid."

Mohit nodded, and they began to pack.

•

Sai had no idea what he was doing; he was just taking orders from Asim and Kavi. It was good they were in charge. They knew what they were doing, and they knew how to compartmentalize. That was something he never was able to do. He could take orders, but he was not able to think on his own and plan everything out. Sai was not a mastermind, and that made him question everything they were doing.

"What happens when we actually get him?" Asim asked. Sai could hear the excitement in his voice. He wanted to get Sultan, and he wanted to kill him. Sai knew it would not be a quick death, but he could not argue with it. He knew what sort of monster Sultan was.

"Who is to say we will actually catch him?" Sai replied cynically. "We all know how sly he is, and even if we did get him, how are we not going to make a spectacle of ourselves? Surely we will draw attention."

Asim's face twisted, but he finally nodded. "You are right Sai; we will draw attention to ourselves. The only thing is the bystanders will not do anything. The moment someone gets involved, they are risking getting in trouble themselves. They will let us go and do whatever we need to do, and they will all assume we have a damn good reason."

Sai could not argue with that. He knew he would have to listen to them. They had been doing this longer than him, and they obviously knew how to go about this in public. He wondered what they had done in public that people looked the other way for.

Grabbing all the materials they were going to need, Sai looked up to all of them. He was going to start everything off, and Sai knew if he messed up even slightly, then Krish might die. However, Sai felt as if Sultan was going to do something. He would be undetected, and he would not go into the crowd. That was what he always did, and that is why Sai knew he would be in the crowd. He would get close to Krish – he would get close to him because killing Krish would be a personal victory.

He looked at the two men. Sai was not going to tell them what his plan was. He refused to let them know, because the moment he told them, they would change their plan. They would not let him get a word in, and it was because they were so set in their ways of operation they would make sure everything went their way and their way only.

"We have an hour before we make our move," Kavi said. "I think we should start getting into position."

Sai nodded, and he was the first one to walk out of the door. He was prepared and he hoped he was right in his assumption as to how Sultan would proceed in his attempt to assassinate Krish. He had to be.

Chapter 55

Raj was still not feeling well, but he was getting better. For the first time, everything seemed to be going right for them. It looked as if they would finally win this war – a war they had been fighting for years. It had been a war he thought he had lost several days before. Yet here he was, still part of the fight, and determined to win.

He walked into the dining room and saw his mother sitting there sipping her coffee. He did not know how he felt about this, and he did not know if he could actually trust her. He didn't even want to trust her. She had lost his trust, and he was sure he was not going to give it back.

Stepping into the kitchen, he opened up the refrigerator and got out the orange juice, setting it down on the counter. He knew she was watching him, and he wondered if she was going to break the silence. He wasn't going to.

"How are you doing this morning?"

Raj glanced over at her and then went to grab a cup. He knew she most likely saw the look of disgust on his face, but she did not flinch. He was pouring his orange juice when he heard her getting up from where she sat.

"Raj, I am your mother and I do genuinely care about how you are doing."

Turning towards her, he shook his head. "Just because you birthed me does not make you my mother. Everything you were has been a façade. You kept up the charade until my father got too close to Chaudhry and you had him killed! So just because you grew a conscience does not mean I will forgive you for the amount of pain you have inflicted on my family."

He saw the pain in her eyes, but he did not care. He would never make her feel the way he felt. It was a feeling of loss, and it was something he still did not want to believe. He did not want Priya and their unborn child to really be gone. He felt as if he was an empty shell that had only dreamed of a girl like Priya. She had been perfect for him and now she was just gone – he did not want her to be gone.

"If I could take it all back Raj, I would. I promise you I would."

"You cannot change the past. You will never be able to change the way I feel. You are a despicable person, and that is probably why Chaudhry loved you so much."

"I am trying to fix everything! I am trying to repair the damage that has been done and I want to be part of your life."

"I do not want to be part of your life though. You had your chance of making everything normal. You threw everything away. Why should I even give you a second chance?"

She was silent for several seconds, and she finally nodded. "I know I am not who you thought I was. I will never be able to make up for everything I did, and I know you will not forgive me. I would just like to have a relationship with my son."

"You have three sons and a daughter," he said evenly. "One of your sons is dead – tortured – when they found his body, they could not identify him. Your other son always wanted to meet you, and he thought you were dead. Your only daughter never got to know you, and that was something she wanted. But with how everything worked out, I am sure none of them really want to have a relationship with you. You got rid of them, claiming it was for their safety, but it was because they were not fathered by the man you wanted."

"The father to my children does not matter!"

Raj threw down the empty glass of orange juice, and he heard it shatter at her bare feet. He was livid, and he pushed past her. She grabbed him, and he turned back towards her. "Do not lie to me," he growled. "Do not try to take back anything that had been said before. You cannot and you will not forge a relationship with any of us."

Raj needed to think, and he went out on the back patio. It was slightly chilly out despite it being afternoon. He turned as he heard the door open behind him. Glancing over his shoulder, he saw Mrs. Wasimrao standing there, her expression placid.

She took a seat, and he knew she was watching him. He knew she wanted to talk to him, and he turned towards her. "What? Did I go about that wrong? Did I say something that was untrue?"

Her hands were on her lap, and she shook her head. "That person you were in there was not you. That was a hurt young boy who does not know how to handle the situation at hand."

"I am a grown man," he said too harshly. "I am not acting any differently than anyone else would be in my situation."

"Do you honestly think she never loved you or your siblings? She loved the wrong man, and she gave her loyalties to a monster. She is trying to fix the wrongs she has made, and she is not going to be able to do that unless you forgive her."

"Would you forgive her? She did not care that her own son had been tortured. She did not care about my father. She had him killed – she gave everything up! Everything! She only cares about what she will gain. She is only looking for someone to love her and that person is not going to be me."

"She is cold, you are not wrong about that. But she is delicate. She was naïve and she loved the wrong person. She grew up thinking everything around her was normal. She was not going to give up the life she had because she did not know how else to live."

Raj was shaking because of how angry he was. "My father was with her for years, and he did nothing but love her! He showed her how life was supposed to be, and she had years to see how her life could be. She threw it all away, and I am not going to forgive that."

"I am not telling you what to do," she said softly. "I just want you to understand that she is a broken woman who was once a broken child. I am sure she did not pretend to love you for all of those years Raj. I am sure she always has loved you. She did return to you, and she brought with her the antidote for ricin. She is trying to fix everything."

"She will not be able to fix anything."

"Do not be selfish about this," she chided. "She is your only mother and she has, and most certainly always will, love you and your siblings."

"No! When I was there it was made very clear why she did not want to keep them and it was because they were Dev's children and not Chaudhry's. She did not care when she learned that Varun had been tortured to death! She is emotionless, and I am pretty sure she was not just pretending to be heartless."

Mrs. Wasimrao stood up, and she walked over towards him and put her arm around him. Raj remembered how his mother, a woman he thought was filled with love, would hold him like this. Before. She would comfort him and tell him everything was going to get better tomorrow. Before. He would never have suspected her of being this person. Someone he detested because everything about her was twisted. But maybe, people could change.

Chapter 56

Sai was walking through the crowd, and he was getting rather close to the first point of contact with Krish. He was looking everywhere and yet he could not find Sultan slinking about. A sickening feeling overcame him. What if he was wrong? He shrugged that off. Sultan was here on the ground, and he was going to get to Krish this way. He would do it because it was a personal kill, and that would make him change his way of doing everything – or so he hoped.

As he pushed past people, he saw the media was here. There was a camera man standing away from the rest of them. He had a camera around his neck, he was not trying to take pictures, and he stood as if he was anticipating a kill. Sai moved closer, and he understood why Sultan had brought cameras here. It was so they could not touch him without being caught by the cameras.

Walking towards him, he saw Krish and Mohit beginning to walk out of the hotel. The hotel's security guards were accompanying them and Sai watched as the lone cameraman stepped closer, and he watched as the man reached under his jacket.

Sai could feel his heart pounding in his chest when he saw the gun. He needed to get closer to Sultan, dammit. He could not see for a moment and as he pushed passed this burly man, he watched as Krish was being pushed closer towards Sultan.

Sai hoped that Sultan would not try and get a shot off. He got behind him, and he watched as one of the security guards made eye contact with him. Of course, there was someone on the inside they were able to use. That was something he should have suspected, and

Sai watched as Sultan turned to face him. Sultan's gun was pointing at his chest and he flinched as a shot went off.

The crowd dispersed quickly, and Sai looked to Sultan's body lying on the pavement. He stared as the streets were thrown into chaos. He saw one hotel security man moving towards Krish. Sai lunged at him and knocked him to the floor. The security guard had his gun out, and he was ready to shoot. Acting upon instinct, Sai grabbed for the gun. They struggled. He heard the gun go off and Sai was finally able to wriggle it out of his hands. Sai looked at the security guard, and he knew he would not be able to kill him. Taking the butt of the gun, he hit him over the head, rendering him unconscious.

Sai heard the sirens, and saw Kavi assisting Krish and Mohit into a car. He motioned for Sai to follow, and he did. As he was getting into the car, he looked at Kavi, unsure of how to feel. He was not supposed to be here. He was supposed to meet them elsewhere. He wondered if they had actually trusted him to get this job done on his own.

The car pulled away from the curb and Sai saw that Asim was the one behind the wheel. He looked at Kavi, and his eyes asked the question he wanted answered.

"We knew you would not go high up," he explained. "You may not have told us your plan, but it was not hard to figure out that you would be doing something entirely different."

"Then why did you not tell me what was going on?"

"Because we did not want you to give away our location. You looked as if you were working alone, and that was what we wanted."

Sai was not angry. He supposed he was supposed to be, but he wasn't. They made perfect sense, and he nodded. "I understand. But who was the one who shot Sultan?"

"Asim did," Kavi said.

"That was not part of our plan."

"No, it was not. But the media was there, and it was not like we could grab him without actually being caught on camera doing so. We improvised."

"He did not deserve a quick death."

"We are not disagreeing with you," Kavi said. "But we saw our chance and we took it. Now," he said as he was facing Krish. "There are a few things we need to talk about."

Krish looked at him and he nodded. Sai knew what Kavi was going to be telling him. However, Sai was sure Krish knew everything. It would not surprise him in the slightest if he knew this entire time that Alka was alive. Sai hoped that Krish was blinded to that fact though, because had he known about her then he could have saved his friend. He could have done so much more, and Sai found himself waiting eagerly for his response.

"What would you like to talk about?"

"Alka Varma. You knew her Krish. You knew her before she was even with Dev. I did some poking around, and you grew up with her and with Vik, and that is something you have never told me or anyone else about for that matter. And you probably knew she is still alive."

Krish was silent, and Sai could see the anger on Kavi's face. "Yes I knew Alka, but not as well as you probably think. We went to school together for some time, but she was not someone I would have considered my friend back then."

"Why is that?"

"Your mother was an introvert who had no self-respect. Her mother mysteriously vanished and every single person knew what her father was doing to her behind closed doors. She was immediately drawn to the one person who made her feel like a queen, and it was that same person who took advantage of her weakness and used it against her. You mostly want to know if I knew she was still alive and the answer is no. I thought she was dead. I thought Vik had killed everyone because Dev was so close to finding evidence against him. Evidence of his trafficking of women and drugs. Dev had all of his schemes listed out and he was ready to bury him, but Vik got to him first."

"I know the story, we all know it. But why would you not tell Dev that the woman he was going to be with was broken?"

Krish laughed madly for a moment, and he shook his head. "I told your father everything Kavi. I told him all that I knew about her but he did not care because he was in love with her. That was something that was not going to change, and it never would change. Even if he knew she was using him. Dev was blindly in love with her and that is something that would not change."

Kavi shook his head, and Sai could see how hurt he was. He resigned himself to patting his friend's shoulder. What else could he do?

•

Chaudhry was sipping at his coffee, and he looked across the table to Tapan. He was furious he was wrong about Alka and her loyalty to him. He was not blind to her; he had never been blind to her or to any person for that matter. He thought he had known her though – he had thought he could trust her, but he was quickly learning that no one could be trusted.

"Stop sulking," Tapan said. "There is nothing you could have done to prevent this, other than killing her back when you killed Dev."

"I am not sulking," he said firmly.

"Sure," he said. "Anyways, did you do what I asked?"

Looking over the rim of his mug he nodded. "They are tracking down Katherine now. I still do not see why you want to get her and that child back."

"She belongs to me, and you understand how possessive I can be. So what do you know?"

"As of now, there is nothing I know other than the fact that she is lying about visiting her grandmother. As far as we can tell, she has no family. She had disappeared and so far they cannot track her down."

Tapan shook his head. "She is doltish, and she would not be able to make a plan to make herself disappear."

"Women are deceitful, as we are learning. Maybe you did not truly know Katherine."

"What could she gain by marrying me and then disappearing?"

"I don't know. But you need to get people on your side for this election. Make a big scene about her disappearance. You will make them side with you."

"I am not quite sure I can do that, especially seeing as how that two faced snake stole the antidote. Krish will get all the glory for rescuing them."

"Do not worry too much Tapan. I will be planning everything for you. All you need to do is be my mouthpiece and everything will work out fine."

Tapan eyed Chaudhry and wondered what he was planning. He had a feeling Chaudhry already had a plan in motion, and all Tapan could do was nod and look back down at the newspaper. The man had spoken and he must obey.

Chapter 57

Siya held her son in her arms, and Navin sat at her bedside. He looked fondly at their child and as she held him in her arms, she felt all her worries melt away. It was just the three of them, and that was all that she needed.

"Have we decided on a name for him?"

She had a name picked out for him. She and Navin had talked about naming him after their fathers but she was not too into that idea. No, she wanted to name him after her brother – after Varun. He was always there when she needed him and he was always doing good things for others, but now he was gone and she missed him dearly. She wanted her son to grow up to be just like him.

"Varun," she said as she cooed at child.

"Varun Carlisle Patel?"

Nodding, she met her husband's eyes. She knew he was always going to be there for her, and that was all she could ask for. Her mind finally wandered, and she wanted to ask how Priya was doing. Navin placed his hand on her forearm and spoke softly. "Priya is fine, sweetheart. If you would like, I can go and check in on her again."

"I would like that very much."

Navin got to his feet, and he slowly walked away. He knew he could not keep this secret from her forever, and he wondered how she would react when she learned he had been keeping this a secret. It was for her sanity. He loved seeing her light up when she was holding their son, and he did not want to break her heart. Despite only knowing Priya for a short amount of time, he knew Siya had grown fond of her.

As he stepped inside Priya's room, he saw something he had not been expecting. He did not know how to react, so he just stood there and he looked at the empty bed.

•

Hari was holding Amala, and Hema was reading her a bedtime story. She was doing great for a single mom, and she had a plan in motion. He did not want her to leave India, but he knew why she needed the distance. He just did not want to say goodbye.

He watched as she began to fall asleep in his arms, and she put down the book and smiled at the two of them. "This seems natural to you."

"In the beginning, I was afraid of dropping her," he admitted. "But now I am used to holding her in my arms."

"When we leave, she is going to miss you. Maybe it is time for you to leave India. You could join me, Hari. We could be a family."

"Hema, we have talked about this. I need to stay here until everything is resolved. Maybe I will meet you in New Zealand."

She walked over towards him, and she picked Amala up in her arms and set her down in her cradle. Hari saw the fondness in her eyes, and he knew why she wanted him to go along. They were all good reasons, but he was not too sure he could leave. This was everything he had ever known, and he was afraid there would be nothing for him in another country. Everything would be foreign to him, and the thought of change did indeed frighten him.

Following Hema out of the room, he knew she had something to say to him. She was relentless, and she finally turned to him. "I need you," she said. "The thought of leaving this all behind frightens me as well, but this is what needs to be done. There are too many bad memories here and once we leave we can start over. We do not need to be here any longer."

He could see the desperation in her eyes. She truly wanted him to leave with her. She needed him and he needed her. For all those years he thought she was dead, and now here she was in front of him. She was a mother and she wanted to start her life over. It was something she deserved, and he knew he had to go.

"When this is over Hema, I give you my word that I will go with you. I need to see this out. I need to finish what has been started."

He watched as she nodded and she walked down the hall. He remained there, and he knew he had made the right decision. He had wanted to stay so that he could take care of other children who had been abandoned. He wanted to make their life better, but he knew someone else would step into his shoes, or at least he hoped so.

"I understand," she finally muttered. "I will wait until this is all over."

Hari smiled at her. There were no words that could describe how he felt. He watched as Hema walked away, and then he headed for the kitchen. He had worked up an appetite. When he saw Raj sitting on a chair, he knew Raj was over thinking (as usual), probably blaming himself for everything that had gone wrong over the past week (as usual), and worrying over what still needed to be done (as usual).

Hari sat down next to him. His food could wait; he needed to be there for Raj. He sat there for a moment waiting for him to say something, and finally he did. "What do you think about the situation?"

"I think that it is unexpected."

Raj picked his head up, and watched him. His face was still bruised and covered in scratches and his fingertips were still raw from trying to get out of the coffin. He had been buried alive, and he was beginning to wonder how he was feeling. Hari was sure Raj was not sure what to do or where to go. He was lost in a sea of uncertainty, and Hari knew no one was going to be able to bring him back.

"What would you do if you were me?"

"As far as what?"

"Forgiving my mother," he said in nearly a whisper.

"I am not too sure. I have no idea how you are feeling right now. Knowing she is alive after all of this time."

"Please do not dodge my question."

"That is my best answer. You know what though? She came back for you, and she brought with her the antidote. We are going to start treating the slums and everyone is going to be all right."

"Or so you say."

"Raj, you cannot remain this angry. It is not healthy and you really need to think about all this. She isn't going away."

"She lied and betrayed my family. How could someone forgive a person for doing something like that?"

"She left behind the dark part of herself. You have to wonder how and why she was the way she was. And you have to also realize she will not be able to get to a better place if she does not have your support."

"I don't need to support her."

"I am not saying you have to. I am just telling you she cared enough about you to start righting all the wrongs she has been a part of. She needs you to understand that."

He was silent for a moment and he shook his head. "I get it, but I am not ready to let this go so easily."

"You are feeling a lot of pain," Hari stated. "Maybe this is what needs to happen. Maybe you need to let go of all of your pain and just take the next step."

"The one person who understood me, who was there when I needed her, is dead. I should have been with her. I should have been protecting her and instead I am here and what have we accomplished so far? Not one damn thing! Chaudhry is still alive, and so are all of the monsters he has under his thumb."

"We are nearing the end of this hellish nightmare Raj. Krish will win this election and we will be able to make our move to eliminate Chaudhry and the others. You will get your revenge."

Raj shook his head. "Killing Chaudhry will not be enough. I have lost everything." And that was the problem. How was one supposed to live without anything to live for?

Chapter 58

Navin stood there dumbfounded. Priya had been here just a few hours ago, and now she was gone. She had vanished into thin air. Looking over his shoulder, he saw a nurse standing behind him, appraising him with curious eyes.

"What happened to the young woman who was in this room?"

"She was moved to the delivery room," she said slowly. It seemed as if she did not trust him. "She went into labor."

He was confused, unsure of what to make of this. "She is not due for several months," he stated firmly. "She could not have possibly have had that baby."

"Of course she did. Her body could no longer carry the child any longer."

"Are they both," he could not get the last word out of his mouth, but it finally passed over his lips. "Dead?"

"I do not know who you are," she said slowly. "And I cannot disclose any information to you."

"Siya told you not to say anything to anyone," he said. "You must be Maggie, one of Siya's friends. I am her husband, and my wife is in the other room with our son. Please tell me that Priya is alright."

He knew he was hoping for too much and the nurse turned towards him. "I will talk to only Siya," she said.

Maggie turned on her heels, and Navin followed her out of the door. He did not know what information would be disclosed to

Siya. He did not want her to know anything, or at least not yet. She did not need to know what had happened to Priya when Siya went into early labor. She did not need to know she was on life support.

Entering her room, Siya looked to the two of them. The look of pure happiness fled from her features and was replaced with dread. "Maggie, is everything alright?"

"It is about Priya," she whispered. "I do not know how to tell you."

Navin could see the tears start in her eyes, and he quickly walked to her side. There was nothing more he could do than to put his hand on her shoulder.

"What happened to her?"

"She went into labor."

Siya looked as if she was going to lose it. "That baby is only seven months old! Is Priya doing okay? Did she wake? Is the baby going to be all right?"

"The baby is under our care. Her lungs are not fully developed, and we are doing all we can to ensure she receives the treatment and the attention she deserves. As for your friend – she woke up. It was a miracle really," she said slowly. "But she has no memory at all. She does not know who she is or where she is. It seems as if she has lost years of her life."

"Is it brain damage that is causing her to forget?"

"Most likely. She did suffer a great deal of head trauma. And," Maggie hesitated but Siya waved her on impatiently, "she did lose oxygen to her brain for about a minute."

"What? When did this all happen?"

Navin could feel her eyes on him. He could not say anything. It was as if he was a deer caught in the headlights of a car at that moment.

"When you went into labor, Priya coded. That was the only reason we found you in her room. Had she not coded, then you could have easily have died. No one is allowed back in that area."

"But overall, she is okay?"

"Yes," Maggie said. "She is under our care, and we are going to do what we can to see about getting her memory back. I am hoping that such a recovery is indeed a possibility."

"Would you be able to bring her back here to see us? Maybe if she was around familiar faces, she would remember something."

Maggie nodded. "I will be back," she promised as she left the room.

Looking to Siya, she did not seem upset with him keeping that secret from her. He bit his lower lip, and he saw that she was looking at him.

"I understand why you didn't say anything," she said. "I am not mad at you. I am merely overwhelmed with concern for Priya. If she does not remember anything, I am not sure we would be able to do anything. Raj would be devastated."

"I know Siya. We will do whatever we can and you know that. For now, I think you should just rest. We will be able to go home in two days."

Siya nodded. She did not want to go home. She knew she had to though. Her son should be there, and she should be taking care of him in the comforts of their home. Although she was not too sure how comfortable it would be after what had happened. It was the event that had triggered all of this. What they were experiencing right now was simply the ripple effect. Siya could not stay in the hospital forever. She needed to face the demons of the dark.

•

She was in pain, and she did not understand what was going on. She did not know where she was, and she did not even know who she was. They called her Priya, but she was not sure if that was her name. How did she end up in this strange place? What she did remember was waking up in sheer pain, and she remembered people swarming around her. They all spoke to one another and they were all afraid and she was not sure why. That was when she saw them holding a child before her. She had only seen her for a moment before they whisked the baby away. Nothing was making sense.

That was when she saw someone walking up to her. She had curly red hair and green eyes and a patch of freckles on her nose. Her name began with an "M," but she did not remember her name. She was really sweet to her and she expressed real concern for her wellbeing. It was as if she knew her, but when she asked, she was told they had never met before.

"Priya," the red-headed woman said. "My name is Maggie, we were talking before."

All she could do was nod her head.

"I have a few people who would like to see you. They know who you are."

"How would they know me?" she asked slowly.

"I am not too sure how they met you, but they were taking care of you in their home. They will be able to explain everything to you."

She was dazed, and she was not too sure she wanted to see people right now. They were strangers, even if they said they knew her. "I will go," she said reluctantly. She was terrified, but maybe they would be able to give her the answers she needed.

Maggie assisted her into a wheelchair, and she looked up at her. "Did I have a baby?"

"Yes Priya. You had a daughter. She is in special care right now."

"Why?"

"You delivered her too early. She is having issues breathing on her own."

Thinking on it for a moment, she realized she remembered being pregnant. She remembered constantly swaying and becoming sick. But if she was pregnant and she just had the baby, who was the father of her child? Why wasn't he here with her?

They had gone down several different hallways, and they finally came to a room they entered. She saw a woman sitting there with a baby in her arms – was that her baby? And there was a man standing next to her. They both seemed to know who she was and she wondered how they knew her.

"Priya," the woman said. She sounded as if a great weight had been lifted off of her. "I am so happy to see that you are alright."

She looked to this woman, and she thought she remembered her. She was not too sure about that. "Why wouldn't I be all right?" she finally demanded.

The two strangers both exchanged looks, and it seemed as if they were trying to piece together the story which she had forgotten.

"Priya do you remember anything?"

"No, I don't remember anything at all."

"My name is Siya, and this is my husband Navin. We took you in because you were in danger."

"Why was I in danger?"

"Because the man you love became a target to a vindictive man. They wanted to kill you because they thought you made him weak."

"Why would they hurt the man I love?"

"It is a very complicated story," Siya said slowly. "But you should know that Raj is trying to fix everything. He wants you and the child you two share to come home to a safe place."

Priya sat there and the name Raj rang in her ears. She remembered a young man who protected her. He held her closely and he made her promises. They had so much in common. They both had suffered through so much pain, but she could not remember what had caused her pain. She could not remember anything about herself, but she did remember him.

"Is he okay? Does he know about everything that happened?"

"No. We told him and everyone else that you were dead to protect you."

"Protect me from what?"

"Someone came to our home and they were after you. They wanted to kill you and that person was almost successful. You went into a coma, and you have been in the hospital ever since."

"So you told the man that loves me that I am dead?"

"Yes."

"Won't that make him reckless?"

Siya was taken aback, but she did realize Priya was right. She had not thought about how Raj would react to the news. He would be reckless because the one person who had shone a light into his darkened abyss was gone. Siya knew she needed to get in touch with him before Raj did something he would regret. He thought he had lost everything and she needed to let him know Priya was all right and nothing had happened. Still, Siya wondered if that would put both Raj and Priya in greater danger.

Chapter 59

Krish had just returned, and Raj could sense that he brought good news. Raj wondered how he felt about all of this. He knew just as much about what Alka had done to their father, and yet he was not angry. If he was, he was concealing it rather well.

"What is going on?" Raj finally asked. He noticed that Asim was not with them. They probably dropped him off at his residence so he could be with his daughters.

"Sultan is dead," Sai said. "They were trying to assassinate Krish, but we were able to figure everything out before anything happened."

Raj was at a loss for words. He had always thought that when they had Sultan they would bring him back here and they would torment him. Give him a taste of his own medicine.

"Are you sure he is dead?"

"Yes," Kavi said. "The shot was clean, and there is no way anyone could survive it. Now we have another task at hand. How are we going to administer the antidote to the slums without exposing what is really going on?"

"Well, the antidote is something we can bake into things," Hema said. "We could go ahead and bring them baked goods, and we can make sure everyone receives something."

"That sounds great and all, but how are we going to remove the ricin from their water supply? We don't even know how much was in there. On top of that, we do not even know how much of it people are ingesting."

They were all silent for a moment. "I think I have an answer for what we can do," Raj said slowly. "We can flatten the slums out."

Before he could finish, he was interrupted. "Isn't that what we sort of saved everyone from having to go through before?"

"Yes," Raj said firmly. "But we can rebuild the slums and give them adequate living spaces. They can all have homes with water pipes run through them and they all can be insulated. We can bring businesses and we can make the slums sustain themselves. Everyone out there is just looking for a way to be able to live their life without worry and to have some form of structure."

"I like the idea," Mohit said. "And I have several business partners who want to expand and they can all come out here. We would be able to create better paying jobs out here for everyone."

"Granted that all sounds wonderful," Krish said. "But I doubt we can get this all done in a good enough time frame for everyone else."

"We can pitch our idea to them and while we do that, we can be passing out the baked goods," Hema chimed in.

"Doesn't this all seem a tad bit too easy?" Sai asked. "After everything we have gone through, why should it be so easy to save the slums now? Every single time we try to accomplish something, another thing pops up, and we are treading dangerous waters. Don't you think Chaudhry will have another plan? Something we have not seen coming?"

"I doubt it," Alka said softly. All eyes were on her and she attempted to make herself invisible.

"Why would you doubt it?" Raj demanded acridly. "Is it because you know him so well?"

"Yes, and I know everything he had up his sleeve."

Raj met her gaze, and he still did not know if he could forgive her. Why would he? He got to his feet, and looked at everyone else in the room. "I need to get some fresh air," he said. "Everyone should think about how we want to proceed, and we should do it before tomorrow. Who knows how many people are infected by now? We should move quickly."

Walking out of the room, he was not surprised when no one followed him. He stepped outside, and he took a seat. He could see the moon above him, and he closed his eyes for a moment. There was still one last thing he had to do in order for his mission to be complete. He still was not sure what he would be doing after it was all over. Where would he go? What would he do? The one person who made his life feel complete was gone.

He heard as the door opened and he did not dare to look over his shoulder when he heard her speak. "What can I do in order to be forgiven Raj?"

Looking over at her, he was still for a moment. He had a good idea as to what she could do for him, but he was sure she would not comply. Tearing his gaze away from her, he could not find the words he wanted to say and he felt it as she touched his arm. He moved away from her, and he realized he was acting as if she had burned him.

"Raj, please tell me what I can do. I want to make this right. You deserve that much Raj. I know I can never make up for what I did, but I want to start doing good with my life."

Letting out a sigh, he finally turned to face her. "Tell me how to get to Chaudhry. That is all I want."

"You do not need to know how to get to him."

He smirked – of course, he thought. "And why is that your decision to make for me?"

"You are a good person and if you become a killer, you will be no better than him."

"He has killed hundreds, and you know that to be true. He does not care about anyone or anything. That is something you know and so long as he is breathing, he will continue to do this, and you know that is true. Sultan is dead and he would be the only one attempting to get revenge if something happened to Chaudhry. No one is standing in my way now."

"This is not who you are. You are no killer, Raj."

"Chaudhry wanted me to be," he said darkly. "If you want me to forgive you, then tell me how to get to him. That is all I want."

"You have no idea how smart he is. He will know you will go to him to try and kill him."

"I am not as predictable as you think I am. Now tell me what I want to know."

Alka looked at him, and she let out a sigh of defeat. Stupid pigheaded men.

Chapter 60

Katherine could not help but feel paranoid. For the past three days, she felt as if someone had been watching her, but every time she looked around, she would see no one there. It was as if she was imagining the entire thing and she was not sure how to handle this. This evening, it was no different. Emery was tucked soundly in bed, and she was beginning to feel anxious. She needed to talk to the one person she trusted.

Grabbing her phone, she dialed his number. She waited for several rings but there was no answer. She knew it was morning there in India, and she was wondering why Mohit was still not back. She was used to his company and now he was absent. Katherine knew she needed him. Something was wrong, and she knew it. The only thing was, she did not understand what was wrong. She had not felt this paranoid in a while, and now she was certain someone was watching her every move. She stopped to think for a minute. The only person who would be looking for her would be Tapan. She had disappeared, and she never called him. Katherine felt sick, but she wondered why he would waste his resources trying to find her. Then she remembered how possessive he was over everything he felt belonged to him.

Walking into the kitchen, she grabbed her weapon of choice. This life was supposed to have been gone. She was raised to be this person, but she did not want to be this person. She wanted to raise her son away from the chaos, and she wanted to be a normal woman. She wanted to be the woman her mother wanted her to be before she died. However, her father raised her. He taught her how to be this way, and she would never want to change who she was. Still, this was not who she wanted to be either.

Sitting on the couch, she knew if someone was watching her, then they would have her routine mastered by now. That was why she was supposed to always change everything, but she had become lazy and reckless. She should have been more cautious. She knew because of her negligence her son might be exposed to the true her. A woman he would no longer see as warm and soft, but would see her as cold and heartless.

Turning off the lights in her home, Katherine felt tonight would be the night that whoever was watching her would make a move. She knew what had to be done, and she knew she most likely would not be able to sleep for the next few nights. Katherine also knew she would not be able to stay here, and she was wondered where they would go next.

Now with all the lights off, she waited there in the darkness. Everything was silent, and she was ready. Silent and deadly.

•

Tapan did not want to believe that Katherine was living another life. He could not believe she was on her own, and he could not help but feel embarrassed. He thought she was ditsy, and he thought she was as controllable as a sock puppet, but it turned out he had been the one who was played. She had been with him for two years and there was no knowing what she had found on him. He did not know if she was going to expose his deeds. He had no idea what she knew and he could not help but feel on edge.

He finally looked to Chaudhry. He was reading through several things, and Tapan did not want to bother asking what was going on. It was not his place, and he truthfully did not care. Chaudhry was always up to something. Tapan cleared his throat.

"What is it?" Chaudhry asked tartly.

"Katherine is not who she claimed to be. She did not exist until she met me. We know where she is though."

"And what do you plan on doing with that information?"

"I want her to die! There is no knowing what she knows about our operations. She had me fooled, and now she is living as if she never knew me or anyone else for that matter."

"How did you find her?"

"I hired someone to do the job for me. Someone we both know is very good in finding people who want to remain hidden."

"You sent DeeGee after her?" Chaudhry asked quizzically.

"Do you not trust the people I send out to do my work?"

He shrugged. "I think it is quite fitting. She detested him, and now you are sending him to get rid of her. It is classic and that little bitch deserves it."

Tapan could not help but think that as well. No one would make a fool out of him.

"Please do me a favor though," Chaudhry said. "Once Katherine is dead, please have DeeGee bring her son back here. We are in need of someone new to learn our ways and to take our places when we meet our end."

"Emery would not be suitable," Tapan said. "There was something wrong with him. He has some sort of disability, and he would not be worth our time of day. We will find you a child that is more suitable."

Chaudhry glanced over at Tapan. Usually he would become furious with the fact that Tapan was talking the way he was, but he knew he was right. Emery was different than most other children, and he probably would not be able to be groomed as their successor.

"What are your plans for the slums?" Tapan asked. "I know there is something you have been planning on doing."

"At this point, I am going to lay back and see what Krish will be doing. After all, we know he has the antidote and he will be curing all of those people. Plus, you are meeting with the press in the morning to talk about your missing wife."

"Do you truly believe that will win people over?"

"There are so many people out there who are weak. They let their emotions dictate how they will act and that is why it will win people over. You need to feel as if you are in love with her, and you need to show that you are genuinely concerned for her wellbeing. By doing so, you should have people eating out of your hands."

Tapan was not too sure he would be able to pull it off, but he nodded. As he looked over at Chaudhry, he knew he was planning something and he was refusing to let him take part in it, but he need not be worried by it. He was already getting enough bad publicity.

•

She was not allowed to touch her daughter, but she was able to see her. Tears were stinging her eyes, and she felt as if she was already a bad mother. Her daughter was in there helpless. She was born at two pounds five ounces and her lungs were not fully developed. All Priya wanted was to be able to hold her child in her arms. She wanted to keep her safe. Priya froze when she heard someone walking behind her.

Standing next to her was Siya. Priya remembered their names, but most of everything was blank. Siya was trying to get her to remember more, but it seemed the harder she tried the more difficult it was to recall certain events in her life. She was frustrated with it, and she was upset.

"Do you know what you would like to name her?"

Priya shook her head. "I do not want to name her without her father being present."

Siya looked to Priya and she wanted to tell her that it was possible Raj would not be able to take part in that. She had called Krish and she had told him she had lied about Priya passing on. He understood, but he had informed her Raj had disappeared into the night and no one had been able to track him down. From that phone call, Siya also learned the woman that birthed her, the woman she thought was dead, was still alive and well. There were so many things going on, and she was not sure how to react to it all. All she knew was she had to keep her composure. There was no need to tell Priya what was going on.

"I am sure Raj would not mind if you named her."

"Do you know when he will be here?"

Siya heard the desperation in her voice. It seemed as if Priya needed him there, and she wondered if it was because she thought that by having him around it would trigger her memories. She could not fathom what it would be like without remembering anything, but maybe it was for the best. Maybe this was her chance of rebuilding herself and becoming the woman she wanted to be.

"I do not know when Raj will be here, but I am sure he will get here as fast as he can." Priya nodded and turned away.

Chapter 61

The symptoms were becoming more prominent in the younger children, Krish realized as they walked through the slums. He could not believe how many of them had the look of lifelessness in their eyes, and he knew there was a chance they were too late in delivering the antidote. He was unsure if it would actually work, but he desperately hoped this would be what they all needed.

They had set up a station about an hour ago and he, along with the others, had been speaking with the people in the slum. Krish told them about what he had wanted to do, but he would not do so without their permission. Some of them were distrusting, but that was something he could understand. The rich never took into consideration the class beneath them. Or at least that was what everyone thought. He could not deny that Raj had a great idea, and it was one he was hoping to get support from the slums in order to achieve. He knew they would be the ones who determined whether or not he was elected. There were more poor men and women than rich.

As he walked among them, he made sure not to wear anything ostentatious. He did not want to show off how much money he had. He wanted to relate to them as much as possible and he was not sure if he would actually be able to do that. Krish had never been poor, and he was not sure how the culture had changed. He had realized they had different forms of communication. It seemed to be something only others they knew seemed to understand.

"Krish," he heard a familiar voice say.

He turned, and standing there was Raj. He was elated to see that he was all right. No one had been able to find him in hours, and Alka had not told them anything. Krish wondered if she had told him how to get to Chaudhry or if he was upset with her and took a long walk. Whatever it was, he was happy to have him back.

"Is everything all right there Raj?"

Krish watched his expression, but he did not see anything there. He could not deny how much he had changed since he had met him. He used to wear his heart on his sleeve the way Dev did, and now he was placid. Krish had not yet decided if that was a good or bad thing and he slowed his pace. He felt it was a bad thing.

"Yes everything is all right. There is just something I need to tell you."

"Actually, there is something I should tell you first," Krish said. "I received a phone call from your sister," he began and then there was a deafening explosion and debris flew everywhere, obscuring everything.

Raj fell to the ground, and he was able to catch a glimpse of what had happened. One of the sections of the slums had exploded, and Raj watched as fire began to consume the poorly constructed slums. He watched as people began to run and panic, could see the smoke beginning to rise. This had all been planned, and he wondered how they knew they were here today. Raj also began to wonder what had made them want to blow up the slums.

Getting to his feet, he saw Krish lying on the ground and he saw that something had caught the side of his face. Picking him off of the ground, he watched as everyone began to flee. Some children had been separated from their parents, and he knew they would be easy targets for anyone cruel enough to hurt them.

As he was helping Krish up to his feet, he saw Sai and Kavi. They were helping clear out the area, and he saw Chaudhry standing away from the madness. He was observing his handiwork, and Raj knew this was the only time to get to him. He also knew that this was too easy. There was something else happening now, and Raj wondered if he knew the fate of Sultan. He wondered if the fact of losing his best assassin had made him snap.

Everyone was quickly getting out of there, and there was no place to go other than the neighboring slums. Raj blinked and when he opened his eyes again, he saw that Chaudhry had disappeared.

•

Tapan had been speaking with the news reporter for nearly an hour now. He had told her about how Katherine had disappeared when she had gone to the states, and that he was desperate for someone to help find her. He could tell she believed him and he realized how easy it was to manipulate an entire group of people. That was when someone came on set and whispered in her ear. Tapan was beginning to wonder if this was the queue Chaudhry was telling him about. The only other thing that would make people get on his side.

"I do apologize, Mr. Batala but there is something that has just happened in the Bandra slums."

He listened as she changed gears and began speaking about what had happened there. It was a mass explosion, and Tapan heard the words he was anticipating.

"With the destruction and loss of their homes, people are all wondering where the residence of the Bandra slums will go."

Tapan grinned. "They can stay with me in my residence. It is big enough to host at least fifty people comfortably. As for the others, I will be able to find a temporary place for them to stay until we can get their homes rebuilt."

He saw the look she gave him, and she turned to the cameras. Chaudhry was a mastermind, but he was not too sure how he felt about having strangers in his own home. It did not matter how good it made him look, because this was not convenient for him. However, he did know he was the hope they needed; even if it was false hope. That hope was what would get him, and not Krish, elected.

Chapter 62

They had stuck with them the entire journey to the other slums. Raj could see how distraught most of them were, and he wondered what he would be able to do for them. He wanted to be able to do something for them. He could not imagine how they all must feel, to not have the familiarity of their homes. It did not matter how extravagant their homes were because the simplest of things could put a smile on the face of the most hardened resident.

Krish sat down when they arrived and Raj looked him in the eyes. "Do you think we can get several cars out here so we can take them to the compound?"

He was out of breath, but he nodded. "Yes. That would be a good idea. We have enough space for several dozen of them."

Raj nodded, and he saw a group of men from the Bandra slums talking to one another and they were eyeing the both of them. It was obvious they were not happy, and Raj was beginning to wonder what they were saying – he was beginning to wonder if they were trying to push the blame on them.

Staying at Krish's side, he watched them all carefully. When Sai and Kavi arrived, it was with seven children. The men smiled as frantic mothers ran towards their children. Raj watched as they sobbed, and they huddled together.

"What do you think happened?" Sai inquired.

"Chaudhry," Raj answered simply. "I saw him standing there on the sidelines, and he was watching as everything was beginning to unfold."

"Do you think he did this out of spite because of what happened to Sultan?"

"I do not think Chaudhry was acting out because of Sultan's death. I doubt he even knows what happened to him."

"So why do you think he did this?"

Krish looked to all of them and he sighed. "We were there talking about wanting to rip the slums apart to rebuild."

"Yes," Raj said. "But that was not something we were planning until last night. There is no way he could possibly know what we are planning. Not that easily."

Kavi shook his head. "He is always one step ahead of us, and it is really getting underneath my skin."

"I think this was about us," Sai said. "By saying this was a way to make us look bad it can be twisted into that, but I doubt they will twist this until later. I mean, if you think about it, Tapan's best way of getting any votes for this election is by getting sympathy points, and he is most likely trying to prove he is caring and he wants to help out. By destroying their homes, he could step up to the plate. Especially since we ruined his original plan. This is his way of getting revenge and winning the election."

Everyone thought about it, and Raj looked back at the group of men. They had dispersed, but Raj could tell they were still eyeing one another. He was beginning to wonder if they were going to act out because they believed they were the reason their slum had been blown up. All they could do at that point was sit and wait and figure out what they were going to do.

●

Chaudhry had returned to the comforts of his home. His skin had blistered, and he had not realized he was standing that close to the explosion. Nevertheless, it was all going to work out according to his plan. He had told Tapan what to say, and he was hoping he was able to keep to the script. He knew Tapan was not an idiot, but it often took a bit of time for his brain to process what was going on. Chaudhry disliked the fact that Tapan was still in this election, and he was not. There was no way he was able to win over the people after what Krish had done, but regardless of that, he knew they would still be able to win this election. And Krish would fail. He grinned manically.

As he was sitting there, he could not help but feel uncomfortable. He felt as if there was something heavy resting upon his chest, and his lungs felt as though they were going to collapse. He felt his heart begin to pound in his chest, and his body was soon covered in sweat. He began to panic when he realized he was dying. What other explanation could there be?

Chapter 63

Several hours had passed, and they had brought several dozen people to the compound. Krish was working on bringing food over for them, and Raj continued to watch over them. He was soon approached by Kavi, and he wondered what Kavi wanted to talk about now. Whatever it was, Raj was not in a talking mood. Kavi stopped in front of him anyway.

"I have a few questions to ask you."

"And I am sure I have a few answers to give."

Kavi was silent for a moment, and then he spoke. "Where did you go last night?"

Raj thought back on it, and he was not too sure he should tell the truth. He met Kavi's gaze, and for a moment he felt as if he was looking at his father, Dev, again. His eyes were stern and yet gentle. As if he wanted the answer, but he was not going to be upset if he did not get it.

"Alka told me what I wanted to know about Chaudhry."

"Which was what?"

He looked around himself for a moment, and when he was confident no one was in earshot, he said "She told me how to get to him without confronting him."

"Wow, her advice sounds helpful."

He knew how it sounded. To get the job done, one usually assumed you needed to be in close range, but he had learned it was not necessary. Raj then inquired thoughtfully, "Have you ever heard of botulism?"

Kavi shook his head, and Raj continued. "It mimics the systems of food poisoning. It is a bacterium that essentially kills if it goes untreated."

"You are talking about a man with unlimited resources. Of course he is going to seek out treatment!"

Raj understood why he was furious and he smiled. "He won't be able to seek out treatment. I found where to get botulism that was active and ready for use."

"I really do not want to know, do I?"

"I don't think so," Raj said. "Anyways, Chaudhry will not be able to live through it. The meal he ordered from his favorite restaurant was laced in it. We made sure he ingested a lot of it and by the time someone finds him, it will already be too late."

Raj noticed how Kavi was watching him and he spoke. "How do you feel knowing he will no longer be around?"

"I don't feel like I am the person I was," he admitted. "I was hoping by doing this I could regain that part of me that is gone. The part of me that died when I learned that Priya was – gone."

Kavi shook his head. "You will never get that part of you back. Even if you succeed in getting your revenge, you will never feel like yourself again."

"Even with Sultan dead you still feel like you lost this war, don't you?"

"Yes. And it is because he took something from me that I will never get back. He took someone away from us that can never be replaced nor forgotten."

"Well," Raj said slowly. "I never knew Varun, so I am not too sure about that. I do admit I wish I had the chance to meet him."

Kavi smiled slightly. "The two of you would have gotten along rather well."

Krish walked up to them, and Raj noted that his face was beginning to blister in some spots that had been exposed. He did not seem to mind, and he spoke. "There was something I was going to tell you before the explosion," he announced. "Siya called me and told me that she lied to all of us."

"What would Siya lie about?" Kavi asked.

"She lied about Priya being dead. She is very much alive, but she has suffered head trauma which has made her forget most things in her life. But," he said trying to sound optimistic. "You are a father to a girl Raj, and you are an uncle to a little boy."

There was nothing Raj could do in that moment other than stand there in silence. He did not know how to feel about any of it. He had thought she was gone, and now Krish was telling him she was alive and well. Raj wanted to believe that to be true, because he had not yet accepted that Priya was gone. He had been told by Chaudhry that she was dead. He knew she was pregnant. His mind was in a whirl, and he did not know what to do. He did not even know what to say.

"Raj," Krish said. "I do not need you here any longer. You are free to go to Priya and be with her now. That is where you have wanted to be after all," he waved a hand, "this."

"The elections are not even finished yet," Raj said. He did not understand why he was arguing. Of course he wanted to leave, but he did not want to seem like he was abandoning Krish. They had not won the war, and there was still so much that needed to be done. Even if his plan to poison Chaudhry worked out, they still had to go against Tapan.

"I understand your concern," Krish said. "But this is all going to be over soon. So go to America and be with the woman you love and the little girl you will raise together. Get your degree, and then if you would like come back, feel free. We'd love for you to see what we were able to do to fix India. Come back later, and see how different your home will be."

He was speechless. He was sure Krish would be able to do what he needed without his assistance. All he wanted was to be able to go and see Priya and their daughter. He knew Siya would be there, and he would be able to meet his nephew. There was a new life ahead of him and he was terrified, but that was good, right?

"I will need to pick up a few things."

"I know. You and Mohit will be able to fly back together. The two of you will end up on different planes towards the end of your journey, but he will be with you when you arrive in the country."

Raj nodded and he saw Mohit talking to several people. He had a pad of paper and a pen. He seemed to be scribbling something down, and he shook each of their hands. That was when he walked over towards them.

"Mohit, you and Raj will be heading back to the house. You two need to get ready for your trip."

"Of course," he said and he gestured for him to follow. Raj was numb. This was all moving too fast, and he was sure he was just dreaming. Maybe he had been knocked unconscious during the explosion. Whatever it was, he felt as if he was getting back the life he thought he had lost.

•

Tapan had arrived back at his residence, and he was rather upset that he was not alone. He had three strangers in his car, and they smelled as if they had never been bathed before. Regardless of the gain, he was beginning to wonder if it was worth it after all.

As he pulled up to the driveway, everyone got out. He was pleased to be able to breathe fresh air. Although he knew there would be more of them joining him within the hour, he was not ready to bring their filth into his residence quite yet.

Stepping inside, no one spoke to him. They all seemed to know he did not want to talk to them. They made him uncomfortable, and as they all walked into the main living space his phone went off. He waved a hand at the strangers to make themselves comfortable and headed to the kitchen.

Quickly, he answered the phone, and listened to the voice on the other end. He felt his blood run cold. "Tapan," she said. It took him a moment to figure out that it was Katherine. She did not sound as fragile as he thought she was. "Did you honestly think sending someone to kill me was a good idea? Well, I hate to tell you, it was not. Now please turn on the television. There are a few things about you that have found their way to the press. And note that if you ever come near me or my son again, it will be you that ends up dead."

He froze as the other end of the line clicked off and he felt as if his heart was sinking. He felt sick, and he did not understand what was going on. He did not know how to process any of it. He turned on the news and watched as all of his misdoings were broadcast for all to see and hear. He would not be able to move past this. His life was over as he knew it.

•

It had been nearly a day, but he was finally pulling up to the hospital, and he saw Siya standing outside. She was holding her son in her arms. There was also a tall man standing at her side, and he did not know what to feel in that moment. He could not believe that this was really happening, and he summoned up the courage to get out of the car.

Siya embraced him, and he was not too sure how he should feel. He had never got the chance to truly meet her. He had been shot, but he was able to recognize her with ease. She was the spitting image of their mother. A woman who gave him what he needed to destroy a monster – a woman who had betrayed him before, but she was now working on becoming the mother he thought she was.

"Raj, it is so good to finally meet you. But I know you did not come here for me," Siya said. "You mostly came here for Priya and your child."

He smiled at her. "Do not sell yourself short," he chided her. "You are my sister, my family. I am here for all of you."

He watched as her face lit up, and she motioned for him to follow. Raj did, and he felt his heart pound in his chest. The walk to where they were heading seemed to take forever, but they finally arrived in a small room and he saw Priya sitting in a chair. She was talking to their child. He knew his daughter was not perfectly healthy, but he trusted that eventually she would be.

As he peered in on her, Siya knocked on the glass and Priya looked up. Raj wondered if she remembered him. As she was walking out to them, she stopped in front of him. He held his breath as he waited for her to say something.

"Raj," she nearly whispered, and he felt her embrace him. This was the feeling he had been wanting, and he did not want to let her go. She was crying into his shirt and he was holding her. There was nobody else but the two of them and the baby he held in his arms.

Six Months Later

After several months of being in the states with Priya, they had quickly realized it was not what they wanted. They both wanted to go back to India. They both wanted to go back to where their lives together started, and they were not the only ones. Siya and Navin had followed them back, and as Raj walked around the slums, he noticed how different everything was.

He was holding his daughter in his arms and Priya was standing next to him. Of all the changes that Krish and the others had made, they had left his home the same. The last time Raj was inside, he had wanted to be captured, but now he was stepping inside to start his life over with his wife and daughter.

"There are many types of people in the world," he told his daughter as his wife looked on. "The ones who could hurt you," he tapped her nose with a finger and she giggled, "and those who could never."

Thank You

Dear Reader,

Thank you for choosing to read my books out of the thousands that merit reading. I recognize that reading takes time and quietness, so I am grateful that you have designed your lives to allow for this enriching endeavor, whatever the book's title and subject.

Now more than ever before, Amazon reviews and Social Media play vital role in helping individuals make their reading choices. If any of my books have moved you, inspired you, or educated you, please share your reactions with others by posting an Amazon review as well as via email, Facebook, Twitter, Goodreads, -- or even old-fashioned face-to-face conversation!

I invite you to connect with me on Facebook:
https://www.facebook.com/AuthorJamesKipling/

With profound gratitude, and with hope for your continued reading pleasure,

James Kipling
Author & Publisher

Printed in Great
Britain
by Amazon

31730559R00210